AN UNFORTUNATE *Alliance*

BROOKE J LOSEE

Published by Golden Camel Press

Paperback ISBN: 978-1-954136-39-7

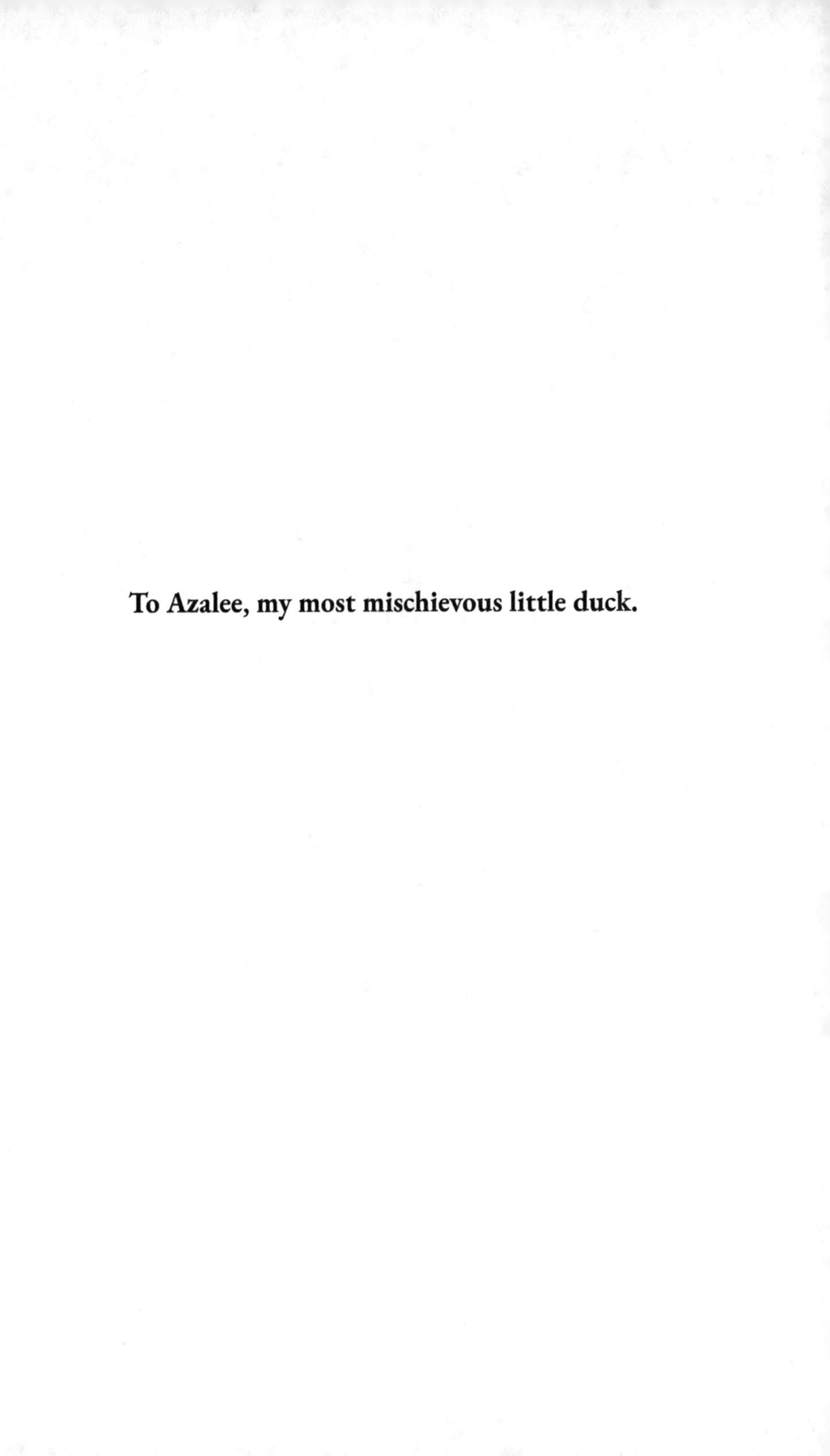

To Azalee, my most mischievous little duck.

Royal Crescent
The Circus
Sydney Gardens
Royal Avenue
George St.
Queen Square
Pulteney Bridge
Bath Abbey
Theatre Royal
York St.
Green Park Road
The River Avon
Lower Bristol Rd.
Ston Easton Park
All Saints Chapel
map of
BATH

Chapter One

London, 1820

GREGORY

Some nights, Lady Fortune wore hearts; tonight, she flaunted diamonds. My heart beat a steady, quick rhythm as I slid more chips across the oak table, placing my bet. I wanted this win.

No, I need it.

The two men tucked against the wall, watching me with critical eyes, were evidence of that.

I held my breath as each punter made their wager and then turned my eyes to our banker, a man with coiffed brown and gray hair and a chubby wide nose. Dressed in deep red, high-fashioned livery, he added to the lavish aesthetic The Sparrow, a gaming hell situated in a back alley off St. James Street, attempted to achieve. Their goal, of course, was to draw the attention and business of high society by creating an atmosphere of leisure and sophistication, despite the illegality of the happenings within. The number of nobility present proved their tactics were successful. Many of the aristocracy frequented the place, and there was no small number of pigeons who returned night after night in hopes of regaining their lost fortunes.

"Are we ready?" asked the banker. He was the dramatic sort, taking his time turning over each card from the deck as if he enjoyed creating the suspense. He reminded me of my mother, eager to put on a show, no matter the situation.

"Deuce for the bank." The banker grinned at the heavy exhale produced by the man at my side. With no luck tonight, I was not surprised when he muttered his intention to leave the game and rose from his seat without waiting for the next reveal.

The banker flipped over the second card, placing it on the left side of the table. "Ten of diamonds."

My heart leapt. I had earned triple my bet. There was a long way to go to get myself out of troubled water, but this was an excellent start.

The game continued until we had gone through the entire deck and onto another. My winnings had grown six-fold by the end of the first hour, and by the fourth, I had won enough to cover my most urgent debts.

"You in for another game, Davis?" Mr. Carlisle, a particularly gruff older gentleman with snowy white hair and icy blue eyes, was a common tablemate for me since we both preferred for the game of faro.

"Too early to quit," I answered. "What is it they say? Fortunes are made long after midnight."

Mr. Carlisle huffed. "Many a fortune is also lost after midnight. A game of chance cares nothing for the time of day. Certainly not for the state in which it leaves its victims."

I chuckled, watching the banker shuffle a new deck of cards. "Fair enough, but I see you are still here, as you are most nights. Being a victim of chance must not be so terrible if it brings you back as often as it does."

Carlisle grunted.

"Why do you continue to spend your nights here, Carlisle?" I asked. "Your expression remains the same whether you win or lose, so I cannot imagine it is purely pleasure. Furthermore, your pockets are not in dire straits. Why, then, do you come?"

"I'm not here to win," he answered simply.

I was never one to pry into another man's reasons for being at the tables. It wasn't my business, but Carlisle's answer ignited my curiosity. "I would hope you are not here to lose, either."

The man heaved a sigh and, removing his attention from the banker, turned to face me directly. "I haven't any care where a bit of my money goes. I've lived a long life; a good one, even. I have no heir of my own, and my wife, who I loved something fierce, has gone from this world. I gamble for the distraction it provides." His brows drew down as his gaze raked over me. "You are young—too young to be wasting your life away in here. There are far better things to engage your time. I wonder what it is you need distracting from."

A humorless laugh escaped me. "I would much prefer a life of luxury where I hadn't any concerns or debt collectors on my heels, but alas, I am not so fortunate. If I am to keep my inheritance and support my mother, then this is where I must spend my time. It is no simple distraction."

Carlisle shook his head. "If you insist, but there are other ways to gain capital to repay debts."

"What? Like marrying an heiress? I believe I will leave that to the gents presently peacocking about the ballrooms of London. I've no interest in marrying some half-witted chit for money. I'd rather rot in debtor's prison."

Not entirely true, but marriage was certainly a last resort. Why should I subject myself to the whims and demands of a wife if I could win the capital I needed on my terms?

Carlisle grunted again, and the game continued without another word.

The other punters placed their bets, and when it came to my turn, I shifted my chips to the six and cocked the card. My stomach knotted with a mixture of anticipation and trepidation, and when the banker revealed a six of diamonds for a *sept et le va*, I leapt from my chair with a cheer. I'd won seven times my initial wager.

One of the other players slapped my shoulder in drunken congratulations, and I couldn't rid my face of my triumph. My body may as well have floated among the clouds. With a long exhale, I reclaimed my seat. The game was nearly done. *I* was nearly done, already safe from the threats that had plagued me for weeks.

Each punter took their turn, and when it came to me, I hesitated. My pulse pounded in my ears as I considered my options. I could walk away now and pay off all my current debts. My winnings were substantial, more substantial, perhaps, than they had ever been. I'd won over four thousand pounds tonight. Though not a complete fix, another round would go a long way toward restoring my estate. There were repairs that needed attention—cracked ceilings and crumbling staircases that required proper care. Those things had been cast aside as the estate floundered, but another win would change all of that. My mother would be free to purchase whatever she stood in want of, and I would not be forced to refuse her. I would not need to release more of my dwindling staff.

Everyone would win, would they not?

I searched my memories, attempting to remember the rounds and what cards had been pulled, an impossible feat given the number of games I had played tonight. Had all four twos been played, or were there still more in the deck? I couldn't remember well enough to increase my odds by probability. No, this round would come down to pure luck.

I slid my tokens onto the knave.

"Are you certain?" The question came not from the banker, but from Carlisle.

"If I were certain, I would be far more heavy in the pockets," I jested.

The man sighed, shaking his head before leaning closer to me and whispering. "Have you made enough to clear your debts?"

I nodded, glancing around the room. I didn't wear my debt on my sleeve, but between the rumors and how frequently we played together, Carlisle could likely guess the extent of my troubles.

"Then why are you continuing?" he asked.

Why?

My stomach tossed with discomfort. I wanted to pay my debts, but I also wanted my estate to flourish as it once had. I wanted to wake up each morning without worrying that I would not have the money to pay my staff or bills. I wanted the luxury of a leisurely life.

But in all honesty, I also enjoyed the exhilaration of winning. I basked in those moments, when all that haunted me seemed to fade from memory.

"You should quit while you are ahead," said Carlisle when I didn't respond. "Gambling to restore your coffers is one thing; doing it for pleasure is another. In my experience, the latter can lead to ruin far more quickly. A man chasing thrills at the expense of logic is bound to find himself without a roof overhead."

"I know when to quit," I spat with indignation. I didn't need someone chiding me. My mother did enough of that. Besides, if I wanted to walk away, or felt my luck had run out, I would leave.

You have failed to walk away before, my mind whispered.

The reminder sent a shiver of guilt coursing through me. Once, I had nearly lost my entire estate in a night of gaming. I'd been fortunate to have those debts forgiven as part of a bargain. But this was different. Tonight would not end the same way. It was one more round. That was all I needed.

The banker placed two fingers on the top of the deck, his expression smug as he built the tension. The anticipation. My gaze flicked to Mr. Carlisle, and the disappointment I saw in his eyes sank my stomach into a deep pit, but I ignored the sensation. I had good reasons to continue and a winning streak on my side. That was logical, was it not?

The banker slapped the next card onto the table. "Knave for the banker!"

Sick. That was the only way to describe the swirling in my gut. I had done so well, and all it had taken was one card to lose. Everything I'd spent the night working for—gone in an instant.

I swallowed the bile in my throat. Although I couldn't meet his eyes, I felt Carlisle's gaze on me. I stood so abruptly, my chair squawked against the wooden floor, then gave a quick bow to excuse myself. Perspiration beaded on my forehead as I slipped outside onto the empty street, stealing glances over my shoulder to see if I was being followed.

The burst of cool air provided an immediate reprieve from the stuffy room I had vacated. This early in the morning, St. James was quiet. Yet with the heavy fog, a looming eeriness settled over the city. Or perhaps that was merely my perception of it after a long night and the dire circumstances that led me to walk beneath the oil-lit lamps, the only light available to combat the darkness.

I glanced again over my shoulder and noted two figures following me. What was I to do now? I could begin anew tomorrow night, but first, I needed to convince my stalkers to *give* me another night. A difficult task, considering my payments were already late and I now owed The Sparrow money too.

Their boots pounded against the cobblestone with increased speed, and my breathing quickened. Debt collectors took their jobs seriously and had no issue with using physical assault to encourage payment. This would not be the first time I had been beaten over money.

"Gregory Davis?"

My body froze. A young man of not more than two and twenty stood before me, blocking my path forward. He wore a silk top hat, and while his attire lent more to that of a servant than upper class, it was clear he was well employed.

"Forgive me, but I am in a hurry," I said, attempting to move past him.

"You won't avoid them by walking the streets."

He was right. I glanced behind me. My stalkers had stopped in the shadows of a building, waiting like hunters. But what else could I do? Even if there was a hackney about at this hour, I hadn't two shillings to rub together. "I have little choice at present."

"I offer one for consideration." The young man gestured toward a carriage down the street from us. "If you don't mind coming with me, sir, my master would like a word. Then he'll see you are driven home."

His master? Unease twisted my stomach, but as the offer had more potential for safety, I followed the young man to the carriage. What awaited me there could not possibly be worse than what waited behind me in the darkness.

He opened the door, and I peered inside. Upon finding it empty, I sent the man a questioning look.

"My master wishes to speak with you in private at his townhome in Mayfair," he said.

"Mayfair?" That gave me pause. Generally speaking, my creditors did not own townhomes in *Mayfair*. But who else would wish me to call on them at this hour? Or know where to find me, for that matter?

I nearly laughed. That last one wasn't so difficult to determine, in truth.

"Aye, sir, Mayfair," the young man responded. "He said if you seemed hesitant to give you this." He handed me a calling card.

"Lord Cartwell?" I asked, reading the embossed name.

I knew of the man, but I had never engaged with him socially. He was at least twice my age of thirty. What could he wish to speak to me about? I looked to the young man for answers, but he merely blinked. It was likely he hadn't any idea of the purpose of the meeting.

"Very well," I said, climbing into the carriage. Perhaps it was unwise, but I was too curious now, and the other option of getting pummeled held no appeal.

We arrived in Mayfair at a quarter past four, and as I stared up at the lavish silhouette of the townhome owned by Lord Cartwell, I felt small and insignificant. I had friends who were members of the nobility, but there was something about the sheer opulence of this particular building that rankled my pride. I could never afford such a place, not even before I'd found myself in my current financial state.

The young man, whose name I had discovered was Thomas, led me inside and up the stairs to the drawing room where I found Lord Cartwell waiting for me. The marquess had little hair left on his head and wore spectacles that caught the flicker of firelight from the hearth, but his coat boasted the finest quality London had to offer. His countenance was a welcoming one, his stance and expression relaxed, easing some of my discomfort.

I bowed to him, and he nodded in acknowledgment. "Thank you for agreeing to come."

"To refuse a marquess is unwise," I said, taking a seat when he gestured for me to make myself comfortable.

"As is spending your nights at The Sparrow." One of his bushy gray brows rose as if daring me to contradict him.

What did this man know of desperation, here in his extravagant townhouse? He would never understand. I forced a smile. "Indeed."

Lord Cartwell sat down on the chaise opposite me. "It is late, and I wish to keep this as brief as possible. I need your help, and in exchange, I will pay off the entirety of your current debts."

My mind stumbled to comprehend his words. "You...what?"

"For the last decade, I have been a man of sound investment. My wealth speaks to that fact. But I have also had my share of disappointments. There is always a risk, to which I am not adverse, but sometimes a failed investment comes down to more than rotten luck. I have reason to believe my most recent venture left me a victim of fraud, and I am determined to see justice is served."

I ran a hand through my hair. I didn't have the money to make investments. Not anymore. It was a form of gambling even I refused to touch. "I'm not certain I understand. What use am I in helping you achieve justice? Your request would be better served to a Runner or the Magistrate."

"Ah, but this snake is too cunning to slither out of his hiding hole. He uses false names to gather investors and then practically disappears. I have a lead, though, for his next scheme. His investment meetings are held in private, by invitation only, and I have made too many inquiries to ever receive one now. But a new face with money ready for the taking? That will appeal to him."

I laughed. "Money ready for the taking? You forget, my lord, where it is your man found me. I cannot even pay my creditors, let alone pretend to have the capital to invest."

Lord Cartwell leaned forward, resting his elbows on his knees. His expression shifted into something more serious and determined. "And if you are given the capital necessary to gain his attention? I want justice, Mr. Davis, and I will have it, whatever the cost."

I swallowed. The man did not jest. I could sense it.

"According to my sources, the next meeting of investors will take place in Bath after the summer Season concludes," he continued. "He's swindled too many London elites to attempt another ruse here for a time."

"And how am I to gain his notice? How would someone like me ever find this man?"

Lord Cartwell swatted the air. "That is the easy part. His many aliases have frequented gaming hells across England over the years. He is sure to do the same in Bath. All you must do is spend time there, toss around a bit of money, and let slip that you have plenty of capital to spare. He will take the bait."

I shook my head. "Let's assume I agree to go along with this plan. How am I to prevent him from discovering who I am? There are too many rumors surrounding my name and even more in regards to my financial state. Surely someone will recognize me."

"You underestimate the power of a good disguise, Mr. Davis. We are all capable of pretending to be someone we are not. Let us not forget that this man has done so for over a decade. Poetic irony that his fall will come under the same guise." Lord Cartwell smiled as if the thought pleased him. "So, here is my proposition in full. I will afford you twenty thousand pounds to—"

"Twenty thousand pounds!" The man was mad.

"Allow me to finish, if you please. Twenty thousand pounds to gain this man's attention. Use it to gamble your way into his circle. Find out where his meeting is to be held and get the evidence I need. Once he has been brought before the courts, I will grant you another twenty thousand for your efforts. In addition, I will see that all current debts are paid. I want nothing to distract you."

My jaw hung slack. What was I to say to this? It sounded too good to be true, and things too good to be true were often not worth the trouble they inevitably created. If this man was, as Lord Cartwell claimed, deeply involved in scandal, he was not a man to be trifled with. There were dangers to consider. Men had been murdered for far less than threatening to expose criminals.

"I…"

"Allow me one last chance to convince you," said Cartwell. "As I stated, this man has gone by many aliases over the last decade, but if I am not mistaken, you might be familiar with one in particular. Does the name Daniel Whitticker mean anything to you?"

My blood ran cold as my mind filled with memories and the familiar guilt that accompanied them. I clenched the armrests of the chair and swallowed hard. "Daniel Whitticker was an alias? And he is still here in England, tricking people out of their money?"

Lord Cartwell's expression softened. "I'm afraid so."

Daniel Whitticker had been the start of my downward spiral, the catalyst to failure after failure and the gradual decline of my family's fortune. For years, I had blamed myself—I always would—but now there was a chance for justice. A chance to finally absolve myself. I had to take it, whatever the danger.

I extended my hand toward the marquess. "Lord Cartwell, you have a deal."

Chapter Two

SABRINA

Immaculate bookkeeping was not on the list of impressive talents my father would have once presented potential suitors, but it had become a skill all the same. Without a husband to manage the finances, it was a necessity, one in which I found enjoyment.. There was something utterly freeing about being in charge of my future.

And also morbidly terrifying.

I stared down at the ledger. The numbers were not as healthy as they had been six months ago. It was not unusual for me to see a decline through the winter months. Families often stood in need of more charity when the harsh, frigid air settled in, and since the majority of my expenditures revolved around that charity, it was only logical that my finances would suffer.

My brows pinched. It was nearly June now, and as such, my spending should have decreased. Instead, I had spent more than expected, despite how warm it had been.

A knock sounded on the door of the small parlor that I had turned into a cozy study, and Helen—my lady's maid, who held additional roles as housekeeper, cook, and my companion— entered with a tray of tea and several biscuits. She and my butler were the only two hired staff.

I glared down at Helen's offering when she placed it on my desk.

"Oh, don't ye make that face," she said, placing both hands on her hips. "Ye haven't eaten a thing today, Your Grace. Didn' touch breakfast. Thought I might tempt ye with these."

I winced at her use of my title, one she only utilized in private when she was cross with me. Helen knew how much I despised it. It didn't suit me given how far I had fallen in the eyes of the *ton*, and besides, those two words brought back memories of my late husband. Memories I would rather forget.

"I am not hungry," I replied. "You may have it, and if you do not want it, I am certain the little Jones boy down the street would gladly accept the biscuits."

Helen tilted her head to one side, glowering. "Ye cannot go without food for days on end. I have already taken your dresses in twice."

I bit my lip. She was correct, though I had no desire to admit it. I could go without for a few days when others went without for weeks at a time.

"Take the biscuits to little Freddy, and I will drink the tea." I quickly continued when Helen opened her mouth to protest. "And I will eat three courses at dinner."

Helen eyed me with suspicion. "Then I'm in charge of the portions tonight. Last night, the servin's you took weren't much at'll."

"Very well," I agreed. "And before you begin dinner preparations, I need to visit Sinclair's."

"You wish to check on Mrs. Barton?" Helen guessed.

"Yes."

Helen nodded. "I'll be in the kitchen until you need me then."

I lifted a brow, my gaze flicking to the biscuits on the tray.

Helen groaned. "I'll be in the kitchen *after* I take little Freddy some biscuits."

"Thank you. And see to it you send extra for his family, please."

My lady's maid sighed and shook her head, but I did not miss the smile she wore as she took the tray with her out of the study. For all Helen's chiding, she was glad of our efforts to help those we could. She had a good heart, a charitable one. It was for that reason I had begged her to come with me to Bath. She'd been my lady's maid since before my debut into society five years previous, but the two of us had grown close over the last two in particular. Whatever formality had once existed between mistress and servant had all but disappeared.

I preferred it that way.

My attention returned to the ledgers resting in front of me, and I pursed my lips. Even before my husband's death and my fall in society, I had never excelled at budgeting. I would spend Father's money on dresses and trimmings—whatever fashionable piece I deemed necessary to impress. Then, I married The Duke of Rochester and spent his money as well, out of habit and per his request that I look the part of his duchess. Now I simply spent all of my own funds—which was quite small given how little my father had asked for on my behalf during the marriage negotiations—though it was no longer on dresses and trimmings.

Well, at least not for myself.

I closed the ledger with a heavy sigh. Regardless of what or who I was spending my money on, the truth of the matter was that sooner or later my coffers would run dry. Sooner, by the looks of things if I remained idle. I had no estate to provide an income. I had no skill in any sort of trade.

But I did have years worth of observing my father's business dealings. While he had not been an example of an upstanding gentleman or businessman, I had learned much from watching his interactions and nosing through his financial records. It was by investing what little I had received from my dowry that I had managed to survive this long.

And by a fair amount of economizing and a great deal of tears.

Still, I was proud to stand on my own, to grasp independence. All I needed now was to find a new investment venture, as I had done multiple times since moving to Bath, to continue my work.

I left the study and, after retrieving my bonnet and reticule, followed the corridor to the foyer. As if he could sense my approach, Mr. Foxgrove met me at the door, his wide smile highlighting the wrinkles forming on his cheeks, forehead, and around his eyes.

"Good morning, Your Grace."

I shot him a glare. "Imagine how much better the morning would be, Fox, if you simply called me Sabrina."

The butler only chuckled. Unlike Helen, Cornelius Foxgrove refused to address me by anything other than my title, no matter how often I pleaded with him to do otherwise.

Were it completely up to me, he would not even be employed in my townhome on Gay Street. My cousin and heir to my father's holdings, Phillip, had insisted that—if I would not accept his offer to stay with him and his young family—he must be permitted to employ a butler on my behalf for safety. Much as I hated to admit it, having a man within the house at night did put me at ease.

This area of Bath, while not the height of wealth, was not particularly prone to criminal activity, but neither I nor Helen, who stood at least half a head shorter than me, would fare well against an intruder. Thus, I had accepted Mr. Foxgrove's role in my life.

And that role happened to come with formal address.

"Shall I call for a hackney, Your Grace?" asked Fox, though why he bothered, I might never understand. I was not one to spare a farthing on a hackney when I could put the money to better use.

"No, Helen and I will walk. I have longed for the summer sun too long to give up the opportunity."

Fox nodded. "Very good, Your Grace. There's not a single cloud in the sky this morning. Your walk should be a pleasant one."

He left then to fetch Helen, and within minutes, the two of us were off to Sinclair's Haberdashery on Milsom Street. The morning air was, to my satisfaction, rather perfect, and the feel of the sun's rays on my skin helped to ease all of my concerns regarding my declining funds. There was something about a warm day that immediately lifted my mood, especially with the scent of blooming flowers floating on the light breeze.

Sinclair's was often quite busy, a testament to the success that offered them a strange sort of status, generally accepted by both the upper and lower classes. There were, of course, members of the *ton* and gentry who would always stick up their noses at a merchant family. My father would have been one of them.

At one time, *I* would have been one of them.

I shook the depressing thought away. It was not with great frequency that I allowed myself to reminisce about the person I once was. That vain and unfeeling woman had gone, or so I hoped, and I was far too busy making up for her past misdeeds to linger on memories.

Helen and I entered the shop and were immediately bombarded by an array of colorful fabrics and ribbons. Penny Sinclair stood near the counter, her copper hair pulled back in a simple chignon, several curls having escaped. They bounced against her cheeks as she spoke animatedly with a patron, the same bright smile fixed on her freckled face as always.

Penny and I were of the same age of four and twenty, and I had liked her immediately when I first moved to Bath. Her spirited personality and ability to see the good in others made me feel welcomed, especially following so much scandal surrounding my father's imprisonment. I had very few friends, and at present, she and Helen were the only two women with whom I would consider myself close. My cousin's wife, Grace, was pleasant enough, but I so rarely saw them or visited London. Stepping foot into a city that still whispered rumors and insults under its breath held no appeal for me.

Helen and I browsed the fabric selections while Penny was occupied, which resulted in me turning down several requests by my lady's maid to purchase said fabric so she could sew me a new dress. Helen was excellent at needlework.

"But this would look lovely on you." Helen held a bolt of pink muslin near my face. "The way it sets off your dark hair and eyes."

"I am not here to shop for myself," I whispered. "You know this. It would flatter you, though."

Helen's brown hair was light compared to mine, an almost black, and I envied her blue eyes.

Helen glanced around us to ensure no one was watching and then forced her lips into a pout. In public, she was careful to act as a proper servant, but within the walls of the haberdashery, when patrons were preoccupied, she sometimes let her guard down. "You never get nothing for yerself. Why not do so this once? You are a duchess."

The word pulled my face tight, and I shushed her before whispering my retort. "A duchess would have an experienced modiste make her gown. When I am ready for a new wardrobe, I will see to it. Right now, the money is better spent on someone who needs it."

"Ye do need it with how slim yer gettin'," Helen muttered.

I heaved an exasperated sigh. "To what end? I do not attend assemblies or go promenading with gentlemen. What good is a new dress to me when the ones I have"—though I mentally admitted they no longer fit in the most flattering way—"are perfectly functional."

Helen's nose wrinkled. "Functional isn't the aim I had in mind. How do ye expect a gentleman to ask to promenade when ye don't let the men in town know ye are here at all? "

That was entirely it. I had no desire for courting or marriage or any interaction with men. I'd had my fill of those things.

Memories of a pair of brilliant green eyes and an easy smile pressed on my mind, unwelcome and altogether jolting. I had not thought of *him* in years. Or was it weeks? Never mind that.

"I do not need another husband," I blurted.

"Never said anythin' about a husband." Helen turned back to the wall of fabric, smiling. "But if that's somethin'—"

"No," I spat a little too loudly. One marriage, short as it had been, was enough to last me a lifetime. The old duke had been more than twice my age and as heartless as my father. I had no desire to live under such circumstances again. "It is not on my mind. It is not even in the vicinity of my mind. It may as well be swimming in The Channel."

Helen nodded, though her smile never faded. "As ye say. I only wish to see ye happy."

Happy? I was happy, was I not? I spent my time however I pleased. I had freedom previously unknown to me. There were no demands to attend parties or balls. No expectations for calling hours and perfect sophistication. Certainly no husband to demand things of me I didn't wish to give. Perhaps I did not live as luxuriously as I once had, but I felt certain I was happier than ever before.

But was that happiness or merely an improvement? Surely the two must go hand in hand.

"I am happy," I said to myself more than to Helen. "But I shall be even happier once I've spoken to Penny about Mrs. Barton. I must know whether her health has improved."

"Alright, then." Helen studied me, a seriousness to her expression that hinted at concern. "Helping people is a grand thing. Heaven knows there be more than a few who owe ye gratitude. Just don't forget to take care of yerself, too."

I swallowed against the dryness in my throat. I was not accustomed to having someone care about me. My father never had, nor the duke, and I could hardly remember my mother ever offering me a hug, let alone deeper affection. Helen's genuine worry for my well-being was foreign but appreciated, even if I didn't believe it was currently warranted. A few loose dresses were nothing to fret over, nor were the brief stints of dizziness that occasionally accosted me.

Once Penny had finished assisting the other patrons, she bounded toward us cheerfully. "Good morning, Your—"

I stopped her with a glare, and both she and Helen giggled.

"Forgive me, Sabrina. I am not accustomed to speaking so informally to a duchess." Penny shook her head. "Or to a duchess at all, really. I may never grow used to it."

"It is no bother," I lied. "Tell me, have you heard from Mrs. Barton? Has she recovered from her fall?"

Last week, Mrs. Barton had tripped over an empty crate in the market and injured her leg. I had sent her family an anonymous basket of food as well as a tincture from the apothecary to help with the pain.

"She is much recovered," said Penny. "Limping, but it does not seem to bother her so severely."

"That is fantastic news." I hesitated briefly before continuing. "Is she in need of anything else?"

"She was in yesterday with the children," said Penny, an uncommon frown filling her expression. "Their clothes are looking more and more tattered. She came for buttons, but I saw the way she eyed the fabric. I know it is months away, but I fear they will not have warm enough clothing for winter. Mr. Barton has yet to return, and they've not heard from him in months."

I nodded, swallowing the familiar guilt that welled within me. Mrs. Barton and her family were not like the other charity cases I took on. "Then I'll see to it they have what they need. A coat for each of them and perhaps a new dress or two for both of the girls."

"That is mighty generous of you." Penny's smile returned.

I turned to face Helen, putting on my best pleading look. I couldn't sew worth a pence, and while I would hire out the work for coats, I could pay Helen extra to do the dresses.

"You could teach me," I added when Helen offered no response. "I would like to learn."

Helen shook her head, but her lips twitched. "A duchess sewin' a dress. I suppose if ye insist. We can make the dresses together, but"—a scheming look overtook her innocent face—"only if ye agree to make one for yourself."

I tried not to grimace. "Very well."

Over the next quarter hour, Helen and I perused the fabrics with the two girls in mind, and I added the pink muslin we'd admired before for myself. This endeavor held my attention until two well-dressed men entered the shop, deep in conversation as they browsed the selection of hats on display.

"So, he is here?" one of them asked, turning a silk hat over in his hand.

His companion glanced about the shop, and I pinned my focus to the display of feathers in front of me, my head slightly cocked.

"Yes. It is my understanding that he arrived in Bath yesterday. The meeting for investors will be held sometime in mid-August."

Investors? My brows lifted. This was precisely the conversation I needed to overhear. Eavesdropping was, perhaps, an unladylike pursuit, but I had gained insight into many investment ventures by listening to men converse. Women were rarely made privy to such information, especially women who, like me, had no husband and lived on their own.

"And how are we to garner an introduction? Arthur Westmore is more elusive than a fox, or so I've heard. He keeps his investors close, and his lack of social presence makes joining his circle difficult."

"True," said his companion. "But I've heard rumors that he intends to frequent The Bottom Ale while here, possibly to recruit. All we need do is spend some time there as well and look the part." The man placed the top hat on his head with a lazy smirk. "Not a difficult task."

As the two men each paid for a new hat, the words rattled around in my mind repeatedly, creating a strange mixture of anticipation and annoyance in my chest.

All we need do is spend some time there as well and look the part.

Such a simple plan, and yet...

I scoffed, scowling at the peacock feather I held. Easy for them, perhaps. As men, they were welcomed into the gambling dens. They were taken seriously when it came to money. And if this Arthur Westmore kept his circle tight, he would likely never consider the inclusion of female investors.

"Look the part," I muttered. "If only—"

The thought melted into something more. Something ridiculous. Something altogether brilliant...

I turned sharply toward Helen, who was attempting to decide which lace trimmings would best suit the pink muslin fabric for my dress. "I have an idea."

"Hmm?" Helen did not so much as lend me her attention.

I continued anyway, dropping my voice to a whisper as I stepped closer to her. "I know how I might get more funds to help the Bartons."

Helen paused, and her face contorted as she considered me. "I shan't like this idea."

She wouldn't, but that would not stop her from helping me. Helen was more than a servant; she was my friend, and I was confident she would agree to this absurd scheme.

A wide grin split my face. "I do believe we may require more fabric."

Chapter Three

GREGORY

A set of familiar green eyes stared back at me from an almost unrecognizable face. I grimaced at my reflection in the looking glass. I was not accustomed to having a beard, and were it not strictly necessary for the mission I was about to undertake, I would not have one now.

Standing in front of the mirror, I tilted my head from side to side and eyed the scruff adorning my face with a mixture of disgust and annoyance. This, decidedly, did not suit me.

But I had little choice in the matter at present. I had arrived in Bath two weeks ago, taking up lodging at the Crescent thanks to Lord Cartwell, and kept within the walls of my rooms until the blasted facial hair grew in. I could not risk anyone recognizing me. So long as I kept away from the more social scenes of the city, the beard should conceal my identity well enough.

Once I had completed my task, I would shave it off.

I tucked a pocket watch into my waistcoat. It had been difficult to order new clothes that were stylistically flat when I usually tended toward bright colors that caught the eye upon entering a room. My closest friend, James, had often called me a dandy, but I preferred to think of myself as fashionably aware. Regardless, my new alias was boring and wore different shades of brown and green, hues that would make me blend in with an old, dirty rug were I to lie on the floor.

Alas, sacrifices had to be made.

Hopefully, between my hairy face and new wardrobe, my false identity would outshine any chance of recognition. The clothing had certainly taken my mother by surprise when I bid her goodbye before she left London to return to our country estate.

She had not been at all happy with my refusal to answer her questions about where *I* intended to go now that the Season had concluded. I would keep this strange dealing with Lord Cartwell from her, just as I kept the state of our finances secret. Lucinda Davis was not easily fooled, however, and she likely suspected our affairs to be in distress to some degree. I had no desire for her to discover the extent of our problems, and with Lord Cartwell's generosity, she never would.

I tugged on my cravat until it came loose so I could redo it. After two attempts, I gave up on the matter and called for Thomas to assist me. While I had accepted my lack of tying skills, I couldn't afford a lopsided knot anymore. Looking the part of a wealthy heir was essential. Cartwell had sent his man with me to Bath, partially, I assumed, to keep an eye on me and partially because I hadn't employed a valet for some time. Yet another reason my mother was likely suspicious.

At least Thomas's presence would ensure my cravat was perfectly knotted.

Tonight marked my first attempt at meeting Mr. Arthur Westmore, the new alias of the man I'd known as Daniel Whitticker. What his real name was, neither I nor Lord Cartwell had yet determined, but it was information I would need if we were to bring him to justice. Gaining that particular detail would require an invitation into his exclusive circle, and according to Cartwell, my best chance of achieving that was to gamble my way in. To make myself appear wealthy and willing to toss about money with reckless abandon.

Not a difficult task with twenty thousand pounds from the marquess at my disposal.

With a final study in the looking glass, I sighed with frustrated acceptance and offered a word of gratitude to Thomas. I collected my hat and made my way out of the townhouse. Though the sun had set, the air still held a warmth to it, and the faint scent of blooming trees within the Crescent gardens tickled my nose.

I hired a hackney and instructed the jarvey to drive me to Beau Street. There was less late-night bustle about the city tonight with those having come from London following the Season already settled. Once the balls began at the assembly halls next week, things would be different, and I would exercise more stealth journeying about town. The likelihood of anyone recognizing me was low as I had never spent time in Bath before now, but still, I would not risk the opportunity Lord Cartwell had afforded me.

His payment would save my estate. I would finally crawl out from beneath my debts and *stay* out.

So, until I could determine whether my disguise was without cracks, I would live in the shadows of the gaming hells by night and keep to my rooms otherwise.

Once on Beau Street, I paid for my hackney and then followed the dimly-lit lamps to the end of the street before turning down a short alley filled with shadows. There, I approached the door of The Bottom Ale, a pub that wore its own sort of disguise, masquerading as an honest place of business to hide the illegal gambling rooms it housed.

I hadn't known which gaming hell Westmore frequented upon my arrival in Bath, but as there were far fewer here than in London, it had not taken long to inquire about the matter and narrow my search. I had no guarantee Westmore would be present tonight, as I'd not found him the previous two nights I had come. Tonight, however, would be different; I could feel it.

I entered the building to find a few tables, mostly empty of patrons, and a maid in a worn, brown dress. The food offered by the pub held little appeal, but it seemed there were a handful of souls brave enough to risk filling their stomachs.

"What can I do for ye?" The maid approached me and, recognizing me from nights previous, offered a toothy grin. "Back for more, Mr. Carrow?"

"Indeed," I said, responding to my alias. "Busy night?"

She took my meaning and stepped closer, lowering her voice. "'E's here tonight, sir."

I nodded and slipped her a farthing for the information. Westmore had come, and anticipation bubbled in my chest. I'd given up hope of facing the man who had tricked me out of so much money, and I wasn't foolish enough to think that my history would make this mission easy. The mere mention of his former alias by Lord Cartwell had dug up anger I had long since buried. Now, it swam leisurely at the surface, and if I was not careful, I would give myself away before finding the evidence I needed to achieve true justice.

I drew in a deep breath, following the long corridor to the back of the building where the card rooms waited. Several tallow candles lit the narrow hall, leaving the space with more shadows than anything and the distinct scent of mutton. The card room was much the same with the added smell of pipe smoke. There were no windows to allow the room extra light, which generally aided the house in its underhanded dealings.

But it would also aid me. Darkness served to protect my identity as well as the hair on my face.

I joined a faro table with two other men, neither of which had the correct build to be Westmore, and once seated, casually took in the room. Would I even recognize the man I'd known as Daniel Whitticker? It had been years, and he likely changed his appearance after each ruse.

Not that it mattered. Even if I did recognize the man, I could not simply walk up to him. No, I would need for Westmore to come to me.

"How much in chips, Mr. Carrow?"

The banker's question snapped my attention back to the table. "Five thousand pounds, please."

The banker nodded and counted out my chips. My heart jolted when he passed me the pile in neat little stacks. It wasn't often I came into possession of so many, and the idea of gambling without the tether of debt sent a thrill through me.

A new deck was cut. Normally, I would begin with a handful of shillings, but tonight, I had a part to play. I slid a hundred pounds worth onto the eight of spades. Once the table had warmed and the deck depleted, I would wager more.

And this time I would be sure to keep better track of the cards.

I may not have a debt to satisfy, but that did not mean I didn't wish to win. After all, Cartwell had not asked for the money to be returned. Whatever profit I turned with it was mine to keep.

Two other punters placed their wagers. The first was a portly man, likely in his late fifties. He laid chips on several cards and leaned back in his chair, smoking his pipe. Relaxed and uncaring were adequate descriptors. He reminded me of Mr. Carlisle. Was he playing for distraction as well?

The second man hesitated to place his wager, his brows furrowed as he stared down at his pile of chips. He had far less to gamble with, but I would not judge him for it. I often wore similar shoes, and having few chips did not mean the night would prove unsuccessful for him.

The fellow was a make weight, far younger than I, and wore overly large spectacles. His hair was mostly hidden within a *passé* brown cap, but a few dark curls peeked out from beneath the rim. There was a wariness to his expression as he slid his chips onto the six, and I wondered if it was the result of a calculating personality or lack of experience in the gambling den.

Perhaps it was a combination of both.

Either way, I needed to stop analyzing my tablemates and focus on my strategy.

Several rounds passed, and having kept my wager low, I found myself without gain or loss. The same could not be said of the other punters, who had both seen a reduction in their chips. The larger man seemed unconcerned by this and continued to bet haphazardly on the five despite it having been revealed four times already.

The smaller man, who the banker had addressed as Mr. Blyth, had not ceased to look uncomfortable since the game began, displaying more hesitancy with each round and chip lost. It was he who stole my attention most often, and not solely due to his obvious lack of skill at the tables and uncanny silence, for he had not spoken a word since I sat down. There was something odd about him that I simply could not put my finger on.

Something familiar?

Nonsense. He was far too young to be the man who had once swindled me, and I'd spent little enough time in ballrooms as of late to be acquainted with a gentleman fresh out of Cambridge or Oxford.

Still, there was something...

I rubbed a hand over my chin and immediately winced at the feel of hair on my skin. I hated this beard.

"How is the game, gents?" A man sat down in the chair to my left, and my stomach lurched. I hadn't been sure I would recognize Daniel Whitticker, and based on looks alone, I might not have.

His features were almost foreign to me—mousey brown hair that curled at the ends with eyes of the same hue, average build, and even the shape of his nose and chin was decidedly ordinary—but his voice...that had haunted me for years, and I knew it instantly.

My portly tablemate grunted. "I've no luck, and neither have these two." He pointed a chubby finger at both me and Mr. Blyth. "The house is hot tonight, and I think I'll take my leave."

Once the man had gone, the newcomer leaned back in his chair and clasped his hands. His gaze wandered over our chips in assessment. "Shame. One never knows when luck will find them. Or when that luck will run dry."

"Indeed," I said. "We can only rely on instinct and hope." I stacked three thousand pounds worth of chips on the seven. This was it—the moment I needed to lure Westmore in. Whether I won or lost this round, it didn't matter. I only needed to display my fortune and willingness to part with it. Westmore would take the bait.

"And you, Mr. Westmore?" asked the banker. "Care to join the game?"

A quiet gasp sounded to my right, and I glanced at Mr. Blyth. His wide eyes were fixated on Westmore. Had he heard of the man?

"Ten thousand in chips," said Westmore. "And I'll match Mr. Carrow's wager on the seven."

He knew my name, which meant he'd inquired after me. If I had already gained his attention, that would bode well for my plans.

"Lucky seven," I said with a more genuine smile. "I have a good feeling about this round."

"All in on the seven." A high tenor voice grated from next to me, and I turned in time to see Mr. Blyth shoving what remained of his chips to the center of the table. It wasn't uncommon for two players to wager on the same card, but three?

My brows drew tight.

"Daring move," said Westmore with a chuckle. "Someone isn't afraid to take a risk."

I glared at Mr. Blyth, who was too busy preening like a peacock at the praise to notice. He reminded me of a woman receiving a compliment on a dress.

The banker drew from the deck, revealing first a king and then a seven.

"Well done!" Westmore clapped, his attention centered on Blyth. "You've made an excellent comeback in one round. We must credit Carrow, though. He chose the card first and received a handsome reward himself. Tell us, Carrow, where shall we place our bets this round?"

My jaw clenched, but I put on a smile as I shifted my chips to the nine. "Here. And I'll add all my earnings from the last round to my bet."

Nine thousand pounds. That sum would grab his attention, surely.

"All in again," said Mr. Blyth, sliding his chips over to the nine.

"Again?" I asked. It was one thing for the fellow to bet everything, but to follow my lead? There was nothing in the rules against it, but the maneuver picked at my annoyance.

"Yes." Mr. Blyth met my gaze briefly, then tucked his chin to his chest. He certainly had rather thick lashes for a man, and they constantly brushed against the inside of his spectacles. Or perhaps the lack of lighting was merely playing tricks on me.

"I believe I'll sit this one out," said Westmore. He slumped back in his chair, arms folded across his chest and amusement written over his face.

The banker drew, first a seven and then a nine. "Winners!"

Westmore clapped dramatically. "Well done, Blyth! Big risk; big reward. No one can claim you a coward."

"Not a coward, but a pest," I muttered.

Despite my quiet tone, Blyth had heard me, and for the first time, met my gaze squarely. A slow smile tugged at his lips, smug and altogether irritating.

Fantastic. I was winning more money than usual, and I couldn't even enjoy it because of the nuisance next to me. He was riding my strategy. He was stealing Westmore's focus.

"Not bad, Blyth," I said with a calm I most certainly did not feel. "Perhaps I should follow you."

There had only been one deuce revealed thus far, giving it high odds of a loss or win. I reminded myself it didn't matter so long as Westmore noticed how much I was willing to throw down. Still, part of me wished to see Blyth lose it all, but by his own volition, not from following my lead.

Which was why I would not place my bet first this time.

I lifted a brow when he hesitated to make a move. We waited long enough that the banker questioned our desire to continue the game.

"Come, don't quit now," said Westmore. "Things are finally getting interesting. Carrow here clearly has an eye for the winning card."

That was all it took—a little praise—to restore my confidence. Blyth might be an opportunist, but I was here to gain Westmore's favor, and I would not bow out before I had achieved my goal.

I leaned forward to shift my chips onto the deuce, but Blyth moved faster, clearly reading my intention and dumping his own chaotically before I could. His chips nearly covered the entire card, and I scowled at him. "That was my pick."

His lips twitched. "Was it? I could argue you are following my lead, as you suggested."

"No, I intended to go there all along." I couldn't hide the indignation in my voice. The last thing I needed was the deuce to win and Blyth to receive the credit. Why did it feel as though the man was attempting to steal Westmore's attention from me? Could he be on a similar mission to garner an invite into Westmore's circle?

Well, I wouldn't back down. The deuce still held good odds, and I would stick with my gut.

I shifted my chips next to Blyth's pile and informed the banker of my wager, then held my breath as the first card was turned over.

My stomach sank as the man called out, "Deuce for the banker!"

Chapter Four

SABRINA

Why anyone would choose to risk their money this way, I would never understand. I had scarcely felt so sick in my entire life. Not only had I lost a sum that would have helped dozens of families for months, but I had also depleted a great portion of my funds.

All in an instant on one lousy game of chance.

I could be angry with Mr. Carrow for choosing the deuce this round, but in reality, the fault rested with me. He had seemed so sure of the winning cards the first two rounds, and since his instinct had proven correct, I had blindly followed him a third time.

Well, mostly followed. I had guessed at his intention to bet on the deuce and beat him to it, which—to my great satisfaction—had aggravated him. Why I took such delight in his frustrations, I could not say, but it had been an added benefit to gaining Mr. Westmore's attention. The drive to impress him and be done with this entire gambling façade is what had pushed me to bet irresponsibly.

Not that betting low and safe had done much to assist me before the man arrived at our table. If I had learned anything tonight, it was that I did not possess much skill when it came to faro.

"Rotten luck," said Westmore, his tone laced with false empathy.

Mr. Carrow shrugged and then asked for a new stack of chips, which he eagerly placed on the four. I nearly guffawed. How could he be so relaxed about losing that much money *and* continue to wager more?

But I hadn't missed the way his face had paled when the banker announced the last card, even in the dim lighting of the candle-lit room and the spectacles that made my vision less than clear. Darkness could only veil so much, and his frustration and concern were two things the shadows failed to conceal.

Why, then, did he keep going? He did seem rather determined to earn Mr. Westmore's praise, and I wondered if we might have similar goals.

"What say you, Blyth?" asked Mr. Carrow, shaking me from my musings. "Care to bet on my number again?"

He was taunting me, and were I dressed as a lady and were we in a ballroom, I might have simply ignored the remark and walked away. I might have given him the cut direct. But we were not in a ballroom, and with my breeches and waistcoat, I most certainly was not dressed like a lady. I was acting as a man, and I had never seen a man back down from a taunt.

"I think I'll take my chances with the queen this time," I said, then asked the banker to supply me with more chips.

Mr. Carrow huffed. "A loss is all that was required to recoup your betting etiquette, I see."

Betting etiquette? I was quite sure no such thing existed. My father had never spoken of gambling *etiquettes*, nor had the late duke, and I had overheard a fair number of their conversations on the matter.

I sat up straighter, lifting my chin. "You are one to talk of etiquette, sir. That beard is far from either flattering or proper."

The jab hit its mark—deeply if the way Mr. Carrow's hand shot to cover his face was any indication. He rubbed over his scruff, wincing all the while as if he himself did not care for the facial hair, then sneered at me. "Not that it is any of your business, but I have no desire to look *proper*. My family is quite strict in their expectations, and I've no wish to conform."

"So the beard is a point of rebellion?" I asked, curious against my will. I didn't precisely care for beards on any gentleman, and neither did the majority of society, but I had never considered it might be used for such a purpose.

"Yes. As is my presence here. Were he alive, my father would have my head." At this, he placed his attention on the banker and lifted a brow. Apparently, the man had been engrossed in our conversation and forgotten his purpose, for he flushed and turned over the next two cards.

The round ended in a wash, as did the ones that followed. The game neared its end, and a quick glance at Mr. Westmore told me he had grown bored of watching us play without failure or success. We were losing him.

I frowned. No, not *we*. I cared nothing about Mr. Carrow's reason for being at the tables, even if it was the same as my own. In fact, it would only complicate matters were it true.

"Thanks for the entertainment, gents." Mr. Westmore stood, and a surge of panic rushed through me. I could not return to this gaming hell again. Every moment spent here put my reputation at risk, or what little remained of it. Acting as a man was not in my repertoire of skills. Eventually, someone would discover the truth.

But what choice did I have? The money gained by a sound investment would give me leave for more charity work, and that was the only way I would ever make up for the misdeeds of my past or my father's. I needed to leave here with what I had come to get, and that was an invitation to Westmore's investment meeting.

I stood abruptly, nearly toppling the chair. All eyes shifted to me.

I cleared my throat, making my tone intentionally deep. "Perhaps a different sort of game would suit me better. Generally, it is business ventures where my money excels."

The statement was too on the nose. I regretted it immediately, but I had spoken in desperation. Mr. Westmore forced a smile, clearly aware of my attempt to inject myself into his business. "Indeed. Such risks can be quite rewarding." He nodded to me, then to Mr. Carrow. "Goodnight, gents. Perhaps we will meet at the tables again."

My heart sank to my toes as I watched him walk away. Meet him at the tables again? I wasn't sure I could handle another night of this. I had lost a significant amount of money. Losing even another pound would hurt more than myself. So many people were depending on me, even if they hadn't any idea I claimed silent responsibility for their welfare.

"Excuse me." My voice came almost as a whisper, and I struggled to maintain composure, tears pricking my eyes. Crying here would do me no favors. I crossed the room and left the address to my townhome on Gay Street, stating it was a temporary residence where the bill could be sent, and then exited the building into the alley.

Darkness filled the streets of Bath, and I immediately felt uneasy to be out this time of night alone. Helen had insisted on coming with me, but I had convinced her, after a great amount of pleading, to stay behind. Men did not walk about town with chaperones, and her presence would have given me away.

But now, alone on the cobblestones beneath the dim, flickering lantern lights, I wished I had not been so convincing. Surely Helen could have waited against the wall or outside?

I shook my head. Neither of those options would have been safe for her. After all, gaming hells were not solely known for their games of chance. Men sought other pleasurable pursuits within those walls, and I would never put Helen in such a risky situation.

"Mr. Blyth!"

I had yet to make it out of the darkened alleyway, and my blood ran cold as footsteps approached from behind. I stopped and slowly turned to face Mr. Carrow, who looked nothing short of flustered. I could not entirely blame the man. Riding on his wins must have annoyed him, but the strategy had worked for a few rounds.

I cleared my throat, deepening my voice to an awkward and uncomfortable level, and adjusted the oversized spectacles on my nose. In truth, they belonged to Fox. Helen had pilfered them since my butler refused to lend them to me—not that I had told him what I needed them for.

Regardless, they distorted the edges of my vision, making the walls of the two buildings we stood between fuzzy, and in the darkness, the man before me appeared as little more than a silhouette with a grumpy frown.

The lack of clarity did nothing to settle my unease. "May I assist you with something?"

Mr. Carrow stopped a few paces in front of me and crossed his thick arms over his chest. Well, thick compared to mine. I was a rather petite sort of man by comparison, yet another thing not in my favor.

"Yes," he snapped. "You can help by staying out of my way from now on."

He was more than annoyed, and my skin prickled with awareness. I'd battled words with men and women alike in ballrooms, but to make an attempt while dressed as a man would not serve me well. I would stand no chance should the argument turn physical.

But I also hadn't decided whether I would give up on my mission to infiltrate Westmore's circle. I needed to invest in a profitable venture, now more than ever, and the only way to do that was by returning another night.

I fought a grimace. How unpleasant that idea was.

"What is it you wish me to do, exactly?" I asked, unwilling to look the coward by backing down. It may not be intelligent to push the man's temper, but it was also foolish to allow myself to be trodden upon. Respect would get me into Westmore's circle, not cowardice. Certainly a fine line to walk. "You cannot expect me to avoid the tables solely at your request."

"Not all tables, no. If you would keep your games away from Westmore and me, that would be appreciated."

Ah. So I had been correct in my suspicions. Mr. Carrow wished to earn Westmore's attention, same as I.

I squared my shoulders, hoping it would add to my presence and hide the niggling of fear swirling in my stomach. "Then I am afraid I cannot heed your request. Westmore is the reason I came to the tables at all."

Mr. Carrow swore and lifted his hat to run a hand through his hair. Between the darkness and degraded vision from the spectacles, I couldn't so much as make out the color of it. Still, the movement sparked a strange familiarity.

"Are you set upon investing with him then?" Mr. Carrow asked.

"That is my goal." Was it unwise to share this information with him? Likely so, but Mr. Carrow, I believed, had already guessed at my intentions, the same as I had guessed at his. Perhaps the shared objectives could benefit us both. We wanted the same thing, did we not?

"I have a proposition for you." I blurted the words before I could truly think them over. What was I doing? The last thing I wanted was to involve a man in my plans. He would ruin everything, never mind how he would react should he discover my identity.

"I'm listening." His curt tone suggested a lack of openness to anything I might say. I considered walking away without a word, but that would not solve our problem. Mr. Carrow would present himself at the tables again, and likely, so would I. Animosity would aid neither of us.

"We could assist each other," I said. "A proper alliance. We both want the same thing."

Mr. Carrow laughed without humor, shaking his head. "I highly doubt that is the case, nor do I think you could help me in any way."

My pride bristled. I had no skill at faro, but that did not mean I was useless. "To make money. Is that not what you hope to achieve by wooing Mr. Westmore? Everyone knows those close to him gain a fortune. Why not work together? Is he not more likely to respond to two gents risking their funds than one?"

Mr. Carrow's jaw tightened. "Not if one of those gents happens to be a poor player." He muttered the rest. "Though, that may prove an enticing lure."

Lure? I was not a piece of bait.

He continued before I could voice my opposition. "But I do not require your help. Had you not been in the way, I would have achieved my goals tonight. Now, I must return and risk even more to gain his attention, which will be difficult with how our conversation ended."

I winced. He was not entirely wrong. My pointed remarks on investments had sent Westmore practically running. I had not been subtle in my hopes of connection, and it had put him off. "I will own that I misspoke, but that does not mean we cannot assist one another."

Again, Mr. Carrow laughed. "I do not need your assistance."

I planted my hands on my hips. "I would wager you won't succeed on your own."

Mr. Carrow eyed me, his gaze drifting to my waist, and it was then I realized my mistake. Men did not generally put their hands on their hips in a display of sheer stubbornness, and not only that, but my voice had lost some of its depth. My arms dropped to my sides, and I fought the urge to shift on my feet. I could not afford such carelessness.

"I would bet two pounds you won't gain his attention tomorrow night," I said, forcing my tone low and hoping the taunt would make him forget my odd behavior.

Mr. Carrow stepped forward until he stood within inches of my boots. The smell of his citrusy soap poured over me, fragrant and strangely pleasing. This close, his height required I look up at him, and his once blurry face grew clear. His hair and beard were a light chestnut color, with curls poking out from beneath his black hat. But it was his eyes that snagged my attention.

Eyes that were a haunting, brilliant green.

My breath caught when he leaned forward, my body frozen with disbelief. Mr. Carrow spoke, his tone somehow both a threat and a warning. "It is in your best interest to stay away from Westmore. If you value whatever funds you possess, you will forget this pursuit."

He did not offer me a chance to respond, moving around me and out of the alleyway. It would not have mattered, anyway. I could not speak, not when my mind insisted on rummaging through memories.

I drew in a steadying breath. It could not be him. It simply couldn't. My mind, exhausted and anxious, had played a trick on me, and I would do well to forever ignore the similarities between Mr. Carrow and the handsome gentleman I could not seem to forget.

Chapter Five

SABRINA

The sky beyond my chamber window filled with the first hints of orange as the violets and deep blues of night faded. Below, a carriage rumbled along the cobblestone of Gay Street, the sound breaking the silence. Watching the sunrise had been a habit long before I moved to Bath, and I recalled the numerous occasions when I observed Father returning home at such an hour. I had wondered then what business pulled him out of our townhome so early.

I knew now the underhanded dealings and scandal he participated in required the veil of nighttime and secrecy.

Father had been a single-minded man with one objective in life: improving his wealth and precedence in society. He could gain neither of those things now that he had been transported to New South Wales. I was likely never to see him again.

The thought did not burden me. I had never meant anything more to him than my value as a bargaining chip. An investment for which he would eventually see a gain. The moment the late Duke of Rochester showed an inkling of interest in me after my debut, Father began the game, weaving a web to ensnare the duke and benefit from his connections.

I had been the web.

As the only child, born a daughter rather than an heir, I had but one useful purpose. Marrying me off to someone who would raise my father's esteem had been the plan since my birth. I'd gone along with it without complaint. Without thought. Why should I not? It was all I had ever known or expected.

I tightened my shawl around me and leaned against the wall, closing my eyes to fight a wave of dizziness. Once it had passed, I peered out the window to the dark street below. The air flowing through the open window held warmth, but a chill had fallen over me upon waking in the early hours, and I could not shake it. Sleep had been impossible the last few nights, and the lack of proper rest showed in the dark circles beneath my eyes and the exhaustion in my muscles.

I had not found the courage to return to The Bottom Ale, even after nearly a sennight of recovering from the outing. Mr. Carrow could not be Gregory Davis; I had spent hours attempting to convince myself of that. Still, those green eyes burned in my thoughts, and the niggling doubt kept me from donning my spectacles and waistcoat again.

A shame, since I had gone so far as to ask Helen to chop off a great portion of my hair for the scheme. I ran my fingers through the short strands and groaned just as Helen tapped lightly on my door. I bid her to enter.

"Up and about, I see." Her gaze wandered the length of my dressing gown, and then back to my head. She grimaced. It had taken nearly an hour of arguing to convince her to cut my hair, and she'd not stopped complaining even after the deed was done.

She approached with a sigh. "Let's get you dressed and downstairs to breakfast."

I nodded, though I hardly felt like eating anything. My failure at gambling and subsequently at gaining access to Mr. Westmore's newest investment venture had killed what little remained of my appetite. I needed a new plan. There had to be a way to reach the man without risking the money I had left.

Or my identity.

"And not because Mr. Carrow is, in actuality, Mr. Davis," I muttered. The idea was ridiculous. As far as I knew, the man never came to Bath. My concerns were an illusion derived from some nearly extinguished hope.

A hope for what, I did not precisely know.

Helen ceased her perusal of my closet and turned to face me. "Mr. Davis?"

"Never mind." I swatted her question away.

My lady's maid narrowed her eyes but did not press the matter. She wasn't unfamiliar with Mr. Davis since I had used the man years ago in an attempt to fulfill my father's wishes. He had demanded I remarry after the duke's death, so I'd set my sights on The Earl of Emerson, Mr. Davis's closest friend. Through extorting Mr. Davis's gambling habits, I'd gained the opportunity to lure the earl into courtship, but the scheme had disintegrated. The earl fell in love with someone else, and I refused to step between them.

That had been my first act of defiance, and my father never forgave me for it. That month spent at Mr. Davis's estate had changed everything.

With Helen's help, I dressed for the day and descended the stairs to the dining room. My rented rooms here were nothing grand, but I lived a comfortable existence. It had taken time to adjust at first, but I found I preferred this small home over the duke's grand estate. Something about the quaint living space brought me relief and security. It had become my haven, a place I could call my own, out of the judgmental eyes of the *ton*.

"The post, Your Grace," said Fox as I exited the dining room. He extended a silver salver to me where a single envelope rested.

My face scrunched, and I offered a simple 'thank you' as I took the missive into my study. Generally, the only letters I received were from my cousin's wife, but this was not written in her hand. My stomach twisted with nervous anticipation as I read.

To Her Grace, Duchess of Rochester

I extend an invitation to a picnic at Lime House to be held on the 7th of June. As I am aware of your current circumstances, I offer you the use of my carriage for conveyance and look forward to your attendance. Please meet at #5, The Circus at eleven sharp.

— Eleanore Anderton

I plopped into the chair at my desk with a heavy sigh. Since moving to Bath, I went out of my way to avoid social functions. That had not stopped women such as Mrs. Anderton from sending invitations. Many came with the hopes of foddering gossip and were not precisely genuine. Regardless, I always respectfully declined. I had no desire to return to the center of gossip. People had the tendency of long memories when it came to scandal.

I slid the invitation to the corner of my desk. Mingling with the upper class no longer appealed to me. That life was in the past.

"Ye did not eat much for breakfast." Helen's chiding tone rang from the doorway, and I looked up to find her scowling at me. She took a step into the room, her hands on her hips. "Ye promised to eat somethin'."

"And I did. I had a slice of honey cake and a cup of chocolate."

"Not nearly enough," said Helen.

"If it were up to you, I would eat enough to fill three grown men. Then you would have to fix my dresses. Again."

"'Twould be better than watching ye shrink," she muttered.

Warmth precipitated by her concern bled through my chest, but now was not the time to linger on it. "We need a new plan. I do not know if I can return to the card tables. It is too risky. I will if I must, but perhaps we can find a safer way for me to interact with Mr. Westmore that wouldn't require me to gamble away a fortune."

Helen looked nothing short of relieved. "Anything to keep ye out of the hells. I do not think my heart will survive another night of worrying whether ye'll return in one piece. What do ye have in mind?"

"Well, the most promising way to gain information, in my experience, is to leave the house. I cannot overhear things if I never abandon these walls."

Helen nodded, appearing far too pleased by this. "An outing, then. The sun would likely do ye some good, too."

I swallowed the urge to argue that I was perfectly well without the sun—or a large breakfast, for that matter—but to do so would waste precious time; Helen would not agree with me, anyway. I needed to find Mr. Westmore and gain his favor before he held his meeting.

Once I had gathered my bonnet and gloves, Helen and I bid Fox farewell and stepped onto the busy street. Several nearby gardens would make for an excellent morning stroll, but they were not my intended destination. There was one place more prone to visiting gossips: The Pump Room.

GREGORY

Talking to birds marked one on the brink of insanity, but so it was that, after days of isolation, I found myself naming the feathered creatures frequenting my window sill. I even had a favorite: James. Why should I not name a pigeon after my closest friend?

Rolling my eyes, I pushed away from the window and paced the length of the parlor to relieve the anxious energy that mounted within me. Confining myself to my rooms at the Crescent grew increasingly difficult, but having found no success in my visits to The Bottom Ale did not help. Each night, I returned home more frustrated than before. Westmore had not made another appearance, and I had discovered no information about his meeting or where I could find him.

"A complete waste," I grumbled, running a hand through my hair.

The motion was followed by a wince. Thomas had styled it for me this morning, and I had undoubtedly ruined his hard work. It took a fair amount of pomade to tame my curls into something presentable, a feat I'd never accomplished on my own. As a result, my appearance had suffered over the last year since letting my valet go. It wounded my pride to catch glimpses of myself in looking glasses or my reflection in windows.

But now, I had Thomas. I merely needed to train myself not to touch my hair.

My pacing resumed. I had no other way to stave off the anxious energy. I could go outside, but that ran the risk of meeting people who might recognize me.

I *missed* people. Balls, assemblies, picnics—they were all things of a former life, one where I hadn't worried about my financial struggles and could enjoy the many entertainments my family's wealth afforded. A life before I had been swindled out of most of my inheritance.

"You will wear a trail through the floor at this rate."

I ceased pacing at the sound of Thomas's voice. He stood at the parlor door, an amused grin on his face. It felt strange having a servant who was not actually in my employment. He seemed a genuinely kind fellow, but how could I trust him fully? I knew he had sent at least one letter to Cartwell since our arrival in Bath. What had it contained? Would Cartwell demand his money returned if Thomas provided a lackluster report?

Our terms had been clear: the money was mine. But I was not so dense as to believe there would not be repercussions if I failed this mission. A marquess had power and influence, and I was in no position to combat either.

"It helps me think." I countered Thomas's amused grin with a clipped tone. "My plan has not gone the way I'd hoped. Westmore hasn't shown for days, and I've no leads as to where I might find him."

Thomas nodded, well aware of my current dilemma. Keeping him informed had been part of Cartwell's deal. "Were ye expectin' it to be easy? Ye didn't think ye would catch the man after one night, did ye?"

I narrowed my eyes at him. Thomas, I had learned, was quite outspoken for someone in his station. Whether he came by the personality naturally or found himself a bit freer in the tongue due to the unusual circumstances and role he presently held, I didn't know. Part of me appreciated our blunt exchanges.

The other part despised it wholeheartedly.

Either way, I was not his employer and had little say in how he behaved. I needed his good opinion since he corresponded with Cartwell.

"No," I said finally. "I did not expect this to be easy."

"That's good." Thomas tilted his head to one side. "What do ye intend to do next?"

"I will discover where Westmore spends his time. Someone in this town must know."

"Certainly. At a minimum, Mr. Westmore knows."

I glared at him. His smug grin had returned. Thomas found too much humor in my struggles. It was not his future on the line.

"I don't suppose you have an idea for how I might go about getting this information?" I asked.

Thomas shrugged. "Servants talk. Gossip passes between houses, but I 'aven't heard nothing about Mr. Westmore. The man is elusive."

Didn't I know it.

"Then I have no choice but to venture somewhere beyond the hells and this forsaken house. Doubly beneficial, as were I to remain here much longer with only you, I would end up in Bedlam."

"You risk exposing your identity going out in the daytime," said Thomas, entirely unoffended by my comment.

"Yes, but I see no other way forward." I lifted my hand and scrubbed it over my face, a better option than leaving my hair in further disarray. Or so I thought. The roughness of my beard scratched against my palm, reminding me of its presence.

Thomas chuckled at my grimace. I had made no secret of my disdain for facial hair, a disdain that had magnified after Mr. Blyth's comments.

Beards were not accepted by the majority of the *ton*, this I knew, but to be called out by a gentleman in a gaming hell seemed the lowest sort of low, especially when he had also stated it did not flatter me. Why should I care what a petite man with oversized spectacles thought, anyway? It was a disguise that did its job.

Thomas crossed the room, retrieved my coat from the back of a chair, and held it out to me.

I shrugged my arms and shoulders into it, both of which were far more masculine than Mr. Blyth's, I might add. At least having no leads on Westmore gave me an excuse to leave the house in daylight, to go somewhere beside an illegal gambling hell where men like Mr. Blyth frequented.

Well, perhaps not Mr. Blyth. I hadn't seen him at The Bottom Ale again, either.

I shook my head, bringing my thoughts back to where they should be. Thomas was correct; going out was a risk. I would need to focus and exercise caution.

"Where do you intend to go?" Thomas asked.

"The Pump Room."

Thomas's brow furrowed. "Will there not be crowds there?"

"It is not yet the fashionable hour, which means fewer crowds. Still, I may find a few gossips about." I straightened my coat and patted down my hair before looking at Thomas. He seemed to sense my need for approval, but I was not to receive it from this man.

"A hat should cover the mess on your head. I'm afraid little can be done for your face."

Perhaps the part of me that wished to throttle him was greater than the part that appreciated his blunt nature. Fortunately for Thomas, he worked for Cartwell. I would do no throttling.

I forced a smile. "Then I shall grab my hat and be off."

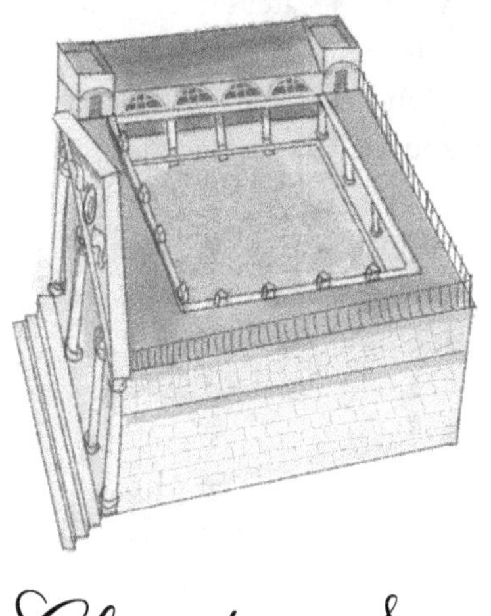

Chapter Six

GREGORY

I stared up at the honey-colored building, its massive columns standing as sentinels to the entrance of The Pump Room. I had visited the place once upon first arriving in Bath, late in the evening when there were few visitors, to pay a subscription to take the waters. I was not convinced hot water that smelled so strongly of boiled eggs could heal any particular ailment, but it was better to pay the monthly fee and pretend, thus blending into society. It gave me a reason to be here.

Besides, I could certainly spare a guinea now.

The noisy streets bustled with life at the start of a new day, but the sounds of carriage wheels and chatter were muffled into near silence once I entered the building into the long Great Room that housed the leaden cistern. A few early risers promenaded the length of the room, and several ladies huddled close beneath the statue of Beau Nash, their voices soft to ensure their conspiratorial whispers went unheard.

I passed a gentleman in a bath chair with wispy gray hair and decades' worth of wrinkles, catching the pungent scent of onions and lard as I did so. He nodded to me in acknowledgment, and then his focus shifted behind me. His aging features did not stop him from making flirtatious remarks to the young ladies who had entered the room.

Near the cistern, a man with a darkened complexion stood next to an elderly woman with white hair, and in the gallery, a small band prepared to play once more visitors arrived.

I wandered closer to the cistern. I had no intention of drinking the water, but I would if it meant opening a conversation. The likelihood of getting the information I needed without leading a discussion in that direction was highly improbable. The difficulty lay in doing so with subtlety. Westmore was careful with his trust. I must be as well.

"Good morning," I said to the man who seemed focused on the elderly woman beside him. She had a slight hunch to her back, and her hands gripped his arm for support. She smiled at me with a short nod of acknowledgment.

His gaze met mine briefly. "Good morning."

That was it then. I would get no more from him without a little push. Fortunately, I had an excellent history in the art of socialization. "Pleasant day, is it not? Fine weather."

"I suppose it is."

My lips pulled to one side. I had never worked to have a conversation with a gentleman. It typically flowed naturally, and if it didn't? Well, I preferred to converse with ladies, anyway.

But I had learned a few things about Daniel Whitticker all those years ago. I may not have realized his intention to trick me out of money, but he had made one thing clear: he did not work with women, no matter how wealthy they may be.

At the time, I had thought little of it. I had never taken an issue with women running their affairs, financial or otherwise, but there was a great portion of the upper class who frowned on any female who preferred to handle things themselves.

Regardless of my thoughts on the matter, the fact that Whitticker—or Westmore—would never allow a woman into his circle of investors reduced my likelihood of gaining information from any of the young misses within the room. That left me with the challenge of getting this man to talk.

But how?

When I wished to steal a woman's attention, I simply flattered her with pretty compliments. I doubted the same would work on a gentleman.

I cleared my throat. "This is my second visit to The Pump Room since moving to Bath. Do you come here often?"

The man eyed me warily, though he put on a smile. "Yes. I come frequently with my mother."

I nodded, my confidence growing. I held out my hand to the man. "Gregory Carrow." Using my Christian name as part of my alias had been a long debate, but the name was common enough that I had little concern about anyone making the connection. It was one less thing I had to remember, too.

"Gabriel Martin." The man shook my hand before gesturing to the woman at his side. "My mother, Mrs. Martha Martin."

"A pleasure," I said with a bow. At least now I was getting somewhere.

"Shall we return home, Mother?" Mr. Martin asked, turning away from me.

Perhaps I was *not* getting anywhere. The man seemed eager to escape. Was it something I had said? No, our exchange was nothing but polite. Then what—

I scowled. My beard. My blasted, deuced beard. I looked too much the scoundrel with all of this scruff. Mr. Martin clearly wanted to protect his frail mother from the hideous beast I was with this mountain of prickle.

Whether it was frustration or desperation, I did not know, but words spilled from my mouth before I could consider them. "My, that is a fine coat, Mr. Martin. Might I inquire as to who your tailor is?"

Mr. Martin, who had been guiding his mother in a direction opposite of me, stopped. He looked over his shoulder, and while that friendly smile was still in place, I could sense his unease. A strange awkwardness settled between us.

"Thank you?" he said, the uncertainty in his voice accompanied by the slight furrow of his brow. "I had it made in London."

I could not blame him. I would not have known how to respond to such a random, pointed compliment from a gentleman either. He certainly didn't preen under the flattery like a lady would have had I complimented a satin dress or frilly bonnet.

Well, if it kept him from leaving, I saw no reason not to continue making a fool of myself. "It compliments your coloring quite well."

Mr. Martin studied me, clearly bemused. "My...coloring?"

"Indeed. I wouldn't mind a new one myself." I patted my shoulder to indicate my own, which was ridiculous given I had worn it but a handful of times. It *was* new.

"All I need is a savvy investment," I continued with a breathy chuckle that sounded nothing like my true laugh. "Then I can dress as sharply as you."

The smile faded from Mr. Martin's face. Confusion lingered, but something I said had put him off completely. I silently berated myself for attempting to force the conversation with such poor success. Had I not chided Mr. Blyth for that very thing with Westmore a week ago?

"Oh!" Mrs. Martin's excitement drew her son's attention back to her. "Look there! It's Her Grace and Miss Colewater. They look lovely today, do they not?"

A strained smile filled Mr. Martin's face. "Of course, Mother."

I bit back a laugh. I knew all too well how it felt to have a mother who wanted nothing more than to see her son matched to a sweet young woman and settled down. The women who approached were certainly handsome enough to tempt the best of us. The more petite of the two possessed light brown hair with eyes to match. She was well dressed, though not completely at the height of fashion or with any sort of extravagance.

My gaze wandered to the second as they drew nearer, and my heart nearly leapt from my chest. Dark eyes peering out from beneath a pale blue bonnet and a confident, comely stride were not rare features among the upper class, but Sabrina Stafford, the dowager Duchess of Rochester, was not a woman I could forget for multiple reasons.

The devil take it. What were the odds that I would run into someone I knew?

I shook the thought away, reminding myself that very few knew Mr. Gregory Carrow, my alias. How could they when he was nothing more than a ghost? So long as my disguise held and I said nothing to jeopardize my true identity, all would be well.

I could not think of a better test for my anonymity than this.

My confidence wavered as the women stopped in front of us, their attention settled on the matron.

"Your Grace, what a delight." Mrs. Martin took Sabrina's hand and gave it several gentle pats. "It has been some time since we've seen you. We have missed our conversations, have we not, son?"

Mr. Martin's smile grew, though I could tell it required great effort. "Indeed, Mother."

Sabrina laughed lightly. "It has been an age. I must make an effort to visit you."

"Yes, you must, dear. I'll be expecting you."

I took a small step backward and then another, hoping no one would notice my departure as their conversation continued. The attempt was in vain, for the movement seemed to trigger Mrs. Martin into remembering my presence.

"Oh! I forget myself. Gabriel and I have just become acquainted with Mr. Carrow. Have you been introduced?"

She gestured to me, and my feet halted their retreat. It was then Sabrina's dark eyes locked with mine. Under her full attention, my heart sped. I could pretend that the possibility of being discovered was the cause, but that was not entirely true. Certainly, I feared it—my entire mission could be in peril should she recognize me—but my heart had responded in this manner the last time I saw her, some years ago in London. The woman was captivating.

Sabrina's eyes widened ever so slightly, and for a moment, I feared she would question my identity. Instead, she curtsied, as did her companion.

"We have not been introduced," said Sabrina. "But it is a pleasure, Mr. Carrow."

I released a breath of relief and bowed. "The pleasure is mine."

Mrs. Martin finished the introductions, and I attempted to act as though I had never met the Duchess of Rochester. Difficult, given our history. I had known the woman since my closest friend, James, courted her. She'd jilted him to marry further up the social ladder, leaving James with a broken heart, a condition rectified indirectly by Sabrina herself after her husband, the duke, died.

Four years ago, I had nearly lost my entire estate to her father over a card game, but the man had offered me a bargain: host a house party in which James and Sabrina were both present, and my debts would be forgiven. He had planned to see the two of them wed out of a selfish desire to further his social standing and connections. I'd agreed to the bargain out of desperation. Guilt had eaten away at me for betraying my friend, but I no longer felt its sting. Things had worked out for the best with James now happily married to someone else. That love match would have never been made had I not gone along with the entire scheme.

"Are you new to Bath, Mr. Carrow?"

Sabrina's question shook me from my thoughts. "Yes. I have visited in the past, but this shall be the first time I have taken up residence."

"You plan to stay for a time then?"

Was I imagining the very pointed interest in her tone or the way her eyes never wavered from mine? She studied me with such intensity that I questioned, again, whether I was safe in my ruse. Beyond her attentiveness, there was nothing to suggest she recognized me. Still, I couldn't help feeling exposed. All it would take was one wrong word to ruin my carefully crafted façade.

I cleared my throat. "I plan to stay for the summer. What I do after that will depend entirely upon the company and entertainment Bath has to offer."

Sabrina smiled slightly and hummed. "I fear if you mean to compare our city with London, you might well be disappointed, though Bath does offer much in the way of entertainment at times. The assembly halls are chief among them, of course. Do you enjoy dancing?"

I clasped my hands behind my back, feeling more at ease. "On occasion, Your Grace. Dancing can prove a suitable source of entertainment."

"I must agree," said Mrs. Martin, nudging her son. "You see? Every gentleman of good standing should see himself to an assembly."

Mr. Martin nodded, though his exasperation was evident. The poor fellow.

"And when not dancing," Sabrina continued, ignoring the whispered conversation between the Martins. "What is it you prefer to do? Attend parties? No, I do not think that is it. I have a talent for reading people." She tapped a finger to her lips, considering me. "It's the gentleman's clubs for you, I should think. You prefer to waste away your fortune and time on cards."

Miss Colewater, who I had learned was Sabrina's lady's maid, gasped and shot her mistress a chiding look, though she said nothing. I took no surprise in Sabrina's blunt assessment. She had never been one to mince words.

"I believe that is a pursuit for most gentlemen of leisure, Your Grace. I shan't deny it."

"The clubs or the cards?" she prodded.

I shrugged. "I deny neither, though I do have a preference between the two."

"Which is the preference?"

"You seem capable of figuring that out on your own. After all, reading people is a talent of yours."

Sabrina's eyes narrowed, and though my stomach was a whirlpool of nerves, I smiled. My reaction seemed to frustrate her, causing her brows to furrow and her lips to purse. Perhaps I was better at hiding my emotions and identity than I thought, for she appeared utterly confounded by our exchange. What I wouldn't have given to hear her thoughts, to know what she thought of me.

"And what of the company in Bath?" I asked. "I presume you have an opinion on that as well?"

"The company I can hardly speak to as I rarely find myself in want of much socialization. Ballrooms and parties have become far too stuffy for me to feel them enjoyable." She turned a soft smile on Mr. Martin. "Would you not agree, Mr. Martin?"

The man nodded but offered nothing more to the conversation, much to his mother's chagrin. The matron sighed with exasperation. "You mustn't encourage him, Your Grace. Already, I have difficulty convincing him to attend social activities. Even responding to Mrs. Anderton's upcoming picnic required pleading on my part. Everyone of importance shall be there."

Everyone of importance. My mind settled on those three words. Would Westmore attend such an event? I had no leads on the man at present, and while I had come to Bath intending to make myself as scarce as possible until my mission was complete, this picnic might be my only chance of gathering the information I needed. Even if Westmore was not in attendance, someone at the picnic would likely know *something*.

The problem was I hadn't received an invitation. The second problem was that attending would put me in the eyes of Bath society. If I was to be recognized, this picnic would be the place.

But my disguise had fooled Sabrina, had it not? If she, a woman who I'd spent time with at length, did not see through my façade, surely no one else would?

"Are you to attend the picnic, Your Grace?" I asked, interrupting Sabrina's conversation with Mrs. Martin. Why I felt the need to know her plans, I could not say. More time in her company could prove a dangerous prospect, increasing my odds of being discovered.

Yes, that must be why I had asked. It was self-preservation, borne out of instinct.

Sabrina hesitated a few moments before answering. "I had not intended to, but I am reconsidering."

I did not miss the delighted surprise that passed over her maid's face, almost as if she welcomed the idea. Did Sabrina truly not attend social functions with regularity? She certainly had in the past, but then, I was not ignorant of the rumors that now surrounded her family's name.

Ballrooms and parties have become far too stuffy for me to feel them enjoyable.

My curiosity was, unfortunately, piqued. That statement went against everything I knew about this woman. Had she changed in the three years since I'd last seen her? Sabrina had been relentless in her pursuit of title and wealth, both during my house party and her first Season in London, but I had come to the conclusion that much of her manipulations and conceitedness stemmed from her father's expectations. Where once I had found her the most intimidating creature of my acquaintance, I now saw beyond the outward display to the vulnerable woman hidden within. One moment, buried deep in our shared pasts, had ensured that.

"Well," I said, "perhaps I shall see you there."

She smiled, and the expression pulled my stomach taut. "Perhaps so."

All I needed now was to procure an invitation.

Chapter Seven

SABRINA

Dear Mrs. Anderton,

I am writing to formally accept your invitation to the picnic. I am pleased to attend and look forward to being within Bath's finest social circles once again. I must also accept your generous offer for conveyance. Thank you again for the invitation. I eagerly await the occasion.

Yours sincerely,

Her Grace, Duchess of Rochester

Mr. Carrow was not a stranger. I had nearly convinced myself the man was not the charming gentleman I knew as Gregory Davis, but his eyes...they had haunted me for years. I could not forget them, especially after visiting The Pump Room.

No matter how I'd instructed my mind to do so.

I sighed, threading my needle with white string. The quiet of the drawing room held a deafening silence, and I would only work on my project for a few more minutes. I could not stand to sit still for so long, especially for this type of activity. Helen, who sat on the opposite end of the settee, was content to work her needle all day.

Perhaps it was talent that made the activity more sufferable. I certainly did not possess it. Only by some miracle would this dress turn out as anything proper to wear.

I shifted on the cushion, my mind wandering again. Meeting Mr. Carrow at The Pump Room three days ago clarified a number of things for me. Not only was I certain of his true identity, but Mrs. Martin's mention of the upcoming picnic had presented my next course of action. I did not know if Mr. Westmore would make an appearance, but there was a chance he would. I saw no sense in ignoring the opportunity, even if it required me to attend a social event.

It seemed Mr. Carrow—Davis—intended to do the same. Why in the heavens was he parading about under a false name, anyway? I knew the man to have a heavy preference for cards. Was that the reason he used an alias? His draw to the tables had played to my advantage in the past. People were far easier to manipulate when one knew their weaknesses.

I grimaced, reminding myself that I was no longer that person, but it was difficult to forget my past, and I poked myself with the needle as a result. I'd been sewing beadwork onto my new gown for an eternity, though according to Helen, it had been but two days. So many other things were preferable to this agonizingly monotonous work.

But I had promised Helen I would adorn the dress in exchange for her making new dresses for the Barton women. They desperately needed the assistance, so I would make the sacrifice.

Or my fingers would, at least.

Unfortunately, such work also left my mind unengaged and un-focused, allowing it to wander to Mr. Carrow with great frequency. Years ago, during my first Season, Father had insisted that I capture several men's attention in case the old duke proved elusive. James Blakely, an earl, had been one such man. I had strung him along, toying with his heart until the duke proposed. I hadn't given his distress upon learning the news a second thought, unattached as I had been. My only concern had been fulfilling Father's demands.

Which was why, after the duke died, I had obeyed Father's demands again. I had won the earl's heart once before; it seemed logical that it would be easy to do so again. But I had broken him, and luring the earl away from his estate seemed an impossible task without help. That was where Mr. Davis came in. As the earl's best friend, I believed he could convince the earl to attend a house party.

And Mr. Davis had, with the threat of losing everything hanging over his head, a situation orchestrated by both me and my father.

I grimaced again. The woman I had been all those years ago was not a woman I took pride in. She'd been heartless, manipulative, and conceited beyond reason. I could blame my father, in part. I'd been raised for one sole purpose and followed the guidelines I'd been given with perfection. It was not until my eyes were opened that I understood how despicable my behavior was.

My eyes had been opened to other things, too. Romance had never been an ideal I considered for myself, but for a brief, fleeting moment...

My stomach swooped oddly, and I shook my head to clear away his image. His eyes. His smile. I was not a woman who romanticized...well, anything. Eyes opened or not, I would do well not to think on the private exchange between Mr. Davis and myself. It was nothing more than a conversation along a quiet road, and while I could admit that it had changed the course of my future, I could not afford to give it more credit than that.

I scoffed at the ridiculous nature of my thoughts, drawing Helen's attention. Her light brown brows furrowed, and she rested her needlework on her lap. "Somethin's bothering ye."

"I am quite well," I said, my tone dismissive.

"Well, perhaps. Different, certainly."

I paused in my efforts to attach another pearl bead and faced my friend. "Whatever does that mean?"

Helen shrugged, but her lips lifted slightly. "Nothin'. Ye just haven't been the same since our outing to The Pump Room, is all. Can't help wonderin' if a gentleman has somethin' to do with it."

I narrowed my eyes. I had not told Helen of my suspicions, nor the conclusions I had come to, about Mr. Davis and Mr. Carrow. She had attended that house party with me all those years ago, but our relationship then had not been what it was now. I hadn't told her of my time with Mr. Davis. I hadn't told her that the man had made me *feel* things.

Things that terrified me, both then and now.

"I cannot know what you mean, Helen," I said, my attention returning to my needle and beads. "Mr. Martin is a fine man, but I've no interest in him. Nor him in me."

"I not be referring to Mr. Martin, and ye well know it. Ye and Mr. Carrow hit it right off. Don't bother denying it. I know ye too well for that."

I frowned. She did know me well, unfortunately. Better than anyone. Even still, I refused to believe I was so easy to read. Besides, my interest in Mr. Davis that day was not the affectionate sort of interest. He merely confused me—first, with his attempt to conceal his true identity, and second, with the reason he would do so at all. Why was he after Mr. Westmore? And why did he chase the man under an alias?

It would drive me mad until I discovered the answers.

"How could there be anything between Mr. Carrow and myself?" I asked. "The two of us have only recently met, and I have never been one to swoon under a man's charm."

Helen's brows furrowed. "No, I suppose not. But he is a handsome man, is he not? Surely that much about him ye can agree with."

I scoffed, despite the way my stomach clenched. Perhaps if I had truly met Mr. Carrow days ago, I could refute her claim. His beard provoked no attraction for me.

But I did know his true identity. I knew what he looked like without that dratted beard, and I also knew the kind man he could be. Never mind the way his green eyes were permanent fixtures in my thoughts.

Regardless, I would tell Helen none of this, else she subject me to more of her nonsensical scheming. I did not need another husband, and even if I wanted one, what man would choose me now? My reputation had set sail with my father, and no man of consequence would ever court me. Had my dowry been something substantial, I might have something to offer, but Father had seen to my disadvantage on that front as well. He had handed me off to the duke for a measly four thousand pounds and negotiated very little on my behalf.

"Well," said Helen, breaking through my melancholy, "I, for one, am glad ye've decided to attend the picnic. It's about time ye get out of this house."

"I go out plenty," I retorted.

Helen passed me a look, and I understood her meaning. I might leave my rooms to venture out into the city, but it was always with the purpose of furthering my work. This picnic would be nothing of the sort.

Not directly, anyway.

With any luck, Mr. Westmore would make an appearance. I would have to fake enjoyment of the social affair in hopes of seeing him there. If I could speak with him, convince him that my money was as good as any gentleman's, perhaps I could cease parading about Bath dressed as a man and attend his investment meeting as myself. That would certainly be preferable and far less risky to what remained of my reputation. Society had already shunned me; I did not need to add to the problem by being caught gambling at some gaming hell.

"If nothing else," said Helen, "Mr. Carrow is likely to attend. Ye could further your acquaintance with him."

Good heavens, would the women ever give up? "I've no need to do that, nor do I believe Mr. Carrow would care to. The man is polite. That is all."

"He looked at you with more than politeness," Helen muttered.

The words spread an unfamiliar warmth through me, but I ignored it. Likely the only reason Gregory Davis looked at me in any particular way was out of caution and judgment. I had acted horribly toward his friend and dragged Mr. Davis into my schemes, forcing him to betray that same friend. He would never trust me.

Memories pushed their way to the forefront of my thoughts—a dirt road leading through a wooded area outside of Cheltenham, fresh tears born from the heavy burden of expectation, and a man who had offered me comfort through a warm embrace. Those arms had made me feel secure in a way I never had, and the sensation of his touch lingered even now, a ghost to haunt me for the remainder of my days.

I tossed my needlework to the side and stood so abruptly that Helen started.

"I need fresh air." I held up a hand when Helen began to rise. "Do not remove yourself from your work. I will only step out for a moment. I shan't go wandering off without you."

"Very well, but be sure to have Mr. Foxgrove wait inside the door."

What she thought might happen to me in the middle of the day on a street as busy as Gay Street, I could not fathom, but I nodded my agreement simply to grasp a moment of privacy. I made my way outside and caught Fox peeking through the window to check on me more than once as I let the sun's rays warm my face, my chin tilted upward so that my bonnet did not hinder its gentle caress. I breathed in deeply and closed my eyes, listening to the thump of carriage wheels and the tap of horse hooves. The noise grounded me.

And I desperately needed to be tethered to reality so my mind would not wander among the clouds where hope resided. A hope I could not make sense of. Meeting Gregory Davis here in Bath had left me in a state of confusion where I battled a deep desire to see him again. To claim time in his company. I hardly knew the man, and yet...

I was inexplicably drawn to him.

To call it curiosity alone would be a lie. Certainly, I wanted to know his aim in taking on an alias and growing a beard, which I assumed was a sort of disguise rather than the act of rebellion he had claimed at the card tables. More than understanding his strange behavior, though, I longed to relive a memory with him. To experience it again.

My face tightened. Vulnerability had no place in my life. I would do well to ignore Gregory Davis, to ignore Mr. Carrow and any urge to discover why he had come to Bath. Some memories were better off forgotten.

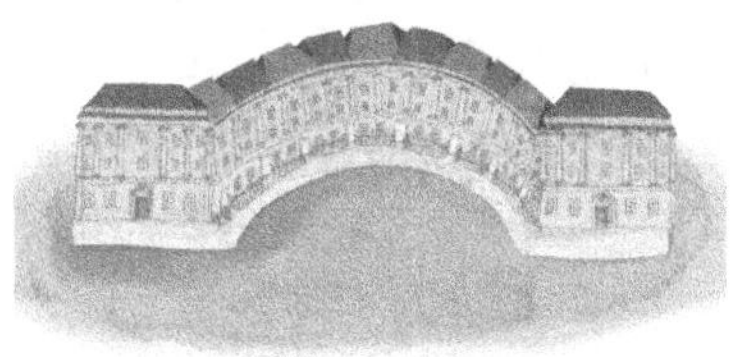

Chapter Eight

GREGORY

The picnic was in four days, and I had yet to find a way to procure an invitation. I glanced down at the floor of my bed chamber, Thomas's jest about creating a trough in the boards due to my incessant pacing fresh in my thoughts. I shook my head in irritation. What was I to do about it, cooped up in this house as I was? My disguise had held up for one social outing, but that did not give me leave to risk going out and about, especially when I had no leads on Westmore to warrant an excursion.

Blast it all, I would go mad hiding away in these rooms!

I crossed to the window and peered down at the street below. The drive following the curve of the Crescent seemed to buzz with activity during the day, which did nothing to curb my appetite for human interaction. The life of a recluse did not suit me at all.

"Still pacing, I see."

My feet halted at Thomas's voice. I hadn't even realized I had begun my march again. "Unless you have a remedy for it that includes information about Westmore, I suggest you keep the observation to yourself."

Thomas merely grinned. He knew I would do nothing, despite the threats I threw at him.

"What do you want?" I asked when Thomas said nothing more. The least he could do was leave me in miserable peace.

Thomas shrugged. "Nothing, sir, except an update on your plan."

To keep Cartwell informed, no doubt. A low growl rumbled from my chest. "The update is that I don't have a plan. I'll inform you the moment I do."

My valet, or more like my spy, entered the room, sweeping his sandy brown hair out of his eyes. "Shall I wait here until you have an epiphany, then?"

"Not unless you wish this room to be your grave."

Thomas chuckled, amused by my threats rather than concerned.

"Sir?"

Thomas and I both turned toward the door. I hadn't employed many staff upon moving to Bath, but Mr. Jenkins served as my butler. I'd also hired a cook, housekeeper, and two maids. In addition to Thomas, that had seemed sufficient for my needs at present.

Mr. Jenkins bowed. He was not precisely old, but his hair had begun to recede to reveal a shiny scalp. "Mrs. Davis has arrived, and I've placed her trunks in the Green Room."

"What?" I sputtered.

My butler blinked, his brows furrowing. "Mrs. Davis has arrived? She said you were expecting her."

What the devil was Mother doing here, and how had she even discovered my location? I glanced at Thomas, wondering if perhaps he was involved in this unfortunate turn of events, but his wide eyes suggested otherwise. The man looked almost panicked.

"Indeed," I said, forcing myself to exude a calm I did not feel. "That will do, Jenkins. If you will direct my...aunt, Mrs. Davis, to the drawing room, I will greet her shortly."

"Already done, sir. She awaits you now."

I released a sigh as he bowed and departed. Other than Thomas, my staff knew me by my alias, and I was relieved that Jenkins had accepted my impromptu explanation that Mother was my aunt and lucky Mother hadn't declared her relationship to me.

Gads, this entire thing was getting out of hand.

"You involved your mother?" asked Thomas.

"No," I snapped. "I haven't any idea how she discovered me. Why would I do something that would complicate matters?"

Thomas nodded slowly, seeming to consider this. "You'd best go speak with her, then. Convince her to play along with the ruse, else word will get out."

He was right, and I hated it. "I will convince her."

Though I wasn't entirely certain *how* I would do it. Not without explaining the entirety of the situation to her. Call it pride, but I had no desire to tell my mother how miserably I had failed our family.

I slipped past Thomas, catching his mumbled whisper of good luck, and took the stairs down to the drawing room. Mother sat on a sea blue settee, sipping tea as she glanced about with a studious gaze. This room was swathed in deep blues, from the curtains to the upholstery. The ceiling boasted intricate carvings, and Roman columns stood sentinel in each corner as well as framing the large hearth on the eastern wall. I wondered what Mother thought of the space. In many ways, it was grander than our townhouse in London, at least in regards to the newer furnishings. We couldn't afford to update it or our country estate.

Couldn't before. That would change after I did Cartwell's bidding. Twenty thousand pounds would go a long way to restoring my holdings to their former glory.

I cleared my throat, drawing her attention. Mother set down her teacup and stood, gently touching her tight coiffure. "Gregory."

Keeping my Christian name had been a wise choice. I congratulated myself on that minor foresight.

I closed the door to the drawing room, which seemed to bewilder her. No matter, she would understand once I explained. The question was how much did I intend to tell her? By the time I had crossed the room and placed a short kiss on her cheek, I still hadn't decided.

"How are you, Mother?" I asked, waiting for her to reclaim her seat before taking the chair opposite her.

Mother scoffed, smoothing out the folds in her hunter-green gown. "How am I? After worrying over you for well over two weeks, wondering where you had run off to and what sort of trouble you'd gotten yourself involved in?" She took a long sip of tea. "I'm positively content. Cannot imagine why I would be anything else."

I rolled my eyes. "I told you I would return to Fallborn after the summer. Is that not enough to ease your concerns? I thought you would enjoy a quiet respite after the London Season concluded."

Mother laughed and placed her teacup on the tray. "Respite? When have I ever required one of those? You know how I enjoy socializing. The time between Seasons is dastardly long and boring. At least when you are home, I have another soul to speak to. I'm entirely lonesome without someone to bother."

Yet we still employed several servants, all of whom were capable of speech.

"My apologies," I said flatly. "I did not realize my purpose in life was for you to bother."

"Oh, stop that." She swatted at the air, making the single slightly grayed chestnut curl that had come loose bounce. "You know I love you, Gregory. I cannot for the life of me understand why you've come to Bath." Her eyes narrowed, studying me in a way that made me shift on the cushions. "Or why you've taken to growing that monstrosity on your face. Ladies are not attracted to beavers."

"Mother!"

"What? 'Tis true. Why have you neglected yourself?"

I bit down on my tongue. Mother had always been rather blunt. Never mind that I agreed with her. This beard had a purpose, no matter how much I hated it. "I am here on an errand for Lord Cartwell."

"Lord Cartwell?" Her face twisted with confusion. "What sort of errand?"

I drew in a sigh. I had to tell her, but it brought me no joy. "The man is a victim of fraud, and he's asked me to help him find the one responsible. The criminal tends to frequent the hells, so I am to go undercover and find him."

"Lord Cartwell has enough money to hire a private investigator for this," said Mother. "Why does he need you?"

I did not completely have an answer to that question, but I did possess a few suspicions. Cartwell knew of my previous dealings with Daniel Whitticker, though how, he'd refused to say. Either way, bringing Westmore to justice provided me with closure.

"Discretion, I suppose, is part of it. He believes I will keep the situation private until the evidence has been gathered. I have experience in the gaming hells as well. I can't deny my familiarity with them. Who better to blend in and play the spy than someone with experience in the arena?"

Mother winced. She knew how much time I spent at the tables, but she had never brought it up. Which was odd, now that I thought about it. She had an opinion about everything, but on this, she remained silent.

"Still," said Mother. "It cannot be safe for you to chase a criminal. I do not like it."

Neither did I in many ways, but she could not understand my motivation. Not unless I told her everything. I settled for a partial truth. "He's offered me twenty thousand pounds to see this through. You know as well as I do Fallborn could use the money. The repairs alone..."

Mother's expression softened. "That sort of sum would go a long way, but no amount of money is worth your safety."

My heart squeezed at her response. Perhaps if she knew precisely how dire our financials had become, and that it was entirely my fault, she would not respond that way.

No, she would. Despite how she irritated me at times, I loved her, and I knew she loved me. That much I had never questioned.

"I promise I am being careful," I said. "I've taken on an alias of my own." I pointed to my face. "Hence the beaver. It is a disguise, and you have my word I shall shave it off the moment this is all over."

Mother hummed. "An alias, you say? And what is this fake name?"

"Gregory Carrow, and I need you to address me that way and not refer to me as your son. I've told my staff you are my aunt."

She pursed her lips, clearly perturbed by the request. I could trust her to successfully fill the role, though. Mother had always been dramatic. Had she not been born the daughter of a wealthy gentleman, she might have found a place on the stage. My only task was to convince her the role was worth taking.

"Very well, I shall call you Nephew or Gregory. The latter shan't be too difficult."

My shoulders sagged with relief. "Thank you, Mother."

She nodded. "Yes, well I have stipulations."

I held back a groan. Of course, she did.

"What are they?" I asked.

"I wish to be kept informed. It will not do to sit in this house and worry about you constantly. My nerves will never recover. You must tell me your plans and where you intend to go."

I laughed without humor. "That won't be difficult. At present, I rarely leave the house. I cannot risk my identity being discovered unless there's a chance an excursion will lead me to information on Westmore—that is the criminal I'm after."

Mother gaped. "You rarely leave? What absolute torture."

"Yes, and I expect you to keep to the house, too, if you intend to stay. No outings and certainly no callers. It would jeopardize my mission."

I had never seen her so appalled. "No callers?"

"None. Not until I have found evidence for Lord Cartwell."

Mother grumbled under her breath. "He could have mentioned all of this."

"What?"

She straightened, lifting her chin. "Never mind, I will agree to use your alias and be your aunt."

"And?"

She heaved a sigh. "And I will not go out or have callers."

I nodded once. "Good, now that we have that settled, I need a favor. There is an upcoming picnic where I might get more traction in all of this, but I have no way of garnering an invitation. Are you familiar with a Mrs. Anderton?"

"Eleanor Anderton?" She continued when I nodded. "I am. We went to school together."

Perfect. Perhaps Mother's arrival was more fortuitous than I'd expected. Which was hardly difficult given I hadn't thought it fortuitous at all minutes ago. "Do you think you could request an invitation from her on my behalf? There is a chance Westmore might be there, but even if he is not, I might pick up information from the gentlemen who are."

The way she glared at me reminded me, in no small way, of the numerous times I'd gotten into trouble as a child. "Let me ensure I understand you correctly. You expect me to abstain from societal functions while you go off to have fun at this picnic?"

Well, when she put it that way, it did seem a touch unfair.

"Furthermore, you expect me to reach out to a dear friend of mine, requesting an invitation for you, but not for myself? And then I am to not even call on her at all while here in town?"

"Mother, it is of the utmost importance—"

"No. I shan't do it. Eleanor will think it the height of rudeness."

I growled in exasperation. "You may call upon her after the picnic. It would not do for us to be seen together when we can avoid it, however. Can you not simply fake an illness that day? She needn't know you never planned to attend."

Mother folded her arms, her lips perched in a pout. I would take that as a no. If Mother was anything, she was stubborn.

"Please," I begged. "The sooner I get information, the sooner this can all end. You may be as social as you like then."

She harrumphed. "I'll consider it."

My jaw clenched. I didn't have time for her to *consider it*. The picnic was in four days. It was bad form to request an invitation in the first place, but to do so this late? Not that I cared, but Mother did. Such a lack of etiquette did nothing to help my odds of persuading her.

"If you do not mind, consider it with haste," I said, rising from my seat. "Now, if you will excuse me, I should inform the rest of my staff that we have a visitor for the foreseeable future. Then, I will hole myself up in my chambers until I've found another way to do this without your interference, as I am no longer optimistic you will help me."

The words were harsh. She didn't deserve my ire, not when she had agreed to play along with my scheme. Still, I stormed from the room, shaking my head. If Mother insisted on being here, why could she not do something to assist me?

It occurred to me as I reached the stairs that I hadn't asked how she had discovered my location to begin with, but something told me she wouldn't reveal her secrets anyway. I swore under my breath. I needed a solution to all of this, and no amount of pacing in my bed chamber would provide it.

But what else could I do?

Chapter Nine

GREGORY

Being stuck inside the same walls day in and day out was torture. Being stuck inside them with my restless mother was...well, we were both destined for Bedlam at this rate. I had even snuck out last night to visit a new gaming hell in hopes of finding Westmore, with no success. The night hadn't been a complete waste, however, as I'd returned several thousand pounds heavier in the pockets.

But I would not tell Mother of the escapade. She would never forgive me. For either leaving the house or for gambling.

Mother heaved a heavy sigh, likely the twentieth one this hour. I'd brought a book down to the drawing room in hopes that it would distract me, though that was a stretch given how much I hated reading. If we were to be cooped up, at least we could do it together, but Mother's subtle moans of complaint while she embroidered a handkerchief were not conducive to silent relaxation. They were constant reminders that we were prisoners.

She pulled my gaze from the page when she stood abruptly, tossing her needlework aside. "I cannot do this."

"It has not even been twenty-four hours since you arrived," I pointed out. "You have stayed home longer than that before."

"Yes, but it was not required for me to do so. The minute the rules are set, I want to break them. I cannot stand to be forcibly caged-in, especially without hope of anyone visiting."

I closed my book and placed it on the table. "You are being dramatic. How do you think I feel having been here for over two weeks? If I can survive that long, surely you can handle more than a day."

"I could if I wanted," she responded defiantly. "But I do not want to."

"You promised," I reminded. "If you jeopardize this—"

"Jeopardize!" Her hands flailed about in exasperation. "An outing or two will not ruin anything. Besides, if I go alone, no one will even associate me with you. Why should I keep holed up for no reason?"

She made valid points. As long as no one saw us together, there was little risk to my plans. Still, I didn't like the idea of her roaming about Bath on her own when I was entangled in this scheme to reel in a criminal. Putting myself in danger was one thing, but to put my mother in the line of fire?

I could not do it.

"Perhaps it would be best if you returned to Fallborn, then. You're miserable here, and as you've said, there is no reason for you to stay."

Mother placed her hands on her hips. "I am not going anywhere." She continued when I lifted a brow. "I am not leaving Bath. I came for a visit, and besides, someone has to keep an eye on you. Always up to trouble. You cannot pretend I am wrong when you sneak out at night."

Blast. She had noticed.

"I was attempting to locate Westmore since I've no leads." I gave her a pointed look. She still hadn't given in to asking Mrs. Anderton for an invitation, which left me sitting at square one.

Mother shrugged. "You haven't provided a good enough reason for me to help with that."

"Besides being your son and asking for assistance?" I scoffed. Incredulous woman.

She ignored my response, tapping a finger to her lips. "You know what could convince me? An outing. Take me to the shops or even on a stroll. I must get out of this house. Doing so will put me in a much better mood."

"And if I escort you on a stroll, you'll request an invitation?" It was far too much to hope for, and I knew it.

"I'll consider it."

"Are you not already doing that?" My voice almost whined. I'd have been embarrassed were we not alone. Not even Thomas had come to the drawing room today to demand an update on my plans.

In fact, I'd only seen him when I changed last night and this morning. Was he hiding from my mother?

Mother grinned, the mischievous sort that put me on edge. "I'd consider it better if I were in a good mood."

I ran a hand through my hair. Exhausting woman. And she wondered why I would not consider marriage. What man in his right mind would choose to deal with this every day?

"Fine," I said. "We will go on a stroll if you promise to really give it some thought." I held up one finger when she opened her mouth. "One hour. I will give you one hour. That is all."

Her grin faded. "Very well. I'll take what I can get. Let's go."

I followed her toward the door, hoping this was not something I would come to regret.

Milsom Street was, in a word, busy. Three-story buildings with mansard roofs and Corinthian columns lined either side of the cobblestone carriageway, and people bustled about, visiting the shops and socializing along the wide pavements. Mother bounced next to me, absolutely giddy with excitement to take in the fresh air, and I could not blame her. Being outside, and not under the guise of night in some illegal establishment, restored something inside me as well.

"Look there!" She grabbed my arm with one hand and pointed with the other toward a perfumery. "I neglected to pack extra perfume. I'm nearly out. Providence, indeed!"

A smile touched my lips at her exuberance as she dragged me forward. It had been a long time since I had escorted Mother to the shops in London or even to those in Cheltenham near our country estate. I had felt too guilty to do so, knowing we could not spare the extra expense such a trip would incur.

But now? Now I had Cartwell's payment in my pocket. I was to use the initial money to catch Westmore's attention, but a few purchases would not hurt. After all, was it not my intention to paint myself as a man of means? I had no guarantee that word of this excursion would reach Westmore, but regardless, Mother deserved something of a treat for being so willing to play along with my ruse.

Besides, I needed her in a good mood, didn't I? What better way to do that than to dote upon her?

I waited patiently in front of the shop, whistling lightly to myself while Mother inquired after a particular scent from the shopkeeper. Mother's mood wasn't the only one improved by being out among people.

As I stood there, my gaze wandered over the other shops as I considered where we might go next. My gaze shifted past a bookshop to Sinclair's Haberdashery, and I added it to my list of choices for places to take Mother. She would enjoy perusing the fabrics and perhaps picking out some lace or beads to adorn a bonnet.

I frowned. Mother hated needlework. Why would my mind even consider that?

It was likely a matter of self-preservation. We might both go mad with nothing to do.

The door to the haberdashery swung open, and the dismal thoughts were forgotten as my attention focused on the woman leaving the shop, her face mostly hidden beneath a pale blue bonnet. I might have questioned her identity were it not for the petite woman following her.

Miss Colewater, Sabrina's lady's maid, stood next to her mistress with a little parcel in hand, the two of them watching the carriages pass by. I concluded they intended to cross the busy street, and after a glance inside the perfumery to note Mother's continued engagement with the shopkeeper, I raced across the cobblestone at the first break on the thoroughfare.

"Your Grace!" I shouted before either lady could step away from the pavement. Sabrina turned to look at me, confirming her identity.

"Good morning, Your Grace," I said, coming to a stop in front of them, slightly out of breath. I bowed to her and gave a nod of acknowledgment to Miss Colewater.

"Lovely to see you, Mr. Carrow." Sabrina tilted her head, and the smile she wore was odd. Not unpleasant, but more...calculating?

"What brings you to Milsom Street today?" she asked before I could fully question the expression.

"My mo—aunt wished to get out of the house. I am her escort."

"Not a very good one, then. I see no aunt on your arm, sir."

I laughed at her jest, shaking my head. "Indeed, I am quite aunt-less at present. She is in the perfumery. I elected to wait outside. All those scents tend to give me a headache, and I'm enjoying the fresh air." I nodded toward the carriageway. "You seemed ready to cross, and I thought I might make myself useful while I waited for her."

I offered Sabrina my arm, and the air in my lungs seemed to grow stale while she debated her response. The anticipation swelling inside me was foreign and strange.

"Well," she said, stepping forward, "we cannot have you being useless, now can we?"

The moment her gloved fingers slid around my arm, a tingling heat spread upward through my shoulder and extended down to my fingertips. Sabrina stared up at me from beneath her bonnet, revealing dark eyes and lashes and even a few strands of black as midnight hair.

I had always thought her a handsome woman. Few would refute that. She had captured the attention of a duke, after all. She'd even turned the head of my friend, The Earl of Emerson, for a time. She possessed everything the *ton* valued—beauty, sophistication, grace, and money.

Or she had, at least.

Regardless, even I knew beauty could run skin-deep. After her manipulations, toying with my life as she had four years ago, perhaps I should have avoided her. Despised her, even. But I found I could not. There was more to Sabrina Stafford than her outer beauty. More to the determined, merciless woman she appeared to be. Once, I'd been offered a glimpse of that person, and the moment was forever burned into my memories. I wanted to see that woman again. I wanted to understand her. Why, I might never know.

I offered my free arm to Miss Colewater, and together, we crossed the street.

"Where are the two of you off to now?" I asked once we'd safely reached the other side.

Sabrina bit her lip and turned away, though kept hold of me, almost as if she were embarrassed to reveal the information. Miss Colewater released my arm and answered for her, holding up the parcel she carried. "We're delivering this to Mrs. Barton. The family has landed on hard times, and Her Grace wished to help them."

Charity work? I watched Sabrina's face turn a light shade of pink. I had known this woman since her debut, and this was the first blush I'd ever seen her wear. It was also the first time I'd heard of her doing anything of this nature. She'd had a reputation even before her father's conviction, and it was not for helping the poor.

"That is kind of you," I said.

"Yes, well, I see no reason to ignore their struggles." She still would not look at me.

"Many would," I countered. "Problems are easier to ignore when they are not our own."

She faced me then, lifting her chin to meet my gaze from beneath her bonnet. "Some of us have a past to make up for."

Make up for? That reeked of guilt and did not sound like the Sabrina I knew. Her answer prodded at my curiosity, but before I could question her further, the door of the perfumery opened, and Mother stepped outside. My heart skipped a few beats. We had a plan to explain our connection, but that did little to put me at ease. Not when Sabrina was on such familiar terms with her.

"They did not have the scent I hoped for, but I found this in—" Mother's words cut off as her gaze landed on Sabrina, who still had my arm. Mother took in the sight and blinked, clearly confused. The expression faded quickly, as her mischievous grin appeared, and then she curtsied. "Your Grace, what a surprise. I hope this man isn't bothering you?"

Sabrina's mouth hung open for a long moment before she seemed to shake herself from her own surprise and dipped into a curtsy. "Not at all. He has been quite the gentleman, escorting us across the street."

"Has he now?"

I did not care for Mother's questioning tone. Not a bit. "Yes, that is what gentlemen do, is it not?"

Mother deemed a response unnecessary. And it was, given the way she stared at me, her eyes full of mischief. Blast it all, she had been here less than a day and was already scheming.

"Mrs. Davis, I have not seen you in years," said Sabrina, oblivious to the silent accusations Mother presently pinned me with. "I hope you are well?"

Mother smiled, sincerely. She was well aware of the things Sabrina had done, of how she had used both me and my friend, James, to get what she wanted. Still, no animosity appeared in her expression.

That had always been Mother's way, though. Quick to forgive and rarely one to hold a grudge.

"I am as well as can be expected," Mother replied. "And you? I know things have been trying the last few years." Her gaze wandered down Sabrina's body and back up again, and her brows creased with the perusal. Not out of judgment, I noted, but concern. What did she see?

"It has," Sabrina responded in a quiet voice, so soft the rumble of carriages and chatter of people nearly drowned her out. Her grip on my arm tightened slightly. "But I've managed well enough."

I almost missed the subtle shake of Miss Colewater's head. Did she disagree with Sabrina's assessment? Had Sabrina lied about her situation? She had gone from being the wife of a duke, living a life of financial security, to once again staying with her father after her husband died. I knew enough of Mr. Perry to guess how stressful such accommodations would be. Indeed, much of Sabrina's actions in the past had stemmed from her father's expectations.

And then news had spread of the man's criminal activity. From what I'd heard, he'd been convicted of fraud and transported to New South Wales. I wasn't certain whether she had been close enough to the man to become distressed over losing him, but his actions had left a blemish on her reputation. The rumors alone were enough to drive anyone out of London, which explained why it had been nearly three years since I saw her last.

"I had no idea Mrs. Davis was your aunt, Mr. Carrow."

Sabrina's pointed remark pulled me from my thoughts. "Oh. Yes, she is."

The Duchess hummed. "And what a coincidence that your Christian name is the same as her son's Christian name."

I swallowed hard. I had not considered this peculiarity, and suddenly, my grand idea to retain my given name seemed rather foolish. Sabrina's dark eyes glistened with sunlight, her amusement clear. Did she know? She had studied me that day at The Pump Room. I had thought myself safe when she gave no indication she doubted my falsehood.

But now, the way she smiled as if entertained by my struggle to find a reasonable explanation...how much did she suspect? The idea that my true identity was vulnerable should have worried me. Instead, I found myself almost hopeful. I wanted her to know the truth.

What was the matter with me?

I turned away, only to catch Mother glancing between us, her attention resting briefly on where Sabrina clung to my arm. Mother's brows lifted in question.

No. I knew precisely what she was thinking and had no time for it.

"My mother and aunt held a fondness for the name, is that not right, *Aunt*?" I silently begged her to cease scheming and do her part.

"Oh, we did. It was a race to see who had a son first and claimed the name. In the end, we both used it." Mother lifted her chin to demonstrate her dramatic superiority over her sister who did not exist. "Still, I won by a fortnight."

I stopped myself from rolling my eyes. At least she had played along.

Both Miss Colewater and Sabrina laughed.

"A victory to be proud of, certainly. I would expect nothing less of you, Mrs. Davis." Sabrina sighed and gestured to the parcel Miss Colewater held, releasing my arm as she did so. "Well, we shan't keep you from shopping. I need to visit the apothecary and deliver this."

"Where does Mrs. Barton live?" I asked for a distraction from the ridiculous absence I felt. It wasn't as though a woman had never been on my arm before.

"Union Street. We'll go there before heading home."

I stopped myself from inquiring where *home* was. That information wasn't important right now, or perhaps shouldn't be at all. Union Street might not be considered a dangerous part of town, but a duchess and her maid had no business going there without a proper escort.

Mother reached the same conclusion. "I believe I've had my fill of shopping. Gregory, why don't you accompany them?"

"Oh, no." Sabrina shifted on her feet. "That is not necessary. I don't wish to inconvenience either of you. We will do fine on our own."

A selfless response, and again, not what I would expect from her. When had she changed so drastically? I couldn't help wondering and wishing to dig deeper. To spend more time with her. Something about the Duchess of Rochester was certainly different.

"Nonsense." Mother swatted her response away. "It is too fine a day to waste. Gregory has nothing better to do, anyway."

I glared at her. She was right, of course, but I did not like the scheming look in her eyes.

"And who will escort you home?" I asked, poking at the obvious hole in her plan.

Mother shrugged. "Hire a hackney for me. Honestly, Gregory, I insist you escort these ladies. I will be a complete bore for the remainder of the day. Perhaps I will take a nap."

"I shan't believe that for a moment. You do not take naps. There is far too much to do to waste time sleeping. Is that not what you always say?"

She shoved a finger into my chest. "Which is why *you*, a spry young man in the first blooms of youth, will not be joining me. I am old. I can waste my time as I please."

I was thirty, not a lad fresh out of Eton, though it also seemed a personal insult to contradict her on the matter.

"Escort them," said Mother with a waggle of her brows. "It might put me in a good mood, and you could benefit from me being in a good mood."

Devious woman.

"Fine, I shall hire you a hackney if Her Grace is not opposed to my company." I turned to face Sabrina and found her grinning, clearly amused by the entire exchange. Spending time with her was not the wisest decision. The more opportunity I gave her to riddle out my identity, the more likely she was to do so. Still, I couldn't ignore the desire to learn all the ways her life had changed over the last few years. The ways *she* had changed.

"We would welcome your company, Mr. Carrow," said Sabrina. She still seemed entertained, but there was a softness to her words.

"Then you have it. Give me but a moment to find a hackney for my mo—aunt, and then we can be on our way."

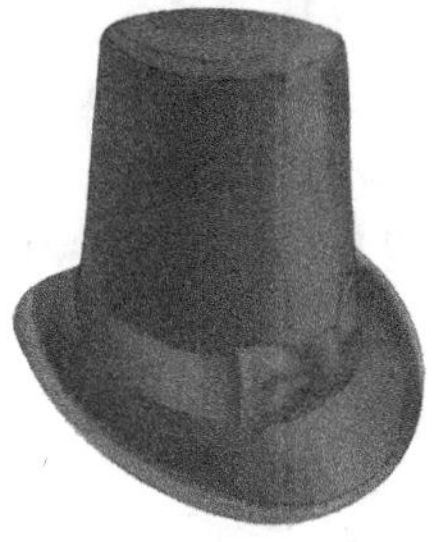

Chapter Ten

SABRINA

Having a man's escort about town was more unusual for me than I cared to admit. Once, years ago, the opposite had been true. Not a day had gone by where I was not being courted or entertained by a gentleman in some way or another. Those days were long behind me. Perhaps my status as a widow and age played some small role in that, but the greater reason rested on the damage Father's conviction had done to my reputation.

I could not blame my sire entirely for the situation, but he did hold a great deal of responsibility for it. Father had spent more time negotiating his benefits from the marriage agreement than ensuring I would be provided for. My dowry had been nothing to brag about, and I had worked hard to stretch it as far as I could.

It was no secret that the duke had left me, financially, with very little after his death, and the ducal family were happy to be rid of me. Not that I blamed them after my actions toward the new Duke of Rochester.

Regardless, all of it had landed me here in Bath with very little to my name and coffers that dried up more and more each day.

Making investments had kept me afloat, but I found inclusion in such ventures difficult. I was a duchess, but the title did me little good when my name held connections to a criminal.

"What is that for?" asked Mr. Davis, nodding to the parcel I had acquired at the apothecary. Thus far, our walk along Milsom Street had gone without much conversation. I wondered if he resented offering his escort. I would not have been surprised. I had, after all, used him quite thoroughly in the past. By all accounts, the man should not trust me.

Then again, he was still playing the part of Mr. Carrow, an alias. Had he only agreed to escort us to keep his false identity intact?

"Your Grace?"

"Forgive me," I said. "I was woolgathering."

Mr. Davis smiled down at me. He hadn't offered his arm again, instead walking at my side with his hands clasped behind him. I hated how much I longed for more contact. To walk arm in arm with a gentleman. It hadn't bothered me for some time to be so forgotten by Society, to live without the callers and parties. Today, I felt it most acutely, and it pricked at my emotions.

"There is nothing to forgive," said Mr. Davis. "I merely wondered what you needed from the apothecary. Is it for Mrs. Barton?"

I nodded. "I heard that one of her girls is struggling. Nothing serious, mind you. A bit of hay fever, which she experiences every summer. Mrs. Barton typically purchases some herbs"—I held up the pouch I carried—"but she has yet to visit the apothecary. I know her funds are low and thought that might be the reason."

"So you purchased them for her?" he asked, though there was little question in his tone.

"Yes."

"That is kind of you."

I stopped walking, as did Mr. Davis. Helen, who had been following close behind, nearly stumbled into us. She backed up a few paces, affording us some privacy, but it did not matter to me. Helen knew everything—my goals and ambitions—and nothing I said would be news to her.

"Mr. Carrow," I began, my tone firm. "I do not need you to acknowledge my actions as kind or helpful or...anything of the sort. I am simply taking these herbs to someone who needs them. I do not need your praise."

His lips twitched. "Much to make up for, as you said earlier."

"Indeed, so I would appreciate less commentary on the matter."

"Your actions warrant it. The words do you no harm and have no effect on your work. What is so wrong with a little praise, Your Grace?"

I faced forward and began walking at a more determined pace. "That is not why I am doing this."

Mr. Davis caught up to me in three long strides. "I never accused you of that."

He hadn't, and perhaps my frustration came down to assuming he would. In the past, it would have been true. I had never helped with charity work unless I had something to gain from it. I had done everything for entirely the wrong reasons, and I would not allow myself to fall into that pattern again. The people I helped deserved better.

With my increased pace, my head grew warm and my balance wavered. The strange dizziness had pressed on me more as of late, and I had no time to address the cause. I slowed down until the feeling subsided. Unfortunately, that allowed my escort to catch up with me.

"Why Mrs. Barton?" Mr. Davis's question caught me off guard, and I struggled to find a reasonable explanation that left me less vulnerable.

"Does it matter? She needs the help, and so, I will give it."

Mr. Davis hummed, but his questions ceased as we rounded the corner onto Union Street. I relaxed the longer we walked without conversation, hoping he would give up on his interrogation. Mrs. Barton did need the help, but that was not the reason I had chosen her family. Not initially, at least.

"Here it is." I stopped in front of an old, two-story apartment. The place wore the years as a beggar might, with patches and holes. The disrepair prodded at me, as it had the first time I had come here. I hadn't known the Barton women then. I did not know them as personally as I would like now, either.

"Shall we knock?" Mr. Davis asked in a hushed voice.

"No." I shook my head. "I will leave it at the door. They will find it."

His brows furrowed. "Whatever for? Surely it would be wiser—"

"Because my assistance is not particularly wanted." A stinging heat brought tears to my eyes. I had made the mistake of revealing my identity the first time I visited. Mrs. Barton had shut the door in my face. Now, I simply left things on the doorstep, too afraid the woman would not accept my assistance otherwise. Penny helped, too, by not disclosing when I paid a bill or requested things on the Bartons' behalf.

I swallowed against my dry throat. "Wait here with Helen."

It was an order, and to my surprise, Mr. Davis obeyed. I could feel his gaze on my back as I approached the house carrying both the parcel from the apothecary and the item I had purchased from Sinclair's. A few seconds was all I needed, then I would make a quick escape. Mrs. Barton would be none the wiser, and her daughter would have the relief she needed.

Gently, I placed both parcels on the ground and retreated backwards several steps, my heart pounding. I had done this more times than I could count, but still, each visit filled me with anticipation and nerves.

With a sigh of relief, I made my way back to the others until a squeaking door and a squeal of delight drew me to a stop. "I've caught you! Our angel!"

Slowly, I turned to face the house, and my stomach sank. The eldest Barton girl, not more than twelve, grinned at me from where she stood at the door holding both parcels. What was I to do? Instinct told me to run. If Mrs. Barton saw me, she would chuck the parcels onto the street.

I backed up another step, and the girl's smile wavered. "Don't leave. We want to thank you."

"I hope that will help your sister." It was enough, and I should have left right then, but I couldn't help but add, "Has your father returned?"

The girl's shoulders fell, and a distressed expression replaced her exuberance. I knew the answer, and guilt burned through my chest like hot coals.

I intended to turn away, but Mrs. Barton appeared in the doorway, standing behind her daughter. They resembled one another with their brown hair and eyes. Even in their rounded chins. Mrs. Barton, though, possessed a far more haggard appearance, the strain of life's struggles heavily pronounced in her sallow skin. Her mouth, drawn into a flat line, spoke of her displeasure to see me.

A silent exchange passed between us, her eyes full of quiet rage and accusation. Apologies perched on the tip of my tongue, but I did not know whether they would make matters better or worse. So, there they stayed until Mrs. Barton pulled her daughter inside and closed the door.

At least the parcels had entered the house with them.

I returned to Helen and Mr. Davis deflated but did my best to hide my dejection. The latter watched my approach, his brows furrowed.

"We will return home now," I said before he could question me. "Your escort was appreciated, Mr. Carrow."

I slipped past him and headed down the street at a quick pace. I had no desire to explain myself to him. It wasn't as though he didn't know about my past. He had been there—been a victim of my callousness. Still, to explain why I needed to help the Bartons specifically despite how little they wanted my assistance...well, I carried enough guilt. I did not need his judgment, too.

"I would prefer to see you safely home."

Mr. Davis's breathy voice startled me. I hadn't expected him to follow. Why was he so adamant about escorting me and Helen? His mother was not here to force the issue. I did not deserve his care and attention and could not understand it.

I glanced over my shoulder and noted Helen struggling to keep up behind us. My pace slowed. "That is not necessary, though I appreciate the consideration."

His lips lifted. "Are you so opposed to my presence that you would not allow me to end the day with a clear conscience? Besides, my mo—aunt will have my head if I abandon you now."

I tried not to smile at his near slip. He had almost called Mrs. Davis his mother a handful of times today. "I am not opposed, sir. I simply have no wish for you to feel obligated."

"I don't."

"No? So you are not escorting us as a gentleman wishing to keep his conscience clear?"

His smile turned into a wide grin. "It is not the only reason, no."

The response made my stomach flutter. Mr. Davis had, on a few occasions, teased me in the past, but there had always been an element of hesitation. As if he did so with fear of how I would respond. A warranted fear given how I had treated him and many others.

But today there was no hesitation about his open flirtation. Nothing guarded about the amusement in his eyes. It unsettled me to be so taken by surprise.

"What are the other reasons?" I asked, my tone even. I would not allow him to hear how his words affected me.

"Curiosity," he answered easily.

"Curiosity?" I narrowed my eyes. "I am nothing to be curious about."

"On the contrary, Your Grace. I find much about you sparks my intrigue." He looked forward, and because the sun was now directly overhead, his hat cast a shadow across his face. The light that did reach beyond the brim highlighted some of the hair on his chin, however, and I noted the slight red undertones hidden between the more prominent browns.

"Why do you have a beard?" The words fell out before I could think better of them, and I bit my lip, heat creeping into my cheeks.

Mr. Davis laughed lightly. "It is not my first choice but a necessity at present."

For his alias. He did not wish to be recognized. I understood yet could say nothing on the matter, not without revealing that I knew his true identity. Would it be so terrible to do so? After all, I knew Mr. Davis was after Arthur Westmore, same as I. We could unite in our efforts.

But I also didn't know how Mr. Davis would feel about a woman pursuing an investment venture. So many of the upper class shunned ladies for dabbling so deeply in financial affairs. To tell him the truth, to tell him my plans, would be to jeopardize them. I could not afford it.

Besides, no gentleman would take well to a woman dressing in men's clothing.

"Are you looking forward to the picnic?" asked Mr. Davis.

I tilted my head from side to side. "I suppose in some ways. I would rather not attend, in truth, but I have a reason to be there."

"Oh? And what reason might that be?"

"Out of necessity," I replied with the lift of my brow. If he would not be forthcoming with his answers, I needn't be either.

Mr. Davis laughed, the sound deep and rich in a way that tightened my chest. "Fair enough, Your Grace. Fair enough. Perhaps you might allow me to guess?"

"We are not so far from Gay Street, sir. You may guess until we have reached my house."

Mr. Davis gave a solid nod, but to my confusion, did not make an attempt right away. We walked in silence for several minutes before he spoke again. "The food. The cook is secretly the best in the whole of England."

"I cannot say I know the extent of the cook's abilities," I answered.

"Then it is not the prospect of eating strawberries until you are ill that appeals to you?"

"Not at all, though enjoying a few will be an added benefit."

Mr. Davis hummed. "At The Pump Room, you stated you are not overly fond of social events, so I can cross socializing off as the reason. Are you hoping to see a particular gentleman there?"

"Yes, but not for the reasons you will assume." I bit my tongue, reminding myself to tread carefully. Mr. Davis may know of my past courtships and efforts to ensnare men of title, but Mr. Carrow did not.

"What assumptions do you assume I've made?" he asked, clearly amused.

"That I seek a match. Marriage. That is not the case. I am perfectly content in my widowhood."

Perfectly might not have been entirely accurate, but Mr. Davis needn't know how often I found myself lonely. How often I longed for the company of others. I may not miss the social obligations I once endured, but spending my days largely on my own was not precisely the life I wanted, either.

"And this gentleman you hope to see but are uninterested in marrying, he will be there?"

"Possibly. I cannot say for certain. I am merely hopeful."

Mr. Davis nodded slowly, as if mulling this over. "And if he is not? What then?"

"Then I will endure as best I can."

He clasped his hands behind his back, and his gaze grew distant as though he were deep in thought. I desperately wished to know what he was thinking. It seemed unfair that he could ask me questions about my life but I could not do the same. Not when he was pretending to be someone else.

"And there is no one else you are hoping to see there?" he asked. "No friends or family?"

I opened my mouth to say *no*, but it stuck to my tongue, a half-truth unwilling to leave. There was one more person I hoped would attend the picnic, and drat it all if he wasn't the one asking the question. The hope was as ludicrous as it was dangerous. I should not want to spend more time in Mr. Davis's company.

I cleared my throat. "I have no family. At least none that I am close to. I don't possess many friends, either. Just Helen and Penny."

"Penny?"

"Penelope Sinclair. Her father owns the haberdashery on Milsom. She hasn't been invited to the picnic, but Helen"—I gestured behind me to my maid—"she will go with me. I suppose that means I'll have one. I shan't be completely friendless."

Mr. Davis tilted his head, and his gaze took on the studious look once again. "You are not what I expected, Your Grace."

I wanted to understand what he meant by that statement. Worse, I wanted to know whether that was a point of favor. Was I not what he expected because he thought I had changed? I wanted that to be true. I wanted to be different from the woman he knew all those years ago. But how could I ask without revealing I knew the truth?

"You've miscounted," he said.

"I beg your pardon?"

"You've miscounted." His lips lifted into another handsome smile as he repeated the words. "You shall have two friends at the picnic, for I plan to attend."

Something inside me twisted, and a fresh wave of burning tears attempted to break free. His words should not have brought me such emotion, but they did. I could not deny I was pleased to know he planned to attend, but having him claim me as a friend...

It was unexpected. It was something I hadn't realized I wanted or needed.

"Thank you," I whispered, taking the last few steps to arrive in front of my townhouse. I gestured to the building, ignoring the pang of disappointment threading through me. "This is it. Home. I must thank you again for your escort, Mr. Carrow. Would you care to come inside for tea?"

He shook his head. "No, I thank you. I should make sure my aunt returned home safely...and that she did not get into trouble during my absence. I would, however, like to offer you an escort again. Unless, of course, you have already arranged transportation to the picnic?"

"Mrs. Anderton has asked us to meet at her townhome at The Circus. From there, she offered a carriage for me and others, but I can send her a note if...I mean to say that, if it would not be too much trouble, I would be glad to ride with you."

Mr. Davis took my hand and brought it to his lips. "Then I will see you there."

My face had never felt so warm, and an unsettling giddiness filled me. These feelings simply would not do. I had too much to accomplish to let myself become distracted by this man's charm. We were friends. That was all, though I could hardly fathom how we had become even that much. Regardless, my focus must remain on finding Mr. Westmore and gaining his favor.

I pulled my hand away with a strained smile. "Thank you, Mr. Carrow. I shall see you on Wednesday, then."

"Wednesday." He backed up a few paces, his smile wide. "I look forward to it."

So did I, and that was entirely unacceptable.

Chapter Eleven

"**I** have come to a decision."

I glanced up from the book I hadn't been reading to look at Mother, who sat across from me. We had settled into the drawing room after supper, she with her needlework and me with a book. I hadn't read a single word, though. Not with how distracted my mind was by a particular duchess. Sabrina had surprised me today, and I couldn't seem to put the changes I saw in her from my mind.

Moreover, why was she so fixated on helping the Bartons? The matron clearly did not want her assistance. The animosity in that glare had been tangible, and the look of disappointment in Sabrina's eyes...

Ridiculous. I should not care as much as I did.

"What decision have you come to?" I asked. There was no sense in hoping this involved an invitation request. Even after I had told Mother about offering Sabrina a ride to the picnic, she still hadn't budged. No, she had grinned and reminded me that I had yet to be invited to the event and that arriving unannounced was bad form. I had thought to force her hand, but Mother was never one to be coerced so easily, especially when she held all the cards.

"I will write to Mrs. Anderton on your behalf," said Mother without looking up from her embroidery.

I sat up straighter, and the book slid from my lap onto the floor. "You will?"

"Yes, but it will cost you."

Of course, it would. Why would my own mother ever do something for me without stipulations? In her defense, she never asked for anything terrible, and it was her way of motivating me to do what I likely already should have been doing. Still, it irked me to no end. "What price must I pay? Another stroll down Milsom?"

She tilted her head and pinned me with an incredulous look. "Have I ever been so easily bribed?"

No. Unfortunately. "What then?"

Mother's gaze dropped back to her needlework, her expression stoic. "You will call on Her Grace twice after the picnic. And you must take her on a walk or ride in addition."

I scoffed, shaking my head. "Why?"

One of Mother's brows raised, but she did not look at me. "That is generally how courtship works."

"I am not courting the Duchess. She has no interest in me."

Mother shrugged. "Call it whatever you prefer, then. My stipulations stand."

"To what end, Mother? You know how she treated James. I cannot think why you would push me toward her of all people."

Her fingers paused, and she seemed to genuinely contemplate my response. "People change, Gregory. Our past misdeeds should not define us when we strive to do better. To *be* better. I would have missed out on many of life's most precious treasures had I clung to old judgments. I suspect Her Grace has grown much over the last few years. Some by the forced changes in her circumstances and some by choice. The latter is often more lasting and true and should be given the chance to shine."

"You have forgiven her, then?" I asked. Mother had always held a fondness for my friend, James. He had been like a second son to her. Mother had been furious when she learned how Sabrina had manipulated him. How the Duchess had left him broken.

But that anger had given way to sympathy. When, I could not say. Perhaps as the rumors about Sabrina's father circulated in London. Perhaps before, at a house party where *I* had seen the first hint of change in the Duchess.

"I do not hold on to the past," Mother replied. "We all make mistakes. Some are worse than others, but it is how we grow from them that should define us, not the mistakes themselves."

She looked at me, and it seemed as though she saw into my soul. I had made my share of mistakes—mistakes Mother remained unaware of. Would she forgive me so easily if she knew? I believed she would. The trouble was I could not forgive myself.

"Besides," Mother continued. "I am worried about her. I think she could use more support in her life."

I nodded. "Her reputation has likely suffered, and it is my understanding that she is not supported, financially or otherwise, by the new Duke of Rochester. Her apartment on Gay Street is modest, but not what one would expect for a duchess."

"I imagine, but that is not what I meant."

My brows furrowed. "Then what do you mean?"

Mother sighed. "Look at her, Gregory. Truly look at her when you take her to the picnic. I think you will see precisely what I mean and why I am concerned."

"Would it not be simpler for you to tell me?"

A light chuckle escaped her. "When have I ever handed you something? Besides, it will be good for you to exercise a bit of observation. Courtships go far better when the gentleman pays attention."

I groaned. "I am not courting her, Mother. I will do as your stipulations require, but it is a means to an end, nothing more."

Mother swatted the comment away. "Name it what you must to sleep at night. So long as you agree to call on her and—"

"Yes, yes, yes. I will call on her twice and take her for a stroll. Now will you write to Mrs. Anderton? Time is of the essence."

Mother set her needlework aside and stood. "I shall do so straight away."

The grin she wore and the giddiness in her step as she left the room made me uneasy. I wasn't oblivious to her goals. She wanted me wed, and for whatever reason, she had chosen the Duchess for the role.

But I could not think of marriage right now, and even if I had the leisure of doing so, Sabrina would never give me a second glance as a suitor.

Would she?

In the past, I had no hope of gaining her favor, but things were different now. *She* was different. Did that mean I had a chance?

The better question was: did I want one?

I shook myself free of the nonsensical thought, removing myself from the settee. Mother was getting inside my head. I had an objective that required all of my focus, and I could not sway from it without risking everything.

No matter how tempting an idea it admittedly was.

Mother was in an excellent mood, and that concerned me. She had been rather helpful the last few days after requesting an invitation to Mrs. Anderton's picnic. The note had arrived this morning, and despite the reminder that I intended to go without her, Mother retained her pleasant demeanor.

Not a single word about the injustice of her exclusion from the upcoming social activity.

I narrowed my eyes, watching her take dainty bites of her breakfast. She had never been one to hold a grudge, but she had also never been slow to voice her complaints to me either.

"You are in a rather good mood this morning," I remarked.

"Why should I not be? It is a lovely day. There is but one thing that could make it better."

"One thing," I repeated. "And what might that be?"

"You could remove that beaver from your face."

I groaned, but Mother wasn't finished. "Honestly, Gregory. How do you expect to woo any lady with that hairy rug covering your handsome features?"

"Mother," I said firmly. "Let me make myself clear. I am not attempting to woo anyone. I know it is your greatest desire to see me wed, but now is simply not the time—"

"Then when?" She huffed. "I want grandchildren. I want to see you settled. I want to know you aren't spending nights on end at those hells!"

I winced, feeling the guilt for having slipped out again last night for that very purpose. I could argue that I still hoped to see Westmore, but his absence had not sent me home. No, I had stayed for hours. Regardless, Mother had never brought up my gambling before. We tiptoed around the subject, but I almost preferred this blunt discussion. At least then I could face her disappointment head-on. Father, too, would have been disappointed in how I had wasted my inheritance, with how I had squandered everything he'd worked hard to build.

But Father was gone. There was no facing his disappointment. Instead, it followed me like a dark cloud that would never clear.

I breathed in and released a slow sigh. "I promise, once I have this money from Cartwell, things will be different. Until then, I can devote no time to courting anyone."

Even as I said it, Sabrina's face appeared in my mind. Her dark eyes and lashes, her soft skin, her smile—those attributes made my heart beat a little quicker, but they were nothing compared to the things I had discovered this week. The kindness, so unexpected from the woman I thought I knew, had lured me in, had piqued my curiosity beyond reason. And then there was the pain and sorrow that filled her features after Mrs. Barton's silent rejection. That had sparked the most intrigue, as well as deep concern. I'd seen the Duchess vulnerable like that once before, and the memory of that moment haunted me. I wanted to alleviate it. To offer comfort.

Who was I to offer a duchess comfort? Never mind that I had done that very thing once before. It had happened so naturally then, without thought. I often wondered if my actions that day had been a mistake.

But mistake or not, I felt no regret.

"So long as you don't forget my stipulations, I will let the hair issue rest for now," said Mother.

"How could I when you remind me every hour?" I muttered.

We finished breakfast in silence, and then I saw to a few matters of business before bidding Mother goodbye, claiming a promise that she would behave in my absence. I left the apartment, and our coachman greeted me from where he stood next to our family carriage, the same conveyance that had brought Mother to Bath.

I nodded once in acknowledgement then settled onto the soft cushions. At least our carriage was in good order, unlike Fallborn. The estate grew into more disrepair with every passing year, and for so long, I had been helpless to keep up.

That would change. It had to.

The drive to The Circus required only minutes, and already there stood a crowd of people patiently awaiting instruction. I was not familiar with Mrs. Anderton, but she introduced herself once I had alighted and expressed her disappointment that Mother had not accompanied me.

"I am afraid my aunt is abed with a terrible headache," I said to ensure the matron took no offense by the absence. "She sends me with her deepest regrets."

At least that much was not a lie. Mother would not have missed such an event were I not insistent she stay behind.

"Let her know I hope she is soon recovered. Perhaps I shall call on her later this week."

I forced a smile. I had no desire for callers at the apartment, but I could not voice it without raising suspicions. Besides, Mrs. Anderton had never met Gregory Davis, therefore she could not truly be a threat to my ruse.

"I am certain she would appreciate that," I said. "And I must also offer my gratitude for the invitation."

Mrs. Anderton barely concealed a grimace, her gaze wandering over my face. "Yes, well, your aunt is a dear friend. She would not have made the request unless you were of good character and a gentleman."

She did not sound entirely convinced, but I put on my most charming smile anyway.

What I wouldn't have given to have shaved this morning. Blasted beard. It put everyone at ill ease. I had instructed Thomas to keep it tidy and trimmed, but society simply did not approve of facial hair, especially on someone of my age.

"I can vouch for Mr. Carrow's character."

My heart immediately responded to Sabrina's voice, picking up pace as she approached with a soft smile. Her eyes were shadowed by the brim of her bonnet, a soft yellow to match the shade of her dress. Both served to compliment the dark curls dangling against her cheeks.

I bowed as she stopped in front of me. "Good morning, Your Grace."

Sabrina curtsied. "Good morning, Mr. Carrow. Mrs. Anderton."

"Lovely to see you, dear. I am so glad you decided to attend." The woman gave Sabrina a warm smile. I wondered at her remark momentarily before I recalled that Sabrina had stated she rarely attended social events anymore. The idea of her turning into a recluse was as perplexing as it was unexpected.

"I thank you for inviting such good company," said Sabrina. "Mr. Carrow is a friend of mine."

She turned to face me, and my stomach tightened. She had meant it, and while I had been the one to suggest we were friends, her acceptance of it still delighted me.

"Fortunate that Mr. Carrow has someone who can introduce him," said Mrs. Anderton. "Given his aunt could not attend. Indeed, I was not even aware Lucinda had a nephew until a few days ago. Or a sister."

I cleared my throat. This conversation was approaching dangerous territory. "Very fortunate, indeed. I trust Her Grace made you aware she intends to ride to Lime House in my carriage?"

"She has, and I have no objections so long as she is properly chaperoned." Mrs. Anderton placed a gentle hand on Sabrina's arm, lowering her voice. "Even as a widow, we must be cautious, yes?"

"Of course." Sabrina gave her an indulgent smile and gestured behind her to where Miss Colewater stood. "My maid will be with us to ensure nothing untoward occurs, but as I said, I can vouch for Mr. Carrow's character. He is a gentleman through and through."

Sabrina had not known me as Mr. Carrow for very long, and her compliments and reassurances pleased me greatly. I wondered, though, if she would offer Gregory Davis the same commendations. I had never done anything to risk her ire, but she certainly knew of my gambling habits and financial struggles. Where did that place me in her eyes? Was I a gentleman or a rogue? Perhaps she had never given me enough thought to care one way or the other.

"Very good," said Mrs. Anderton. "If you will excuse me, then. I must see that all of my guests have transportation so we can be on our way."

Once the matron had gone, I offered my hand to Sabrina. "Shall we?"

She accepted it, her petite, gloved fingers fitting securely in mine. We were mere steps from my carriage, but even so, my pulse pounded as I guided her over and handed her inside. Once I had helped Miss Colewater as well, I joined the two women, sitting opposite them. Sabrina's gaze was fixed on the window, and she paid my entrance no notice, her eyes searching the movement outside.

"Do you see him?" I asked.

Her head snapped toward me, her brows furrowed.

"The man you are not interested in marrying," I clarified. "I wondered if you had spotted him yet."

"Oh. No, I haven't."

"He will come," I reassured, though truthfully, I could make no such promise. My curiosity burned to know who this man was and what business she had with him, but I kept the questions to myself. We were friends, but only blossoming ones.

My attention shifted to the window, too. After all, I was also looking for a certain man. Would Westmore attend? I had almost asked Mother to inquire about whether he had been invited, but that seemed too pointed a question.

The carriage pulled forward once all the guests were ready. With no sign of Westmore, I could only hope that I had either missed him or that he intended to arrive by his own conveyance. Staring out the window would do me little good now, so I turned my attention to Sabrina. She still watched through the glass, though her expression hinted at her disappointment. Rather than inquire more about the man she hoped would attend, I seized the moment to study her without the eyes of society to judge me for it.

After all, Mother had instructed me to look at her.

Yet, I saw what I had always seen. Sabrina was as lovely now as the day she debuted, perhaps more so. I admired the way her dark hair and eyes were set off by her smooth, pale skin. Her figure, the epitome of perfection with its curves, was enough to drive a man mad.

What else did Mother see? Truly look, she had said.

My brows furrowed with concentration. Next to Miss Colewater, Sabrina was more than simply pale-skinned. In fact, her coloring was almost sickly were I to compare the two of them. Had she always been that way or was it merely the result of being indoors so much over the winter season?

My focus moved to her sunken cheeks and the sharp curve of her jaw, then down to where her collarbone was exposed. It seemed to protrude more than it should, a characteristic I had seen among the lower class where money was tighter than even I'd experienced.

Destitution. Sabrina had once told me that I was not the only one who faced that sort of future. I hadn't given the comment adequate thought until now. She had lost financial stability, despite marrying a duke, and with her father now imprisoned, I imagined her life was not without difficulty.

But destitution? Had she fallen so low?

How desperately I wished to ask more about her present circumstances, to understand all that she had endured the past three years. The words waited to be spoken, but how was I to broach such a complicated and sensitive topic?

"Are you well, Mr. Carrow?"

I blinked, meeting Sabrina's gaze. "I am."

She tilted her head, a mixture of disbelief and worry playing over her features.

"I am," I reassured. "A few unpleasant thoughts, but nothing some fresh strawberries won't cure."

Whether she believed me or not, our conversation shifted to safer topics, and we arrived at Lime House shortly thereafter. The home was quite modest but boasted a large horse stable to the north and the land surrounding it was decorated with tenant farms. The area was peaceful compared to the bustle in town, and I found that it reminded me much of Fallborn.

A pang of longing coursed through me. Generally, I preferred the busy life of town to my country estate, but I couldn't deny the yearning I felt for home. Perhaps it was more the desire to finally see to the estate's needs, to return it to its former glory. Fallborn was modest in its own right, but still, it had been in my family for several generations.

It was home.

I wanted it to remain as such.

Upon arriving, the guests were immediately given baskets and directed west of the house to the strawberry patches. We all climbed the hill and made the short walk in eager anticipation and good humor. I stuck close to Sabrina's side, which went largely unnoticed by the Duchess as she studied the crowd, presumably still searching for this *man* of hers. Westmore was also nowhere to be spotted.

I swallowed my frustrations. If I could not find him socializing with Bath's upper class or at the gaming hells, then what was I supposed to do? What if the man had left town completely? The situation stoked my ire, but I did my best to hide it. I was already here. I might as well enjoy the picnic. Besides, I still had the possibility of gaining information from the other guests.

A quick sweep informed me I did recognize one other person in our group. Mr. Martin met my gaze, and I offered a nod of acknowledgment. He reluctantly returned the gesture with a wary expression. Our conversation in The Pump Room had not been productive, but second chances always proved more valuable, did they not?

Sabrina stepped away to search through a patch shaded by the nearby towering oak trees, and on impulse, I made to follow her, ramming into something solid as I did so. A sharp squeal followed, and with a quick hand, I steadied a young woman before she fell over.

"My apologies, miss."

"Hanaway."

"I beg your pardon?" I asked, retrieving her basket from the ground.

"My name," she said. "My name is Ruth Hanaway."

Ah. I had heard of Miss Hanaway, a wealthy heiress fresh from the American continent. Her debut in London had been...well, I may not have participated in balls and parties last Season, but the rumors of the acerbic way she dealt with any suitor bold enough to declare himself had been plenty, even within the lesser clubs such as The Sparrow.

I held the basket toward her. "My apologies, Miss Hanaway. I was not looking where I was going."

Miss Hanaway accepted it and studied me, unabashedly. Her gaze roamed my face and landed on what I could only guess was my beard. Her nose scrunched slightly. "Apology accepted, sir."

"Gregory Carrow," I said. It wasn't a proper introduction, but I hadn't precisely asked for one either.

Miss Hanaway blinked a few times, and it seemed to me that she came to some conclusion, her brows furrowed and her smile forced as she dipped a quick curtsy. She scurried off without another word, and I shook my head.

Blasted beard.

Not that I truly wished for a more intimate acquaintance. That was not my purpose here.

My eyes immediately searched the strawberry patch, and not for Westmore as they ought to have. He was my sole purpose for attending this picnic, and yet, it was Sabrina's lithe form my attention settled upon. She sat next to another young woman, happily engaged in conversation, a genuine smile filling her expression.

I joined them, kneeling near enough to catch both of their attention. "Good afternoon. Might you introduce me to your friend, Your Grace?"

"Of course," said Sabrina. "This is Penelope Sinclair. Her father owns the haberdashery on Milsom Street. Penny, this is Mr. Gregory Carrow."

"A pleasure," I said with a cordial dip of my head.

"I came for a delivery and was invited to stay," said Miss Sinclair as if she felt the need to explain her presence. "Mrs. Anderton is most kind."

"I do not know our host well, but I must agree given she offered me an invitation at the last minute." I avoided Sabrina's eye, but I could see the quizzical look she wore in my periphery. "Regardless, I am glad you could join us."

"Thank you, sir." Miss Sinclair's response was quiet. I imagined she did not receive the same welcome from everyone.

It was odd that the daughter of a merchant would be welcome here among Bath's high society, but that is not what I found the most curious. I still struggled to understand this drastic change in Sabrina. Four years ago, she never would have associated with the daughter of a merchant beyond whatever interactions were required for purchasing goods or services, let alone have such an intimate friendship with one.

But friends they were, as was evident in their continued exchanges as we picked strawberries.

"There are many here I'm not acquainted with," said Sabrina, adding several berries to her basket as she looked over the large group. "Do either of you know who that gentleman is?"

I followed where she pointed and shook my head when I didn't recognize the man. He was quite tall with a broad frame, and his tan skin suggested he spent a great deal of time out of doors. His most prominent feature, though, was his tight scowl.

"That is Mr. Williamson," said Miss Sinclair. "He has recently come from the American continent."

Sabrina grimaced. "He looks as though he has eaten something rather sour."

"Perhaps it is merely his disposition that is sour," I said, stuffing another strawberry into my mouth. "Not all of us can be sweet and charming, like these strawberries."

"He is not sour." Miss Sinclair glowered at me. "He is likely exhausted from his travels."

"You know what else he is?" Sabrina asked. "Handsome."

Her words sent a prickle of jealousy through me until she continued with a wide grin. "Are the two of you acquainted, Penny? He seems to catch your eye with great frequency."

Miss Sinclair's cheeks turned rosy. "He does not catch my eye and certainly not with frequency. We met when he came to buy new clothes, that is all."

"And you did not tell me? I should know if a man claims my friend's attention."

"He has not...you have no room to talk." Miss Sinclair glanced at me, then lowered her voice, though not so low that I could not hear. "You arrived with a man who is not your relation. Explain that."

"He's a friend," Sabrina defended, though her cheeks were now closer to the color of the strawberries.

What was I, a fly on the wall? The two of them prattled on about me as if I were not sitting right here. It was, admittedly, entertaining to overhear.

One of Miss Sinclair's brows rose, but she said nothing more, and neither did Sabrina. Both of them focused on harvesting berries, and I was left to ponder on Sabrina's blush. Our arrival together could certainly be misconstrued. Was she embarrassed by the possibility?

Once my current area had been completely harvested, I shifted farther toward the trees, bringing me right next to Sabrina. I leaned forward, and my arm brushed hers, sending a rush of heat down to my fingertips.

"You know," she said in a light tone, "I have already cleared that area."

"Have you? Then you won't mind if I check your work. Make sure you haven't missed any."

She lifted her chin to meet my gaze from beneath her bonnet and passed me a playful glare. "I did not miss any."

"You are so certain. Perhaps we should make a game of it. If I find a berry, you owe me a favor."

Sabrina scoffed. "What sort of favor—not that I believe you will find anything."

"A simple favor to be determined at a later date," I answered.

"And if you do not find a berry? What do I get?"

"A favor from me, naturally."

She considered this for several moments before giving a firm nod. "Very well, but I am very thorough. You shan't win."

Thorough was, unfortunately, accurate. Minutes passed, and I found not a single berry. It was worth the loss to catch Sabrina's grin and the way she shook her head with amusement. It was worth each brush of my arm against hers as I meticulously searched the spot she had vacated.

"Well, my basket is nearly full," she said, sitting back on her heels.

I reached inside and stole a bit of her hard work, then threw it into my mouth with a dramatic hum of delight. Sabrina slapped my hand away when I went for another.

"Eat the berries from your basket. I won't have you stealing mine and making me look lazy."

"Yours is full enough no one will notice if I eat a few," I countered. "Besides, is that not what we are here for? To pick and eat strawberries."

"Some of us apparently," she muttered, brushing her skirts as she stood.

I stood and, plucking a large berry from my basket, offered it to her. "Try one. They are delightful."

"I will wait until they announce the picnic is ready."

"Oh, come now, Your Grace. One strawberry will not fill you." I pressed the berry closer, ignoring the way Miss Sinclair watched us from the other side of the patch.

Sabrina sighed with feigned exasperation and set down her basket. "Fine. I'll have one, and that is all for now. I had a rather large breakfast."

I watched as she put the red fruit to her lips, and the hum of chatter around us seemed to fade. I had never observed a woman eating with such...interest before. My gaze was attached to her lips and the way her tongue ran over them on occasion to catch the juice before it slipped onto her chin. The air had been warm when we arrived, but I felt a sudden surge of heat from within. Thomas had tied my cravat far too tight.

"You were right," she said, oblivious to her effect on me. "They are rather *delightful*." Her voice dipped low on the last word, mimicking me. Something about it struck a cord of familiarity.

I nodded, and without a word, offered her another berry from my basket. Sabrina glared at me and dramatically propped a hand on her hip. "I said one, Mr. Carrow."

But I hardly heard the teasing words that followed, too fixated on the way she stood, and not due to how particularly attractive a pose it was. No, in that one movement, Sabrina had unlocked something in my mind, and the pieces began to fit together like a puzzle I hadn't meant to solve. That voice, the stance, those dark lashes, and even the way her lips lifted in a crooked smile...

I had seen and heard all of it before while having a discussion with a gentleman in a dark alley outside a gaming hell. A gentleman who possessed dark hair, thick lashes, and a rather feminine physique. A gentleman whose characteristics were not unlike Sabrina's.

I chuckled, the notion almost beyond my comprehension. "You are Mr. Blyth."

Chapter Twelve

SABRINA

My stomach sank to my toes at Mr. Davis's proclamation, and I froze. How could he have possibly figured out my ruse? I had said nothing of Mr. Westmore—nothing of investments. We had been discussing strawberries, for heaven's sake.

Regardless, it would not do for him to know the truth. I wanted to trust Mr. Davis, but instinct insisted I tread cautiously. After all, few men in my life had ever proven themselves trustworthy. My cousin, Phillip, was perhaps the only exception, but I wouldn't burden my cousin with this secret. I hadn't any idea how he would respond to me dressing as a man and entering an illegal gaming establishment.

On second thought, I *did* know how my stuffy cousin would respond. He would demand I move in with his family so he could keep an eye on me and all sense of freedom would vanish. I did not need someone ordering me about, not when I had left behind all the expectations and chains of the past.

Have you left all the chains behind? my mind whispered.

I ignored it. I was more free now than I had ever been. That was the truth of it, and I would not allow my secret to get out so easily. Not when it had the potential to take away every ounce of my independence.

I furrowed my brows and forced my expression into one of utter confusion. "I beg your pardon?"

Mr. Davis grinned, his eyes lit with amusement. "You're him. Do not deny it. You were there that night at The—"

I rushed forward, my basket swinging so precariously that several berries fell out, and grabbed his arm. "Shush! I do not know what you're on about, Mr. Carrow, but accusing me of being a *him* is not going to do my reputation any favors. You must know by now that I have been shunned by a decent portion of society, especially in London."

Not that I truly cared about that.

I glanced around us, noting Penny had gone elsewhere. Fortunately, most of the party were either busy filling their baskets or conversing in the shade, too preoccupied to have overheard anything.

Mr. Davis stepped closer, so close his coat brushed my arm. He lowered his voice to a whisper. "I am aware that you have suffered the past three years, Your Grace, though not aware to the extent that I would like. However, that has no bearing on what I have only just come to realize: you have been parading about Bath under an alias."

I had two options. I could continue to argue against his *realizations*, pretend I hadn't any notion of who Mr. Blyth was, or I could accept that the truth was out and confess, hoping beyond measure Mr. Davis would keep the knowledge to himself. The latter was far too risky for my tastes. So long as there was a chance Mr. Davis would believe himself mistaken, I would not give in.

"I have never paraded about Bath, sir," I said firmly, stepping closer to him. "And certainly not under an alias."

"You have," he insisted.

"You insult me. Why would I do such a thing? Why would I put my reputation in more jeopardy? The entire idea is...is...nonsensical. I am a duchess." It was not without effort that I kept myself from wincing. I hated referring to my title.

"Why would you do it, indeed?" His eyes rounded. "You were hoping to see Westmore today. Is that not who you have searched for since the moment we arrived—nay, before we even left The Circus?"

"I am not acquainted with a *Westmore*." That wasn't a lie, at least. Sabrina Stafford had never met Arthur Westmore. Only Mr. Blyth had that privilege.

Mr. Davis scoffed. "Not well acquainted, you mean. Not after you chased him off, ruining both our chances with him."

My mouth dropped. "I will not take all of the blame for that. If you hadn't pouted about me playing on your card choices—"

"Ah, hah!" He held up a finger, a triumphant grin pulling his cheeks. "How could you possibly know about that unless you are Mr. Blyth?"

Drat this man. He'd tricked me, praying upon my pride. What could I do now? There was clearly no dissuading him, and the failure stoked my anger—anger that stemmed from the past. I would not be in the situation were it not for Father or even the late duke, but the greatest blame rested on me. I had made the decisions that led me here. I could have refused the duke's offer. I could have sought a different way to gain capital instead of dressing up as a man and pretending.

I could have...

Tears pricked at my eyes. As much as I wished to change my choices, I could not. Even if I could, what would I have done differently? At the time, I hadn't seen another option. Disobeying Father had held its own consequences, just as desperation had driven me to manipulate Mr. Davis during his house party. That same desperation drove me to become Mr. Blyth. It seemed I was always swimming in deep water, struggling to remain afloat. At what point would I exhaust myself and lose the battle?

"Your Grace?" Mr. Davis's voice fell over me, soft and gentle. I met his gaze and saw concern in his eyes. Those brilliant green eyes that had haunted me for so long. They had looked at me this way before, and the memory of this man's embrace was so vivid I could almost feel it now, enveloping me in a cocoon of warmth and security.

How I longed to be in his arms again, as illogical and dangerous as such a thing would be.

Mr. Davis reached forward as though to touch my cheek, perhaps to wipe away the tear that had escaped, but I stepped back to evade him. My bonnet snagged on a low tree branch and was snatched off my head with the hasty movement. It landed on the ground at my feet, and I quickly gathered the fabric in my hands, loosened the strings, and replaced it on my head.

Not before Mr. Davis caught a glimpse of my hair. His shocked expression suggested that, despite the way Helen had pinned and curled my dark locks, he could see how short it was.

Drat it all. This was yet more evidence against me. There would be no convincing Mr. Davis now.

"Well," I said, retrying the bow to keep my bonnet in place, "I suppose I shan't deny it anymore. Instead, I must ask that you keep the information to yourself."

He studied me for a long moment. "I'm not certain I can do that, not if you intend to continue the charade. You have no business—"

"No business?" My voice raised enough to catch the attention of Mrs. Anderton and several others. I waited until their attention was once again engaged before continuing in a whisper. "My business is my business, Mr. *Davis*, and I expect you to stay out of it."

I marched away, leaving him and his panicked expression behind.

GREGORY

Sabrina knew. It should not have surprised me that the woman had figured it out. We weren't precisely close, but we did have a history. I suspected seeing me escort Mother around Milsom had not helped my case.

I watched her stomp away, inclined to rush after her, but arguing when others were around to hear would do neither of us any favors. Dressing as a man would damage her reputation more than it already was, and if word got out that I was here under a false name, my mission would flounder. All the money Cartwell promised would be yanked from my hands.

And I dared not think how he would react to learn I had spent half his initial payment with nothing to show for it. Certainly, some had gone toward catching Westmore's attention, but not all of my gambling had been for the sake of the cause.

I had to ensure Sabrina would keep quiet.

Mrs. Anderton announced it was time for the picnic, and the group gathered their baskets and headed down the hill toward the house. Perhaps I could find a way to get Sabrina alone long enough to finish our conversation. We would have the carriage ride home, but that might be too late should she decide to spread the truth among those at the picnic.

Not that she was likely to do that. Exposing me would, inadvertently, expose her. Still, I would feel better knowing we were of the same understanding.

I walked quickly with my near-empty basket. A servant took it from me once we had reached the picnic area, and I rushed toward Sabrina as she sat down at one of the tables, a bit too hastily as I rattled some of the dinnerware and startled the Duchess.

"What are you doing?" she whispered with a frustrated tone.

"I'm about to eat. What are you doing?"

She glared at me, and while things between us were clearly on rocky ground, I couldn't help my smile.

"Must you sit here?" she spat and received a censored look from several elderly ladies down the table.

"I must sit here," I answered as I began to fill my plate. The spread over the table was impressive. Ham, greens, warm turnovers—all of it made my stomach grumble. "You and I are not finished."

"We are. I have nothing more to say about our discussion."

"Really? Because I have quite a lot to say. Firstly, I have no intention of telling anyone about your recent escapades or about the way you dress for your evenings out. I hope you will afford me the same courtesy."

"I—"

"Secondly, but in no way less important, I feel it is my duty to encourage you to cease your late-night activities and pursue more proper entertainments."

"Entertainments? Is that what you think? That I did all of that—risked so much—for entertainment?"

I had said the wrong thing. That much was clear given the fire that burned in her dark eyes. I hadn't meant the comment to come off as offensive; I'd merely hoped to ease the tension between us by teasing her. "Either way, it is not safe. Your reputation aside—"

"You think I do not know that? I am no stranger to what goes on at the clubs. You forget, sir, that I had a father who dabbled in all sorts of illegal business. You forget that I was married to a duke who, if you must know, was no more loyal to me than he was his first wife. I am not naïve or oblivious to the ways of men."

My jaw clenched. How could a man wed a woman more than half his age and still seek company outside his marriage? Indeed, why would any man married to the woman next to me require more at all? Sabrina had been married to the duke for less than a year when he died. That the man could not even remain loyal to her for that short amount of time bothered me.

"Regardless of what you know, it is not safe for you to be there," I said.

"And it is not your job to worry about my safety."

She turned away from me and began filling her plate. She wasn't entirely wrong; it wasn't my job to worry after her. That responsibility rested with her family, but Sabrina had so little support in her life, as Mother had aptly stated. The Duke's family had no interest in her at all, casting her aside after her husband's death, and her father had been shipped away from England completely. To my knowledge, her only close male relative was her cousin, Phillip Montfert, who had inherited, and I hadn't any idea of the extent of their relationship.

Whose job, then, was it to worry after her, to serve as her protector? Sabrina was a widow, but that did not mean she should be left on her own.

"Perhaps it is not my job," I muttered, "but I cannot help worrying anyway." Why, I might never know. I could admit my attraction to the woman, but this concern ran deeper than outward appreciation of her beauty. It was rooted so far inside me that I couldn't have torn it out even if I wanted. It had been there since that day outside of Cheltenham.

I closed my eyes, and the memory flooded back to me. Sabrina had received a letter that morning, one that had upset her, though she'd tried to hide it. But she had also been determined to coerce my best friend into marriage. Thinking James might grow jealous if I escorted her into town, we set off. The plan had been doomed to fail before it began, for James had taken a fancy to someone else, and after Sabrina had jilted him to marry the duke...well, my friend had no desire to speak to the Duchess let alone court her.

Stubborn as she was, Sabrina refused to see reason. It was not until our ride home that I decided to push the matter, to ask about the letter. I had expected her ire for prying, but what I did not expect was her vulnerability. I caught a glimpse of her then, a true, unveiled glimpse. It sparked my compassion and concern. My desire to comfort.

Never had I wished to offer a connection so intimate to any woman but my Mother.

Sabrina had ended up in my arms, her quiet sobs a testament to how much she had needed that comfort, to feel cared for. And I had never forgotten the feeling of having her there, brief as the encounter had been, nor the feeling of adequacy that followed. As if I had finally done something right after failing in so many other aspects of my life.

Truly, it made little sense that I should care about a woman who had used me so shamelessly, but I did. Both then and now. I could not turn a blind eye to her struggles.

With the remainder of the party now settled around the table, our conversation dropped. This was no place for it given the risk to us both. Sabrina conversed with those around her but never touched her food. If she had landed on hard times financially, and basic needs were not being met, would she not jump at the chance for a free meal?

From the corner of my eye, I once again studied her figure. Her clothing did not fit her properly, hanging loose in places. She was certainly more thin than I remembered. Why had I not noticed before now?

Someone suggested a game of Blind Man's Bluff sometime later, but I stayed rooted to my chair. I was in no mood for games, and if enough people vacated the table, I might have the opportunity for another conversation with Sabrina.

I tapped my finger against the table. My purpose here was to get information about Westmore, and that was deucedly difficult when I spent my time smoothing things over with the Duchess. And worrying about her.

Attending this activity was turning out to have been pointless.

Movement next to me drew my attention. Sabrina shifted to the edge of her chair, her gaze on the others gathering for the game. Did she intend to play?

In a bout of panic, I reached for her wrist before she stood, halting her. "Wait."

Sabrina glared at me. "For what, Mr. Carrow? I told you. I have nothing else—"

"I need your word that you will keep what you know to yourself."

The Sabrina I had known before would not have hesitated to use any secret she had against another person as a weapon. I had no reassurance that she would not do so now. My entire mission relied on her silence, and I could do little more than plead for it. I might possess one of her secrets too, but I would never consider using it to force her cooperation. Manipulation through secrets never yielded good results, and I would not trick someone the way I had been by Daniel Whitticker.

"Please," I whispered.

Her expression softened, and as she pulled out of my grasp, she nodded.

Relief washed over me. Perhaps I should not have been so quick to trust her, but I did. Ever since Sabrina had stood up to her father at my house party, I had believed her capable of sympathy. My secret was not the first she had agreed to keep, but both were evidence of change.

"Thank you," I said.

She did not respond, pushing herself up from the table. I expected her to make her way toward the open lawn where the others were gathering, but instead, Sabrina stood there, unmoving.

I glanced up and noted her pinched expression and closed eyes. Her fingers gripped the edge of the table, and when her body swayed, I jumped from my chair. My arms wrapped around her waist, taking on her weight and steadily guiding her to the ground. A few gasps of surprise sounded around me, but I paid them no heed, pushing Sabrina's bonnet from her head until it hung behind her.

"Your Grace?" I spoke softly despite the concern building within me, brushing strands of her dark hair from her face. "Your Grace, can you hear me?"

My heart pounded when she gave no response. Was she ill? Or had I overwhelmed her—pushed her to a fit of nerves?

One of the other gentlemen kneeled next to him and picked up Sabrina's hand, feeling her pulse. "Don't worry. She's only fainted. She'll be right in a moment."

Was he a doctor?

As if to prove the man correct, Sabrina's lashes fluttered, and when her eyes opened, she stared up at me with confusion. "What happened?"

What, indeed.

"You swooned. Are you feeling unwell?" I removed my glove and pressed the back of my hand to her forehead. It was improper, perhaps, with the number of people surrounding us, but at the moment, I did not care. "You were rather pale before, but much of your color has returned. And you do not feel feverish."

Stating those things out loud was more for my benefit than hers. I helped her sit up, watching her closely for signs of…well, anything.

Sabrina massaged her temple, her face scrunched in a wince. "I have quite the headache."

"Perhaps you ought to lie down." Mrs. Anderton stood over us, concern for her guest wrinkling her expression. "I can have a room prepared for you.

I opened my mouth to agree, but Sabrina shook her head. "No, I think it may be best if I returned home to rest." She met my gaze and gave me a pleading look.

She needn't have. I would have acquiesced without complaint.

"If someone could have my carriage readied and find Miss Colewater, that would be most appreciated," I said. "I will take Her Grace home."

The gentleman—who I realized was Mr. Anderton, the son of our hostess—volunteered while I assisted Sabrina to her feet. Her balance had returned, at least, and she seemed no worse for the wear beyond the grimace that I could only assume had resulted from her headache.

I tucked her hand around my arm and pulled her closer than I normally would have dared, guiding her around to the front of the house. She made no effort to resist, which was hardly comforting considering how at odds we had been minutes ago.

"There will be talk," she whispered.

"Do not concern yourself over that now. There is always talk of some sort."

She paused when I handed her into the carriage, her grip on my hand tight. "Thank you." Her voice was weak, but she smiled slightly as though to put me at ease before entering.

"Mr. Carrow!"

I turned to see Miss Colewater rushing toward us, her skirts held up as she ran.

"Is she well?" she asked when she had reached my side.

"She is now," I said. "I am not certain what caused her to swoon. She stood up after the picnic and lost her balance."

Miss Colewater's jaw tightened. "I take it she did not eat anythin' during the picnic?"

I gaped. How had the woman known?

"I'm right." She glanced toward the carriage and, seeming to note the open door, lowered her voice. "Her Grace has not eaten anythin' in two days. Nay, barely a cup of tea."

I could have chided the woman for gossiping about her mistress, but I saw the situation for what it was. Miss Colewater was worried, and she felt comfortable confiding in me. I appreciated that more than she knew.

"Are you certain?" I asked in a whisper. "She told me she had a large breakfast."

Miss Colewater scoffed. Sabrina had lied. Her fainting spell was likely the direct result of not eating for so long. *Why* was the question, and the only person who could truly give me an answer was Sabrina.

The lady's maid accepted my hand and climbed into the carriage. I stared at the gig for several moments before joining them. It was high time I got some answers.

Chapter Thirteen

SABRINA

I kept my gaze trained out the window as Mr. Davis entered the carriage, my emotions a whirlwind of chaos. The headache did nothing to help, but at least the dizziness had, for the most part, faded. I was still frustrated by his insistence that I cease dressing as a man and entering the gaming hells.

Not that I had done so more than once, but Mr. Davis was unaware of that. Regardless, his ordering me about made me wish to do it again. My freedom from men who would demand my obedience had been hard won. I was not about to give it up.

But then, I also could not erase his tender look of concern from my mind. The ghost of his touch lingered on my skin. I could not deny that the man genuinely cared about my well-being, which made staying frustrated with him difficult.

The carriage door closed, and the moment the conveyance lurched forward, Mr. Davis spoke. "Why are you not eating?"

The question caught me by surprise, and I turned to face him. "I beg your pardon?"

"You have not been eating," he said. "I want to know why. Is there a heavy burden on your finances?"

I must have looked appalled by the question, for he continued. "I realize the impertinence of this conversation, but I expect an answer nonetheless."

"Expect?" I repeated, shaking my head. "Your expectations are your problem. Not mine. They do not mean I am required to oblige. How do you know I do not eat anyway?"

His eyes flicked, briefly, to Helen—the traitor.

I shot her a glare, and she had the decency to appear apologetic.

Mr. Davis's knee bumped mine as he scooted forward on the seat. "Do not be angry with her. I noticed you ate nothing at the picnic, and besides that, you are..."

"I am what?"

His gaze trailed down my body, igniting my cheeks with heat. Mr. Davis swallowed. "Thin. You were not this thin last I saw you."

I shifted on the seat, uncertain how to respond. Or feel, for that matter. His statement implied he paid attention to my figure. Not just now, but years ago, too. Many men had taken notice of me before, but none of their attentions had ever felt this flattering.

Well, as flattering as him implying I was too thin could be.

"Tell me why," he said, softly this time.

"I told you before; it is not your job to worry about me. I eat when I am hungry, and I have sufficient funds to ensure I do not go without." I held up my chin as if my statement was final and would put an end to our discussion. It did not.

"If you will not explain about your lack of appetite, then perhaps you can educate me as to why you are after Westmore. Why are you putting your reputation at risk by dressing like a man?"

Next to me, Helen gasped.

"Yet another thing that is of no concern to you," I answered, ignoring my maid. She would demand a full report once we returned home, no doubt.

"It is my concern, considering you interfered with my plans."

There it was, then. The reason he expressed any interest in my façade was because it had interrupted his own. Perhaps I was wrong. Perhaps he did not care about me as much as I'd allowed myself to believe.

"I could ask you the same question. Why are you running around Bath using a false surname?" My focus settled on his facial hair.

"And why are you trying to prevent recognition by growing that monstrosity on your face?"

Mr. Davis winced. I gathered he did not particularly care for his disguise any more than I did.

Not that it mattered to me. He could grow a beard if he wanted, to go with his fake name.

"It is best if you don't know," he said.

"Then it is best that we both mind our own business." I sat back on the seat and crossed my arms. If he had no intention of explaining himself, I would do him the same courtesy.

Mr. Davis scrubbed a hand over his face, and only then did I realize one of his gloves was missing. His bare skin had pressed against my forehead after I swooned, I assumed, to see if I had a fever. Apparently, he had not recovered the accessory afterward.

"It is not safe for you to continue what you're doing." He leaned forward, resting his elbows on his knees. The proximity made my heart flutter, and the look of determination in his eyes did nothing to help. "No woman is safe entering the hells, but especially a woman of your standing. It is in your best interest to never go again."

How redundant. The same argument we'd engaged in at the picnic. Who was this man to say what was best for me? He knew little of my circumstances and even less of my motivations. I needed to secure an investment. I needed to get close to Mr. Westmore.

"I do not expect you to understand," I said. "A gentleman with an estate that earns an income. A man who can go where he pleases whenever he wishes. You can make connections far easier than I."

"Women can make connections," he retorted.

Not the kind that mattered when it came to investing. He hadn't any idea how difficult it was to get a man of business to take me seriously, especially with my reputation in tatters.

"On the former," he continued, "perhaps I would understand if you gave me the chance. If you would confide in me."

"You refuse to confide in me," I pointed out.

"For your safety. It is not the same—"

"Then we are at an impasse."

I smiled sweetly, and Mr. Davis muttered something under his breath that sounded much like 'stubborn woman' as he shrank back against the seat. What did he expect? Trust went both ways, and unless he was willing to divulge his secrets, I wouldn't be exposing mine. After all, I knew how much power secrets could hold. At one time, I'd eagerly used them to manipulate and control those around me. I would not allow someone to do the same to me.

The last bit of sunlight dissipated, leaving Beau Street in darkness. I had not been back to this part of town in weeks and had forgotten the eerie feeling of being out so late, unaccompanied and without protection. Dressed as a man, I should not need it, but that did not stop the hair on my neck from prickling with every sound.

I adjusted the spectacles on my nose, wholeheartedly regretting that I had made them part of my disguise. They did nothing to put me at ease when they blurred my vision. It wasn't horribly muddled, but in the darkness, every shadow seemed like a monster ready to pounce.

I had been nervous my first time dressing as a man and entering a gaming hell, too, but tonight, my anxiety was far worse. Mr. Davis's advice of caution repeated through my mind, unsettling me. I knew he was right—this ruse was both foolish and dangerous—and perhaps that alone kept me from forgetting his words.

Entering the establishment, I was immediately bombarded by the smell of drink. With a single nod to the maid clearing the tables, I followed the long corridor to the back of the building. The dimly lit space was rank with the smell of mutton, and I held my breath until I reached the end and entered the massive room decorated with tables.

Thick cigar smoke seized my lungs with each inhale, and I closed my eyes, breathing slowly until I could adjust to this strange environment, barely keeping a cough at bay. Once I had grown accustomed to the tainted air, my gaze searched the room for any sign of Mr. Westmore.

I spotted him in a far corner, casually conversing with several men, and my stomach tightened. He was here, and this time, I wouldn't blow my chance.

Picking my way across the room, I weaved through men who were three sheets to the wind and sat down at a table close enough to gain Mr. Westmore's notice but far enough not to appear suspicious. The banker asked how many chips I wanted and passed me the requested amount. I stared down at the stacks. They looked so unassuming, as if my future did not rely on keeping them.

I blew a slow breath past my lips to calm myself. It didn't work, my heart pounding so loud I was certain the other players could hear it.

"Not a good sign to already be so worried, Mr. Blyth," a low voice said beside me.

Turning, I barely controlled my gasp of surprise to discover I had sat down right next to Mr. Davis. His eyes bore into mine, his expression giving nothing of his emotions away. He knew who I was, which left me feeling vulnerable, as if his solid stare would reveal my ruse to everyone else in the room.

"I—"

"Do not speak," he whispered, leaning slightly toward me as the banker shuffled the deck to begin a new game. "The more you talk, the more likely you are to out yourself."

A quiet scoff escaped. "My voice had you fooled well enough last time."

Mr. Davis's jaw clenched. "Perhaps."

Incorrigible man. There was no perhaps about it. He had not suspected me of being anything but a gentleman that first night. Granted, I had kept speaking to a minimum, but I did not like being told to do so.

"You may place your bets," the banker called out.

Mr. Davis swiveled in his chair to look at me, his knees brushing against my thigh and a smug grin stamped to his lips. "Care to take the lead this time, Mr. Blyth?"

So, this is how it would be, then? Neither of us was going to get what we wanted if he spent the entire game baiting me with taunts. Why couldn't he simply play as if he did not know me or my secret? Why could he not keep his nose out of where it did not belong?

I plopped several chips onto the nine and raised a brow, daring him. His grin never faltered as he placed three of his chips next to mine.

"Really?" I muttered while the remaining punters placed their wagers.

"Really." That was all he said until the banker declared us winners that round. "My, my, Mr. Blyth has good luck. Tell me, where do you intend to bet next?"

"If I had good luck," I said, forcing my voice low, "I would not have seated myself next to you."

"Fortunate for me," he answered. "I do intend to keep my eye on you—on your wagers, I mean. I suspect tonight will be interesting. An adventure some would deem foolish. Outlandish, even."

I wanted to whack him. "You have made your opinions quite clear, Mr. Carrow. They require no repetition."

Mr. Davis slid his chips onto the eight. "They do since they were not heeded."

The banker looked at me, waiting for me to place my bet. Part of me wished to follow Mr. Davis's lead and annoy him as I had our first night of cards, but stoking his irritation had done me no favors then. It would do me none now.

I placed my chips on the knave. To my surprise, the man next to me said nothing for several rounds, which proved a blessing since my luck—though I was hardly convinced that I had any—had run out. I lost three rounds, then the next two were a wash. After losing another and watching Mr. Davis's pile of chips grow, I gave up the idea of fending for myself. It ate at my pride, but when the banker called for bets again, I waited for Mr. Davis to place his wager and followed suit.

"Ah, tired of losing already?" he asked without looking at me. Probably a smart move on his part. I was sorely tempted to slap the smirk from his face.

I shrugged. "Sometimes, a change in tactic is required for success."

He nodded with a soft hum. The banker called out the cards. A win for both of us. How was it possible that my confidence and irritation were bolstered at the same time? Mr. Davis placed his next bet, and I copied him, despite the stab to my pride. And then I did so again.

Over and over for several rounds, I followed his lead. Where before he had grown irritated by me mirroring his plays, this time Mr. Davis seemed amused, passing me a grin each time we won. Eventually, those grins turned into shouts of mutual celebration and laughter.

"Hah! You and I have found our stride," he said, shifting toward me after another win. His leg pressed against mine, and under the weight of his full smile, I felt airy. And warm. Whatever nerves I had experienced upon arriving seemed a distant memory now, a strange sense of security developing with each turn I took with Mr. Davis at my side.

I would give him his due credit. While much of the game relied on chance, there was an element of skill involved. He possessed it; I did not.

"That we have," I said with a wide grin of my own. "At this rate, we both might walk out of here a little heavier in the pockets."

Which I would not complain about. I had been far more cautious with my bets this evening, but even so, I had won enough to recoup what I'd lost last time. This thrill of success was intoxicating, and I could finally see why so many gentlemen became addicted to it. Why they returned night upon night and fortunes were put in jeopardy. It was easy to get caught up in the excitement and forget that victory was just one side of the coin. The other side was far less forgiving, though equally as probable.

The men at the table ordered brandy, including Mr. Davis, and not wishing to bring attention upon myself, I did the same. I needed to fit in to maintain my ruse, after all, especially when I had finally found a path to success.

"Do you typically enjoy brandy, Mr. Blyth?"

I ignored the tease in Mr. Davis's voice. "Don't all men enjoy it?"

"Many," he said. "Not all of us do. It is not an *expectation* for our sex."

He lifted his brow. A subtle statement.

I shot him a glare. "I do not abide by expectations anymore. I will drink brandy if I wish." Now I had two reasons to guzzle the stuff: to maintain my cover and to oppose more of Mr. Davis's objections. My life was not his to mold as he saw fit.

I gripped my cup and brought it to my lips. My betting companion eyed me with another one of his amused smiles as I took a large swallow and nearly choked, the liquid burning my throat. By the third gulp, I had nearly grown used to it.

Nearly.

The game continued, and I lost track of time. Much of it passed in a haze, but it seemed to me my cup never ran dry no matter how much I drank. More than once, Mr. Davis insisted, through whispers and subtle looks, that I stop.

It fueled me to continue.

The next round began, and with it came another win. The other players cheered and congratulated us, and my enthusiasm continued to build. I shot to my feet in a shout of celebration, my balance teetering. Mr. Davis chuckled next to me, steadying me by the arm and tugging me back into my seat.

I reached for my cup, but he removed it from my fingers before it reached my lips. "I think you ought to slow down, my friend."

My friend? He and Sabrina were friends...at least, I had thought so until he ordered me about. Regardless, Mr. Blyth was not his friend. Or, hadn't been before tonight. We were getting along smashingly well at present.

"I do not need to ssslow down." My brows furrowed. "Ssslooow." Laughter burst from me. "That word sounds rather odd, does it not? I had never consssidered it before."

"Mmm, well, I think you've had some help with your considerations." Mr. Davis shoved my cup across the table out of my reach. "Too much help. Perhaps your night is at an end."

I scoffed and held up a finger. "I am not done yet. I have...reasons."

Although, I was having a difficult time remembering precisely what they were.

"Reasons," Mr. Davis repeated with a glance at the banker. "Those will still be here tomor—"

I leaned forward abruptly, intending to press my finger to his lips and stop him from speaking but missed his face entirely. My body slid from the chair, and I landed on the floor, knocking my cap somewhat askew. I blinked, but the room spun, and even peering over the rims of my glasses did not clear the blurriness of my vision.

Warmth spread over my head as the cap there was shifted back into place, then onto my shoulders, and the smell of oranges and something distinctly masculine wafted over me. It was more appealing than the smoke from the tallow candles or cigars. I had inhaled that scent before. But where? Not on my husband, the duke. No, he had smelled...old and strongly of alcohol. Like a musty room that hadn't seen sunshine in years. Was it the scent of a suitor instead, perhaps? A faint memory of a time when men had sought to court me? There had been a number of them.

"Let me assist you, Mr. Blyth," said Mr. Davis, his voice loud and firm.

I allowed it, mostly because I realized any effort made on my own would land me back in a heap on the floor. I could hardly stand, and the card table appeared to sit on a slope, with the men around it ready to fall out of their seats.

"I believe my friend is finished for tonight," Mr. Davis continued. I assumed he addressed the banker and other players. "I think I should see him home."

Home? Yes, home seemed like a good idea, but was I not forgetting something? I had come here for a reason. I hated going out and returning without the thing I had left my rooms for. Such a waste of time.

"Wait," I demanded, though my feet carried me forward. With a great deal of help from the broad figure guiding me.

"We cannot wait." Mr. Davis's warm breath caressed my ear. "I must get you home before..." His words trailed off, but with them, my foggy brain pieced together my memories. I *had* come here for a reason.

"Wesssmore." The word sounded sloshed even to my ears.

"Shhh. You are in no condition to speak with him."

Why was he still whispering? And why was he so...so *close*? My feet tripped over each other, and Mr. Davis stopped my tumble forward with an arm pressed into my stomach. A wave of nausea roiled within me, but I kept the brandy down.

Ah, yes, the brandy; that was the cause for Mr. Davis's proximity. I had, admittedly, worked too hard to fit in with the men at the card table.

Mr. Davis's grip returned to my shoulders, firm but not harsh. His arm draped across my back, his coat brushing the hairs on my neck and sending a chill through me. I doubted I could have walked across the room without the assistance, but I was torn between ripping out of his grasp and slinking farther into him.

Hmm. The latter would likely meet with objection given my current style of dress.

Not that I would slump into Mr. Davis's arms anyway. The idea was preposterous.

We reached the door, by which Mr. Westmore stood with three other gentlemen, glasses of brandy in their hands. I narrowed my eyes at them. Why could I not get Mr. Westmore's attention? I had never had to work for a man's attention.

Well, that was not entirely true. The Earl of Emerson had rejected me once, but that was neither here nor there.

I rolled out of Mr. Davis's grasp and wobbled toward them. Mr. Westmore's gaze wandered over me with a raised brow, and his lip curled into a grin. "Enjoy yourself, Mr. Blyth?"

I stopped in front of them. "Enjoyed myself immensssely."

"I see that." The man's smile grew when a set of hands fell to my shoulders again. "And won quite the sum, from what I hear."

"Did I? What is it you men say? Capital! Yes, capital, indeed."

Mr. Davis patted my shoulder. Not gently like one would a child, but as if we were old chaps from Oxford. "Blyth and I are walking away happy tonight. More funds to throw down another day."

"Fuuundsss." The word slithered from my tongue as if it were the longest snake at the menagerie in London, and then I smacked my lips together. "So many funds."

"Well," said Mr. Westmore with a light chuckle, "perhaps I will see the two of you here next week. I usually frequent this establishment on Fridays. Perhaps, we might discuss the best ways to utilize such funds?"

"A tantalizing offer," said Mr. Davis before I could respond. "Hopefully we will see you in a sennight. Until then, I believe I should get my friend here to his bed."

I hummed with the delightful thought of curling up in my soft blankets, only half aware of Mr. Davis leading me out of The Bottom Ale and onto the darkened streets of Bath.

Chapter Fourteen

GREGORY

Never had I thought someone drunk as a wheelbarrow was adorable, but Her Grace was precisely that. She babbled endlessly, her words a slurry of incoherence as we haphazardly traversed the quiet streets of Bath. Once beyond Beau Street, we were fortunate to find an enclosed hackney willing to drive us to Gay Street.

With great effort, I assisted the Duchess into the conveyance, and she tumbled onto the seat with a giggle. At least the feminine noise could be attributed to her drunken state rather than a woman roaming about Bath dressed as a man. I sat next to her, keeping as much distance as I could in the small cab at first, but once the hackney set into motion, it became clear she would end up on the floor without support.

I slid closer, pressing my leg against hers and draping my arm over her shoulder. "What were you thinking?"

I did not expect an answer. The woman was hardly lucid enough for a conversation. She surprised me, though, with a proper response, albeit still slurred. "Not drinking would have appeared suspicious."

"As I told you, not every man drinks brandy," I said in response. Initially, I had been amused by Sabrina's stubbornness. I had found her loosened tongue and relaxed demeanor intriguing. She had always been so calculating, so properly poised, and so careful to shield her true self from everyone. She wore a shield that no one, to my knowledge, had ever fully penetrated.

But tonight, I had seen another glimpse of what lay below that shield, just as I had that day near Cheltenham. That curiosity and amusement had kept me from stopping her in the beginning. Certainly, I had advised against it, but I could have said more.

Done more.

What if she had let her guard down and forgotten her ruse? What if she had ceased using her masculine voice?

Or rather her attempt at using one. It might have fooled me at first, but the more she spoke, the more flawed I found her efforts. No, she was fortunate that tonight had ended without severe consequences.

Sabrina shifted, her leg further pressing into mine, and scowled up at me. "Why do you order me about? I hate when men order me about."

A niggle of guilt prodded at me, but I pushed it aside. "I am trying to keep you safe. What you're doing is foolish."

She scoffed and shoved against my chest, though there was little strength behind it. The movement was almost playful. "Foolish? Maybe so, but I will do what I must." Her voice dropped to a whisper. "Must."

"Why do you need to gain Westmore's attention?" I asked.

Her head shook slowly. "It is the only way. I need to help the Bartons. They need help. It's his fault. It's *his* fault."

"Who's?"

"Father's. It's his fault, but he is gone. He cannot fix it, so I must. I must fix all of it." She looked up at me again, her dark eyes warm and full of sincerity. "He is gone. They sent him away, and I am glad."

My arm tightened around her. I could not blame her for being glad. Mr. Perry was a despicable man. He had little respect for women as a whole, but I had seen firsthand the way he treated his daughter. She had been nothing more than a pawn to him, one he could order around as he pleased. It was little wonder she opposed any advice from a man, whether given out of concern or not.

Her shoulders slumped, and before I could take another breath, she leaned against me, her head resting on my chest. "Does it make me a terrible daughter to feel happy he is gone?"

I swallowed, my throat suddenly dry and my heart...my heart beat erratically, a deeper awareness of our proximity in such a tight space thrumming through my veins. I had always found this woman attractive; that was not something I could deny. But having her cuddled against me, having her so near, fanned that attraction until it grew into a raging inferno.

You like having her in your arms for more reasons than her beauty. My mind whispered the truth—a truth altogether terrifying. I did like it, far too much for my own good.

"No," my voice rasped. "It does not make you a terrible daughter."

"That is good. I was a terrible person before. I do not wish to be anymore."

"And that is why you do so much charity work?"

"I must." She shifted again, putting more of her weight against me with a sigh. "But it will never be enough. We made too many mistakes."

We? I wanted to ask for clarity, but the hackney rolled to a stop. Sabrina did not seem to notice, her head still resting near the lapels of my coat, her eyes closed.

"We've arrived, Your Grace." I squeezed her shoulder, and she sat up, her eyes droopy and unfocused. I would have to see her into the house before returning home myself.

I assisted a tipsy Sabrina onto the pavement and paid the hackney. The carriage left us alone in the darkness, standing in front of Sabrina's townhouse. I kept my arm around her back, my hand resting on her waist to keep her steady, and she leaned into me, much as she had in the carriage.

You like holding her. You like having someone rely on you.

I did, and both were folly. No one had any business relying on me. Not when I so often failed.

"Come," I said. "Let's get you to bed."

We climbed the stairs, and I lifted my hand to knock, but Sabrina grabbed my arm. "No. We mustn't do that. My Fox does not know about this." She gestured over herself, and I took it to mean her masculine disguise.

"Your fox?"

"Yes. My Fox will tell Phillip if he sees me like this. Phillip cannot know. He will drag me back to London. I have no wish to live in London."

"I see." I didn't. How much of what Sabrina sputtered was drunken nonsense? Her fox? What could she possibly mean by that?

Instead of questioning her, which would do little good in her current state, I reached for the door handle, but it was no use. The house had been locked. "How do you propose we get inside?"

Her brows furrowed, creating an endearing crinkle above her nose. "Helen. Helen will be asleep in the parlor. I am meant to knock on the window upon my return, and she will let me in. We mustn't wake my Fox."

"Right." I nodded in feigned understanding. "We cannot wake your fox." I shifted her closer to the door until she could rest against it. "Wait right here, and I shall go knock on the parlor window. Which one is it?"

"That one." She pointed to the left. To a street lamp rather than a window. It seemed I would need to do this on my own.

"Very well. Wait here, Your Grace."

"Do not wake my Fox," she whispered as I walked away.

A large shrub blocked the first window, and I had to press into the branches to peer through the tiny gap between the curtains. In the dark, I could not make out much of anything, but it did look as though it might be the parlor.

Deciding a light tap was worth the risk of waking the household, I rapped my knuckles gently against the glass. A minute of silence followed, but upon my second attempt, the curtains flew open to reveal the petite form of Miss Colewater. Her eyes went wide at the sight of me.

I gestured toward the front door. She hesitated for a brief moment, then released the curtains. I scrambled out of the shrub and rushed back to the door. Sabrina had slid down it, sitting with her back pressed against the wood. I had no time to help her move before the door swung open.

Sabrina tipped backward, landing flat on her back.

"Your Grace!" Miss Colewater shouted with surprise. "What—"

"Shhh." Sabrina pressed a finger to her lips, giggling. "Quiet. We cannot wake Fox."

Miss Colewater turned to me, confusion lining her expression. Whether it was Sabrina's insistence we not wake the fox or because of her present state, I wasn't sure. I could alleviate one of those questions, though.

"She had brandy," I whispered. "Far too much brandy."

Miss Colewater glared at me. "And I don't suppose ye thought to stop her? She could have been discovered."

"I did stop her...eventually. But you have no place to talk. You should have stopped her from going out dressed like this in the first place."

She scoffed. "As if I could have. I am a maid, sir, and besides that, Her Grace is..."

"I am determined," Sabrina finished.

Stubborn, more like. Or perhaps both.

With a heavy sigh, I approached and reached for her hand. "Allow me to help you up."

Sabrina accepted my assistance, her balance wavering the moment she was on her feet. I tugged her against me again and escorted her inside, all under the watchful, considering eyes of Miss Colewater.

"We must get her upstairs to her chamber," the maid said. "I am the only staff member aware of the disguise. It would not do for anyone else to learn of it."

I glanced up at the open staircase. The bed chambers were generally on the second floor, which meant Sabrina would need to climb two flights of stairs. Without waking anyone. That was hopeless.

I peered down at her, and Sabrina seemed to sense my gaze on her, looking up at me. Her head tilted to one side, her dark eyes studiously traveling over my face. "You look as though you have a bowel astriction." She lowered her voice to what she likely believed was a whisper only I could hear. "Excessive costiveness is a serious condition. You should see a doctor, Mr. Davis."

Miss Colewater giggled but quickly covered her mouth with her hand.

Perhaps I ought to ask Mr. Anderton his opinion. He seemed to know what he was about, though that would be an awkward conversation. I grinned. "I thank you for your concern about my costiveness, Your Grace, and take it under full advisement."

Sabrina nodded and gave my hand a sympathetic pat.

"Now," I said, "I do not think you will fare well on the stairs. Would it be alright if I carried you, Your Grace?"

Her brows furrowed, and I thought she would deny the request. Instead, she tapped a finger against my chest. "Only if you cease calling me Your Grace. I despise it."

She despised it? Would this woman ever cease to surprise me? "What would you have me call you then?"

She rolled her eyes, her tone laced with annoyance as if the answer were obvious. "Sabrina."

I swallowed, reminding myself that this woman was under the heavy influence of alcohol and that such a request said nothing about our connection. It did not imply any sort of familiarity. She had been Sabrina in my head since my house party all those years ago, since that moment along the road, but that was hardly the same as openly addressing her as such. I would oblige her tonight, and that was all.

"Very well, Sabrina. May I carry you to your chamber?"

She lifted her chin in triumph. "You may, sir."

Despite giving her permission, she gasped when I scooped her into my arms, her own flinging around my neck. Her forehead pressed against my skin, and I sucked in a deep breath. The scent of whatever cologne she'd used to solidify her disguise tickled my nose, but underneath it, there was still a hint of something more delicate and floral.

Miss Colewater led the way up the stairs, and I had to shush Sabrina more than once, reminding her that we did not wish to wake her fox. I wondered if I would ever know the meaning of that particular insistence.

I entered Sabrina's bedchamber, a room much smaller than my own at the Crescent and decorated far simpler. It was cozy and so ironically barren for the titled woman I carried that I wanted to laugh. Everything I thought I knew about the Duchess was being overturned.

"What can I do to help her?" Miss Colewater asked as I placed Sabrina on her bed. "She'll feel the consequences of the brandy tomorrow, and I'm not accustomed to...attending to that."

I chuckled, watching Sabrina remove her cap and toss it across the room. She lay down, and her dark hair fanned out over her pillow and down her cheeks.

"There is little to be done. Some tea to help her stomach will be adequate. Peppermint and Chamomile if you have them."

Miss Colewater nodded. "We do. Should I give her some now?"

"It would not hurt."

The maid crossed the room to Sabrina and removed the Duchess's spectacles before turning to face me. "I need to return these and make the tea. Can I trust ye to stay with her and...and behave like a gentleman while I'm gone?"

"You may trust me, Miss Colewater," I said gently.

She nodded, her shoulders sagging with relief. If I had any ill intentions, I could have executed them long before now—at The Bottom Ale, in the hackney, or even during our drive to Cheltenham years ago. Miss Colewater seemed to understand that. If memory served, she had been Sabrina's lady's maid for quite some time, and Miss Colewater knew my true identity. She'd been in the carriage when Sabrina questioned me.

The maid left the room, leaving the door open wide. It was improper for me to be in here, especially at this hour, but with Sabrina's current state, someone had to keep an eye on her. The last thing she needed was for the entire household to discover her secret because she decided to leave her chamber.

"How are you feeling?" I asked, keeping some distance between myself and the bed.

"Grand. Light as a feather." She lifted her arms, then let them drop back onto the bed with a thump.

She was light as a feather, but stating that would earn me another glare. Once I'd noticed how thin she'd become, I could not unsee it. I could not stop the worry. In the carriage, she had been forthcoming with information, even if it hadn't all made sense to me. Was it wrong for me to ask her more questions, knowing she would not give me answers were she lucid?

I scoffed lightly. Wrong or not, I needed to understand.

Three long strides brought me to her bed. I sat down on the edge of it, Sabrina watching me with glazed eyes. "Why are you not eating?"

Her brows furrowed. "I am not hungry. I think perhaps I drank too much." She patted her stomach as if to verify its fullness.

I smiled. "You did drink too much, but I'm not speaking of tonight. Miss Colewater says you often refuse to eat anything."

"Helen worries too much," Sabrina grumbled. She was silent for a moment, then without warning, sat up straight. It brought her far closer to me than I had anticipated, and my heart jolted. Sabrina continued, oblivious to my internal reaction. "She always worries too much. And maybe she is right to do so."

"Why is she right to worry?" I asked gently.

Sabrina fiddled with the folds of the blanket beneath her. "Every time I eat, I feel...guilty. Why should I enjoy a bountiful meal when so many have nothing? It isn't fair. A-and whatever is not eaten, I direct Helen to donate to those in need. The less I eat, the more they have. The Bartons need more."

The Bartons seemed very important to her for whatever reason, and while I admired this new Sabrina—admired her eagerness to serve those less fortunate—her fixation on this charity work came at a cost. Something told me Miss Colewater had attempted a similar discussion with her mistress, for I had seen the lines of worry in her expression that day at the picnic. I doubted Sabrina would listen to me any more than she did her maid, a woman she seemed to respect despite her station.

But I had to try.

Slowly, I reached for Sabrina's hand and removed the glove she wore. I enveloped her petite fingers within mine and waited until she looked at me before I spoke. "Helping others is a noble cause, but it should not be done at our own expense. You need not feel guilty for eating, Sabrina. You must take care of yourself."

"I do," she argued. "I eat enough. I sleep relatively well. And—"

"But you don't. You swooned at the picnic because you hadn't eaten in some time. That shows it is not enough. You do not need to punish yourself to help others."

"I should be punished," she whispered. "We were horrible people."

There was that we again. I would never understand until I got to the bottom of that particular phrasing. "Who is we? You mean yourself and...?"

Her gaze fell to where my hand held hers. "Father. He hurt so many people. He hurt the Bartons. I must make it right."

Her father? Mr. Perry had hurt a great number of people. The man had been carted away on charges of fraud, after all. Was Sabrina attempting to make up for his misdeeds? It explained everything. Sabrina felt guilty for the way she had acted in the past, but her guilt ran deeper than her own mistakes. She carried the burden of her father's as well.

I stared at her, this unfamiliar woman with wild dark hair and contrite, shimmering eyes. She was not the Sabrina I had known, and yet, she had been there all along. Buried, perhaps, beneath a hardened exterior shaped by expectations and demands. She was still the same beautiful, determined creature, but the Duchess had changed from utterly self-absorbed to this. This soft, caring woman who wanted to right the wrongs of the past. This outspoken lady whose determination could not be quenched.

I reached forward and lifted her chin until her sorrow-filled eyes met mine. "Your father's mistakes are his alone. They are not yours to carry."

"Father is gone. Who else *is* there to carry them?" Her voice broke, and a single tear slipped down her cheek.

I brushed it away, then lowered my hand. "Sabrina, you cannot continue to carry all of that alone. You are withering away because of it. At some point, you must let it go. And not just your father's misdeeds, but your own as well. I suspect you have more than made up for them. You must forgive yourself."

She said nothing in response. Her eyes had grown droopy, and I wondered if the alcohol was finally pulling her toward sleep. She may not even remember this conversation come morning.

"You should lie down and rest," I said. "You will wake with an awful headache tomorrow."

She grinned at that, and I thought she might listen to me for once. Instead, she brought her hand to my cheek and slid her bare fingers over my beard. I stiffened, and my pulse sped. Warmth spread over my skin when she pressed her palm against my face, her thumb slowly caressing the hair right next to my mouth.

"I do not like your beard," she blurted but continued to stroke it.

"Neither do I," I croaked. Did she realize what she was doing? How inappropriate this was? I should pull away. Miss Colewater could return at any moment. But I found myself incapable. Or, perhaps, unwilling was a better word.

Her gaze climbed to my eyes, and she seemed to stare into my very soul. What did she see? The man she had once blackmailed into hosting a house party? A man who had failed his family and squandered most of his inheritance? I wanted her to see so much more than that, but how could she when I couldn't?

"I do like your eyes, though," she whispered. "I dream about them."

"Dream about them?" I asked, the words breathless.

"Yes. I thought I would forget them, but three years has not been enough."

My breath caught. Years? She had dreamed about my eyes for *years*?

Her finger trailed over my forehead, brushing at my hair. Lightning skittered across my skin, a surge of desire to pull her into my arms following in its wake. I had held this woman close before, and that memory remained as vivid now as the day it happened. A ghostly sensation that longed to be replicated.

Sabrina leaned forward, her nose nearly touching mine. "Do you know what else I have dreamed of?"

I swallowed. Was it wise for me to know the answer to that? I strove to be a gentleman. If I could not honor my father's legacy by maintaining our wealth, the least I could do was not act like a cad. Sabrina's confession might jeopardize that decency, especially given the way her gaze had fallen to my lips.

The trouble was I wanted to know—desperately. So I remained silent, patiently waiting for her to offer the information.

But she did not offer it with words. Instead, her lips met mine, briefly, before she replaced the space between us.

Briefly, though, was more than enough to overwhelm my thoughts and encourage a response. I slid my hand behind her neck, bringing her back to me. She came willingly. Eagerly. This time our kiss was not so one-sided and certainly not so short. My fingers wound through her hair as I slowly explored her lips—lips that still tasted like brandy.

Brandy.

I shot away from her, removing myself from the bed. My chest heaved. Sabrina stared at me in confusion, with hurt, but I could not kiss her like this. Not when she couldn't truly give permission. I had forgotten her foxed state during our conversation, forgotten the reason I was in her bedchamber in the first place.

"I have the tea," Miss Colewater said as she entered the room, her voice hushed. Her brows furrowed when she looked at me. I imagined my expression reflected the horror I felt within. If she suspected anything, though, she did not mention it. "Thank ye for staying with her, Mr. Davis. I can take things from here."

I nodded. "I will call tomorrow to check on her."

And do whatever I could to forget that kiss in the meantime.

Chapter Fifteen

SABRINA

A knock sounded at my door, but I ignored it. Since I had given up socializing upon moving to Bath, I had no reason to rise early. I could sleep all day if I so wanted. Today I certainly did. My head pounded with what was perhaps the worst megrim I had ever experienced, and nothing could convince me to leave my bed.

The knock came again, and I groaned, yanking the covers over my head as if that would prevent the sound from reaching my ears. The knocking was the least of my troubles, however, for after a third attempt, Helen entered without permission.

"Ye must get up," she said, her tone calm and even. From beneath the blanket, I couldn't see her, but the slight squeak of my wardrobe and the subsequent rustle of fabric indicated her search through my clothing.

"I wish to remain abed," I grumbled. "There is no reason for me to get up."

"Oh, but there is," Helen responded, an odd cheer to her voice that made me suspicious. "Cook has made yer favorite tarts."

"*You* are the cook and should know by now that making tarts will not coax me from bed. I am not hungry."

The wardrobe door squeaked again. "I did not make them for ye."

My brows furrowed. "Then who did you make them for?"

Something settled over my legs as if Helen had placed an extra blanket on me. It was likely whatever dress she'd chosen. "Yer special guest o' course."

"I do not have a guest. Especially not a special one."

"Ye do."

"I do not."

"Ye do. He's waitin' in the drawing room."

I threw the covers off my head, my pulse suddenly very alive. "He?"

Helen grinned, and her eyes danced with mischief. "Ye have a caller."

"No, I don't." I shook my head but ceased when the movement made my head throb even worse. "I do not get callers. Ever. Nor do I want them."

Helen shrugged. "Ye have one all the same."

"Then send him away with my deepest apologies. I am clearly in no state to entertain anyone." I sat up and gestured over myself, trying to ignore the way my heart beat hard within my chest, prodded by an illogical sense of hope. I did not want a caller, and certainly not one by the name of Gregory Davis, no matter what odd sensation stirred within me.

"I told him ye were still asleep," said Helen, "but he insisted on waitin'. He's been here over an hour." She sighed wistfully. "I will give Mr. Davis credit. He can match yer stubbornness."

No, no, no! Why must it be him waiting in my drawing room? Though, on second thought, I could think of no other gentleman I would prefer to see me this way. He had seen me dressed like a man. This could not possibly be worse.

Not that I had any intention of going downstairs.

"Did he say what he wanted?" I asked, massaging my temples.

"No, but I imagine he has come to check on ye after what happened last night. He did mention he would."

"Last night?" I repeated. What had happened last night?

I rubbed my forehead, attempting to recall the evening, but it was hazy. I had donned my disguise and returned to The Bottom Ale. Mr. Davis had been there, seated next to me. Then, the men had all ordered brandy, including me. The rest was…well, I could recall little that happened during the game and nothing about returning home. That did not bode well.

I met Helen's gaze. "How embarrassed should I be?"

Her expression softened, but she still smiled. "Ye might be better off to focus on how fortunate ye were to have Mr. Davis lookin' out for ye. He was kind enough to see that ye made it home safely. I'm grateful to him for that."

I groaned again. Mr. Davis had escorted me home, and the fact that I could not recall it meant I had drunk a great deal of brandy. Who knew what I had done or said under the influence of alcohol, and not just in Mr. Davis's presence. Had I given myself away? Was my reputation more tattered than before?

Helen rushed to my bedside and sat down next to me. "Ye look unwell."

"I feel unwell. Can you truly not rid us of Mr. Davis? I'm not certain I can face him like this."

She considered the request for a moment. "I think ye should speak to him. He knows yer secret, and while I don't think he intends to do ye harm, it would be best to understand his motives. And thank him. I don't think ye would have made it home on yer own."

She was right; I owed the man my gratitude for seeing me home.

I heaved a sigh. "Very well, help me dress."

Helen smiled. "Yes, Your Grace. Don't ye worry about a thing. I'll get ye looking right proper."

Right proper? I scoffed lightly. Mr. Davis had already seen me at my worst—apparently—and would not expect perfectly proper from me this morning.

That, however, did not stop me from insisting Helen try her best over the course of the next half hour.

GREGORY

I would not generally consider myself a patient man. Heaven knew how often I escaped my residences, whether in London or at my country estate, to avoid Mother's nagging. I loved her dearly, but oftentimes she wore down what little reserves of patience I possessed. I also rarely found myself sitting still. I hated the quiet I'd endured these last few weeks, trapped in my rooms at the Crescent with little to entertain me.

I was a busybody, and busybodies needed to stay...well, busy.

Yet, waiting for Sabrina to come down from her bedchamber was oddly easy. She could take all afternoon, and I would wait. Perhaps this patience was born out of pure concern, the need to be reassured of her well-being, but I suspected something more was afoot. Anticipation for this call had greeted me the moment I awoke and had not left me since.

It was somewhat concerning.

Mentally, I'd made the excuse that I was here to fulfill a promise. I had agreed to call on Sabrina twice after the picnic and escort her on a walk. Mother had reminded me of her terms at breakfast. My grumbles of complaint in response had only been half-hearted, though.

I stood near the window of the drawing room, the one above the very window I had knocked on last night to gain Miss Colewater's attention. The memory of the events that followed brought a smile to my lips unbidden. How much of our time together would Sabrina remember this morning?

I had drunk to excess a time or two myself. I typically remembered very little. At the moment, I could not decide whether Sabrina's forgetting was for the best or not. Part of me wished for her to remember our conversation. Our kiss.

The other, more sensible part, hoped she would not recall any of it.

"Good morning, Mr. Carrow."

My heart leapt at the sound of Sabrina's voice, and I turned to face her. She stood in the entry, her smile somewhat hesitant. She looked a vision in her lavender gown, momentarily stealing my breath. Without a bonnet, her dark curls were visible and no less lovely for how short they were.

I bowed deeply, my gaze never straying from her. "Good morning, Your Grace."

Sabrina winced but did not correct the address. Did she remember permitting me to use her Christian name? Likely not.

"Forgive me for my lack of curtsy, but I fear my balance remains a bit shaky." Her cheeks tinted a lovely shade of pink.

I crossed the room and offered her my arm. "Then allow me to provide support."

Her smile turned genuine, and she accepted my help. I guided her to the settee nearest the window and sat down next to her. She had given me plenty of time to prepare as I waited for her to come down, time to consider how I might begin a conversation about the night before, but I still struggled to start.

"We should—"

"I must—"

I smiled, holding out my palm. "Please, go ahead."

"It seems I owe you a great debt." Her tone was so quiet, so lacking in the confidence she typically carried. I wished to reach for her hand and offer reassurance that I would not betray her secrets. She could trust my discretion.

I kept my hands firmly on my knees. Just because one kiss had disassembled a formal wall between us, that did not mean I could go about holding her hand. Sabrina would not welcome it, especially if she had forgotten what occurred between us. We were friends, yes, but our relationship hardly justified more intimate exchanges.

"You owe me nothing," I said. "I merely wanted to ensure you arrived home safely."

She glanced from me to the open drawing room door. Only Miss Colewater knew of Sabrina's ruse, which made having a conversation, even in the privacy of her drawing room, difficult.

I cleared my throat. "Miss Colewater is fetching a breakfast tray for you. Once she returns, perhaps we can prevail upon her to serve as chaperone so we may talk more freely with the door closed. Until then, might you tell me how you fare this morning?"

"My head feels as though it might explode."

I chuckled. "I can understand, having experienced such an ailment myself."

She tilted her head, studying me. "Is it an ailment you experience often?"

"No, not at all. I prefer to have my wits about me, especially when risking large sums."

Her cheeks pinked again. I was starting to crave seeing that color on her skin. It was far better than the sallow appearance they held otherwise.

"Last night…" She whispered the words, shaking her head slowly. "I haven't any idea what came over me. Tell me, am I to expect an article about the incident in the papers? Am I ruined?" She pursed her lips, and my attention fell to them. I had kissed those.

"You do not remember, I take it?" I asked, dragging my gaze back up to her eyes.

"Another symptom of this ailment I would love to be rid of. Helen has given me the shallow details, but I am afraid the last thing I remember is drinking the brandy."

So, she did not remember the vulnerability she had expressed or our kiss. I swallowed my disappointment. It was for the best. "Allow me to set you at ease. Your reputation is…well, it is in the same state as it has been since your father's trial. Your ruse is intact, and if that news isn't fortunate enough, you and I won a great deal of money last night."

Her eyes rounded with excitement. "We did?"

I shushed her. "Yes. The night ended quite well, all things considered."

Miss Colewater entered with a wide tea tray and set it on the table in front of us. All manner of appetizing food adorned the surface—ham, fruit, and two different tarts, among other things. "Breakfast, Your Grace." She cut Sabrina's protest off. "Ye need to eat somethin'. It will help ye get over yer upset stomach."

Sabrina glanced at me, and I nodded. "She's right. You should eat."

"What about you? There is more than enough for both of us."

I shook my head. "Thank you for the offer, but I have eaten."

While Sabrina begrudgingly picked at some fruit, I instructed Miss Colewater to close the door and join us. I had gotten very little sleep after returning home to my apartment. My thoughts had been far too consumed by the lady next to me. I had kissed women before, but none of them had ever elicited the feelings I'd experienced last night.

The lingering yearning.

Aside from that, my mind had been plagued with what to do next. Westmore had told us to return to The Bottom Ale in a sennight, a positive prospect, but my body writhed at the idea of Sabrina entering that hell again. Too many things could go wrong. We truly had come away fortunate last night, and tempting fate with another round was beyond foolish.

But I also knew Sabrina. She was stubborn and wouldn't give up without convincing. Her well-being, as I had learned, was not the key to that since she fully disregarded her health as it was. No, the only thing that might keep her from pursuing Westmore was the truth.

"I have a secret to tell you," I said.

The statement immediately drew her attention, and she ceased nibbling at her food. "A secret besides you going about under a false name?"

"Yes, but I will only tell you if you keep eating." I nodded to the tray of food. If I was going to persuade her to stop dressing like a man, I might as well utilize every ounce of curiosity she expressed as well. The woman was not taking care of herself, and until last night, I hadn't understood why. Now that I knew, I could not simply ignore it.

Miss Colewater giggled, apparently pleased with my scheming, and took up some needlework in a chair near the window.

Sabrina glared at me but added a lemon tart to her tiny plate. "Continue."

My lips twitched. "I know you believe getting close to Westmore is the quickest way to find an investment venture, but you are wrong." I held up my hand when she opened her mouth to protest. "Eat, and I will explain."

And so, I told her about my meeting with Cartwell and my many attempts to find Westmore in Bath. The only details I left out were regarding my personal experience with the man. Such information was irrelevant. Sabrina listened with rapt attention, and I did not miss the solemn disappointment that flashed over her features when I revealed her plan to gain capital was nothing more than a dead end.

"So you see, investing with the man will bring you nothing but misfortune," I said. "Some of his ventures are profitable, no doubt. He must have some success to pull off his scheme before moving on to a new alias. But I believe this will be his last under this name, which means anyone caught in the web stands to lose a great deal of money. I do not wish to see you entangled in it, to see you taken advantage of by that snake, let alone the risk it poses to your reputation."

Sabrina sighed, and her shoulders sagged with the movement. "Truly? You are certain Lord Cartwell is right in all of this?"

On impulse, I took the empty plate from Sabrina, placed it on the table, and then claimed her hands with my own. She wore no gloves, likely forgotten in her haste to ready herself and come down to the drawing room, and while my own prevented me from feeling the smoothness of her skin, the fabric between us did little to settle the fluttering in my chest.

"I am certain Cartwell is right," I said softly. I could explain further—I could tell her how Westmore had swindled me out of money not long after my father's passing—but I hesitated. How could I expect Sabrina to trust me if she learned how foolishly I had acted? How easily I had been tricked and persuaded by Daniel Whitticker?

Worse, I didn't relish the idea of how it would change her view of me. The last thing I wanted was to see her disappointed, for her to know the depth of my failures.

I squeezed her hands and then, remembering the watchful eyes of Miss Colewater, released them. "Trust me on this. Westmore is a scoundrel, but I will bring him to justice."

Her brows furrowed. "If he is as you say, is this not dangerous for you as well? The man will not take kindly to a trial or prison sentence. My father certainly didn't."

The concern in her dark eyes burrowed into me. Sabrina *cared*. About me. Those flutters in my chest intensified.

"I won't tell you it is not dangerous, but I have to do this. That man needs to be behind bars, not out in the public where he is free to continue this scheme. He has harmed too many people as it is."

Sabrina studied me for a long moment, and then slowly nodded as if she understood my motivations. Perhaps she did. She was driven to help those harmed by her father's actions, almost to an obsessive degree. That kind of determination was admirable. It was beautiful. It was...

I stood and took several steps away from the settee. Now was not the time to allow my thoughts to stray. "Before we left, Westmore mentioned he would return to The Bottom Ale in a sennight. It was practically an invitation. A subtle one, but an invitation nonetheless. After watching us drop the money we did, and recklessly"—I gave her a pointed look, and she once again colored with embarrassment— "I believe we might have our in."

"It is good to know getting foxed was not without reward," Sabrina said, her tone full of sarcasm. "What do we do next? What's our plan?"

"We...wait, no. *We* are not doing anything. You are going to stay out of this."

"I most certainly am not. I want to see this man taken down as much as you do."

I highly doubted that. "You've risked enough as it is. I told you everything so you would understand why there is no benefit to continuing your ruse. You will need to find another investment. Another way to gain capital."

"Hang the capital!" Sabrina stood, wobbly a little before gaining her balance, a fire in her eyes like I'd never seen. Three steps brought her to me, within arms reach. "I want to help. I spent years watching my father ruin lives, and I did nothing to stop him. I have a real chance to help—to take another criminal off the streets."

I took a step closer. "While the resolve to see justice served is estimable, I cannot let you—"

"Let me? You cannot *stop* me. You have no say over my actions." She lifted her chin, bringing her face closer to mine. At some point during our argument, my breathing had grown ragged, and her proximity was doing nothing to help. My thoughts swarmed with a mixture of worry and desire, attraction and frustration. This woman was a stoked fire, uncontrollable, chaotic, and mesmerizing.

My gaze fell to her lips, memories of the previous night forcing their way into my mind. What would it be like to kiss her absent the influence of brandy? To hold this spitfire in my arms?

I'd likely end up incinerated, but part of me believed it would be worth it.

I stepped backward so abruptly Sabrina started. Being near her with our kiss fresh in my mind was not ideal. Clearly, my mind needed time to process and forget.

The latter seemed impossible, but a man could hope.

"Stay out of this, Your Grace," I said. "Please."

"And if I don't?" Sabrina planted a hand on her hip, drawing my attention to her curves. Blast the woman.

"Then..." I hadn't any idea what I would do. I was too befuddled at present to think coherently. "Then Miss Colewater will inform me."

The maid, who still sat on a chair near the window, gave me a look of reproach. Deserved, given I had just asked her to betray her mistress.

"Because we both want to keep Her Grace safe," I added. "Yes?"

Miss Colewater grimaced. "Yes, sir."

I threw a fake, triumphant grin at Sabrina. Her brows were raised. She hadn't bought my pretended confidence for a second, but it was all I had at present.

"And even if Helen informed you—which she won't—what would you do?"

I narrowed my eyes. What I wanted to do was kiss the smug grin right off her face, but that seemed a terrible idea. Or unlikely to help the problem. It was a tempting option, all the same.

"I will see myself out now. Your Grace, Miss Colewater." After a quick bow and a sharp turn, I marched to the door. Sabrina would not let this go, of that, I had no doubt. But at the moment, I saw no way to convince her. I needed time to think. To plan.

I thanked the butler for retrieving my hat and greatcoat, then left the house. Explaining the entirety of the situation with Westmore to Sabrina had done nothing to help. In fact, I was certain I had dug myself into a deeper hole than before.

And unless I found a shovel to dig myself back out, Sabrina might wind up Westmore's next victim.

Chapter Sixteen

SABRINA

I walked in silence with Helen down Union Street, attempting to keep up a happy façade. It was difficult to maintain after being rejected by Mrs. Barton. I had hoped to learn whether she had received word from her husband, but the woman had refused to speak on the matter.

Or at all really. She had closed the door in my face.

The twist of her features at my question, however, had said more than enough. Mr. Barton still had not returned. The longer he was away, the more I worried about the family. Mrs. Barton worked as a maid, but such pay was not enough to sustain her and the children.

My brows furrowed as Mrs. Barton's expression filled my mind. There had been more than frustration at my question. I had seen her worry. Her fear. Where was Mr. Barton?

I huffed in irritation. One would think, given my title, I would have the means and resources to find the man. Thus far, I had gotten nowhere. I hadn't the respect or money to pursue the problem, and it ate away at me.

Mr. Barton had struggled to find work these past few years and failed at no fault of his own. At least, not entirely. My father had hired him years ago when the family still lived in London. Mr. Barton knew my father's business dealings well, despite his lowly origins. He knew them because he was directly involved with the fraudulent activity.

I hadn't understood the reason Father had chosen a man of such little consequence to run our family's business dealings until I had asked Mr. Barton for evidence against my father. I had suspected Mr. Barton was a good man and didn't truly wish to be involved in illegal activities. That instinct had been right. Threats against him and his family had pushed Mr. Barton into doing my father's bidding, and after thorough convincing, Mr. Barton delivered the evidence needed to have my father arrested.

My eyes stung, and I blinked back tears. I had thought that, after my father's trial, Mr. Barton would be free. Phillip and I had testified on his behalf and convinced the courts to forgo punishment, after all. Instead, I had sentenced him. Perhaps not to death, but with his reputation ruined, his prospects for finding work dried up. No one would hire him. In time, he disappeared from London completely to escape the scandal.

I had chosen Bath specifically after learning that was where the Bartons had gone. I needed to make things right. The man had helped me, and what did he have to show for it? A ruined life. His family living in destitution.

And now, Mr. Barton was missing altogether.

Your father's mistakes are his alone. They are not yours to carry. The words echoed through my mind, and not for the first time today, but I could not determine where I had heard them. For whatever reason, they came with Mr. Davis's voice, which irked me greatly. Why could I not escape the man even when he was not around?

"Your Grace! What a fine surprise."

My feet halted, and I dragged my gaze up from the pavement. Mrs. Davis stood in front of me, smiling from beneath a deep red, wide-brimmed bonnet. Her dress was of a similar shade, and the beadwork along the sleeves caught the sunlight. I dipped a curtsy, and she did the same.

"It's lovely to see you again, Mrs. Davis," I said, leaning slightly to see around her. Not that I hoped a certain gentleman had accompanied her. I was checking to make sure he *wasn't* there. I had no desire to speak to him. My thoughts did that on their own.

"He's not with me, dear," Mrs. Davis said as if reading my mind, then shifted closer, lowering her voice. "I gave him the slip. He's going to be furious." Mrs. Davis tittered, clearly finding the prospect of her son's anger entertaining.

I would be a hypocrite to chide her for it. I had found annoying Mr. Davis entertaining on several occasions.

"What has you out and about on this fine day?" she asked.

"Oh, I was visiting a...friend. I am for home now, though."

"As am I. Gregory is likely pacing the drawing room as we speak. He does not like me to go out on my own, you know. Thinks I will listen to him, the poor boy."

I scoffed. "Yes, he assumes everyone will simply obey him when he makes demands. Even when the matter is none of his business. So typical of men."

The amusement in Mrs. Davis's face dissipated. "You sound as though you have experience. He called on you yesterday, did he not?"

I shifted on my feet. How much had he told his mother? I didn't relish the idea of Mrs. Davis learning my secret. She couldn't have a high opinion of me anyway after what I had done in the past, but I saw no reason to cement that opinion further.

"Yes," I answered slowly. "He called yesterday."

"And you had an argument? He told you to do something you didn't wish to do?" She held up a finger before I could respond. "No, a determined woman like you? It must be the opposite. He told you *not* to do something you wish to do."

Well, it seemed she wasn't aware of my late-night activities. "You are not wrong. He thinks he can control me, but it is not his place to monitor my every move or berate me for my actions."

Mrs. Davis stepped to my side and slid her arm around my own. We began walking toward Gay Street at a slow pace. "I know it seems that way, but Gregory is not as controlling as you think. If he demands something of me, or anyone else, it is likely out of concern. He has never been a man to make many attachments, but when he does, he gives everything. He cares very deeply for those he calls friends, and he wants nothing more than to prove himself capable. I'm not saying he's not misguided at times in his concerns, but he means well."

"So, you think he considers me a friend?" I asked. Mr. Davis had said as much, and he had certainly helped me when I most needed it. Still, friends were a commodity I was not accustomed to having. I had Helen and Penny, but no man in my life had ever truly *cared* about me.

An image of my cousin, Phillip, popped into my mind, and I winced. Perhaps Phillip did care, but we had never been very close. I hadn't believed I could trust my father's heir, not until I finally understood Phillip would be nothing like him.

"Of course, he does," said Mrs. Davis. "He called on you. That is more than he's done for any woman in over a year. He thinks I am blind to his actions, but I know where he usually spends his time."

"I don't—" I closed my mouth. The only *woman*. What did Mrs. Davis think? That her son was interested in courting me? He hadn't called on me for that purpose, but I couldn't precisely correct her without outing myself. And anyway, the idea was laughable.

Laughable until the memories came barreling back. Me on my bed in a darkened chamber, me stroking Mr. Davis's beard, my lips brushing his. And then, the warmth of his hand on my neck, the chills racing over my skin as his fingers wove through my hair, and his kiss...oh, his kiss had been everything I'd imagined it would be. Soft and gentle and passionate. Just for a moment, I had felt treasured. I had felt loved.

The moment had ended too quickly, and even now, I could recall his horror-struck face.

Foolish, foolish, foolish.

In my drunken state, I had initiated all of it, and Mr. Davis was too much of a gentleman to take advantage of what I offered. He did not want me like I wanted him.

I wanted him. The truth settled over me, heavy and laden with more emotion than I knew how to handle. I *wanted* him. It was so plain to see and too easy to accept. There had been an undeniable tug toward him since that wretched house party, and now...now I had acted on the pull. Allowed myself to fall without knowing how deep the hole was or if I could climb out.

"Did you hear me, dear?" asked Mrs. Davis.

"Forgive me. I'm afraid I have much on my mind today." I gave her an apologetic smile.

She patted my arm, and her lips rose in a wide grin. "Well, as much as I enjoy tormenting Gregory, I do love him and should get back.

Why don't you take tea with me? The company would be nice, and I would very much like someone around to temper Gregory's anger."

"You would be better off choosing someone else for the task," I said. "Seeing me might make him more angry." Even as I said it, I wondered how much truth the words held. Mr. Davis had kissed me, but more than that, he had cared enough to see me home and had called to check on me the next day, as any good friend would do.

I shook my head. "As I said, we argued yesterday. I doubt he will want to see me of all people."

Mrs. Davis studied me for a moment. "Not so, Your Grace. Come along now, and I shall prove it."

GREGORY

Thomas watched me pace across the drawing room with an amused smile despite the number of scowls I had thrown at him. How easy it would be to stand there without concern if my future wasn't on the line. But, no. Thomas did not have a mother wandering about Bath, risking his secrets.

I yanked my pocket watch out and checked the time. "Where is she?"

"Likely shopping," said Thomas. "Or visiting someone."

"If you cannot be helpful, then you may keep quiet," I snapped. "I told her not to go out without me. Does she know how irritating she can be?"

Thomas shrugged, his lips twitching. "I imagine she's well aware. Indeed, the knowledge may even be used to exasperate you intentionally."

That was likely true. Mother enjoyed vexing me. I might call it her favorite hobby.

"The end is in sight, Thomas. I am to meet with Westmore in six days. Could she not hold out until then? I would have taken her shopping again had she asked."

"Can't say I understand women enough to answer that," Thomas replied. "I am glad you have made progress, though. Lord Cartwell shall be pleased to learn it."

I nodded absently as I stopped in front of the window and peered outside down to the street below. I could blame Mother for much of my irritation, but in truth, I had woken up with the majority of it. Every time I thought about my argument with the Duchess, it welled within me, expanding until I felt ready to burst. Stubborn woman. Why could she not simply heed my instruction?

Or, advice, rather. I hadn't demanded it. Not really.

Had I?

Perhaps I could have delivered my argument a bit gentler. Sabrina had lived most of her life under the thumb of her father and then a year under the late Duke's. Why should I expect her to listen to me after she'd finally gained her freedom?

I ran a hand through my hair. If one thing had become clear to me in the early hours of morning when I couldn't sleep, it was that Sabrina had every intention of returning to The Bottom Ale next Friday night. I might have warned her away from investing with Westmore, but that hadn't deterred her determination for justice, even if she had no prior involvement with the man. She had seen too many suffer because of fraudulent activity firsthand.

A soft smile tugged at my lips. Never would I have imagined Sabrina would develop a resolve to right those wrongs. I could see it in her eyes—the fierce determination to fix what her father had destroyed. An impossible task, especially for a widow with a tarnished reputation and little funds, which was why I admired her so much. Sabrina never backed away from a challenge.

"What's that about?" Thomas asked.

I glanced at him. "What?"

He twirled his finger in a circle. "That silly grin on your face."

"I'm not grinning, and if I were, it certainly wouldn't be silly."

Thomas hummed. And nodded. I didn't know what he was thinking, and that made my irritation grow. "Just spit it out."

"What? I'm not eatin' anything. Besides, sir, that would be mighty rude to yer maids. They work hard to keep things clean for ye."

My eyes narrowed. Sometimes, Thomas's responses came with a heavy lower-class accent, and other times... I shook my head. Perhaps I merely imagined it. I likely did not pay him as much attention as I should, especially given he communicated with Lord Cartwell.

"You've got a look about you," I said. "As if you do not believe me. I don't like it."

"I don't believe ye. Does it make ye feel better for me to say it with words instead of my face?"

A growl rumbled from my throat. Thomas ignored me, continuing. "I think ye have a distraction. Lord Cartwell told ye not to have any of those, did he not?"

"I'm not distracted."

Thomas lifted his brows, his grin smug, but the expression quickly faded with the sound of chatter at the front door. Mother had returned.

Thomas practically flew from the room, and his boots tapped rapidly up the stairs. The man never stuck around with my mother nearby, an oddity I couldn't account for. They had never met. Why should he fear her so?

"Gregory! I knew I would find you here." Mother entered the drawing room and rushed toward me, her face flushed with the exertion of climbing the stairs. And from walking to wherever she'd gone this morning.

"Where have you been?" I asked with a pointed look when she stopped in front of me. "You promised not to leave."

"Never mind that right now; we can discuss it later. We have a guest."

A guest? Yet another thing I had forbade Mother.

I looked to the entry where a woman stood. My heart nearly stopped. Dark curls peeked out from beneath a white bonnet adorned with deep blue flowers. Her cheeks held a rosy hue, though whether from exercise or embarrassment, I couldn't say. Either way, her skin appeared healthier than I had seen it since coming to Bath, and I hoped that meant she had started eating properly again.

Sabrina stared at me with hesitation, as though uncertain whether she should fully enter the room.

A hard thump smacked against my chest.

"Ow!" I rubbed the spot, glaring at the perpetrator.

"Do not stand there gawking," Mother demanded. "Escort the lady. Invite her in!"

I gave Mother a pointed look that she merely chuckled at, then crossed the room.

"Good afternoon, Your Grace," I said with a deep bow. Sabrina returned a curtsy, though she said nothing. It seemed our argument had left us in a strange place that neither of us knew how to navigate.

I offered her my arm. "Will you join us for tea?"

Sabrina bit her lip. "I do not wish to intrude. Your mother invited me, but if—"

"No." I scooped up her gloved hand and settled it on my arm. "It is no intrusion. Please stay."

My insistence would fill Mother with glee, but I had motives that did not involve courtship. I needed to convince Sabrina to stay away from Westmore, and time in her company was the only way to do that. There was nothing more to my actions than that.

Sabrina accepted my arm, and I led her across the room and deposited her in an empty chair. Yesterday, I sat next to her, and it did not take long for me to regret the proximity. I could think of little else but our kiss when seated so close to her. Besides, sharing the settee would further give Mother the wrong impression.

A maid brought the refreshments, and our conversation trekked through all the vacuous topics one would expect from a morning call. This sort of surface-level exchange would typically bore me out the door, but instead, I took my time sipping tea and stealing glances at Sabrina. To my relief, she partook of the tea and sandwiches without encouragement. For the most part, she appeared comfortable and perfectly poised, as any duchess would be, but on the occasions when I caught her glancing at me, her cheeks would tint and her gaze would dart away. I had never seen this woman act shyly, and it gave me cause to wonder if her memory had returned.

I desperately wished to ask, so I might explain myself—and apologize, even. Sabrina may have initiated that kiss, but it had been me who responded. Me who kissed her back with far more passion.

But I could not get the answers I wanted with Mother in the room. She was the last person I wished to learn of that kiss. The banns would be posted within the hour should she discover it.

I ignored the giddy feeling the thought struck in me. Marriage had always been something I intended to avoid, at least until my financial state had been rectified. Even then, I had looked at matrimony as a simple agreement, without notions of romance. While I hated to admit it, the prospect of exchanging vows had shifted from something I dreaded to something...different.

"Well." Sabrina set her teacup on the tray and smiled. "I should be going. I believe my time is past spent."

"Oh, posh." Mother waved her comment away. "I never understood the rules for morning calls. If I wish to spend time with my friends, the clock need not dictate how long it lasts. Half an hour is hardly enough, especially when I am intent on coming to know you better. Do stay."

Sabrina's brows drew together slightly. "You wish to know me better?"

"Of course I do!" Mother said with a heavy dose of feigned indignation. "Why should I not? Do you think me so terrible?"

"Not at all," Sabrina quickly assured. "It is only that...well, I should not see why you would want to. In the past, I have not been the kindest person toward you or your son." She met my gaze, briefly, then shifted in her chair. "I do not want to force the acquaintance—on either of you—that is all."

"Nothing has been forced, dear." Mother's tone softened. "We welcome your company. Both of us." She turned to face me with a lifted brow. Normally, her attempts to pressure me into polite socialization sparked my ire, but not today.

"I could not agree more," I said. "Though I would like to add that we would not wish to force you to stay, either."

Mother gasped, and I continued before she could argue. "So, perhaps I might extend a dinner invitation, instead. We would be pleased for you to join us tonight if you've no prior engagement."

"A dinner party?" Sabrina asked, her hesitation returning. "I do not know if—"

"Not a party. Just us. And I promise to make it worth your while if you agree to come."

Her eyes narrowed, and I grinned. Sabrina and I had at least one thing in common—our curiosity easily got the better of us. "Very well, I will come."

"We look forward to seeing you then." Which meant I had mere hours to devise a way to convince her to stay away from Westmore.

Chapter Seventeen

GREGORY

Sabrina was never going to stay away from Westmore, and there was no sense in denying it anymore.

I heaved a sigh and took a seat so Thomas could style my hair before dinner. I'd spent hours in my bedchamber, and the dozens of scrap foolscaps I'd scribbled on were evidence of how fruitless my efforts had proven. No matter how many reasons I'd contrived since she left after tea, I knew none of them would convince her. The Duchess planted stubborn roots that went too deep to simply pull out. Once she set her mind on something, I doubted anyone could talk her out of it.

So, I had come up with a different plan. If Sabrina refused to stay out of this mess with Westmore, then the next best thing would be to keep her close. She had no protector here in Bath, and whether she liked it or not, I was going to take on the role.

"Word below stairs is we have a guest coming to dinner tonight," said Thomas as he added a significant dollop of pomade to my unruly curls. "What would that be about?"

"It's nothing." I couldn't even blame Mother this time since I had been the one to invite Sabrina. Mother's giddy delight once the Duchess left nearly sent me to Bedlam. Try as I might, I had not convinced her I had no intention of courting Sabrina. Perhaps my powers of persuasion were nonexistent seeing as I had no luck persuading the women in my life to do anything.

"Word is she's also a duchess. And a widow."

I met Thomas's gaze in the mirror. "And? What of it? Though why you are so concerned about the gossip below stairs is beyond me."

"Ye've a nice sum coming to ye soon," Thomas continued. "Can't help wonderin' if the lady knows about it." He tilted his head to one side. "Or if perhaps yer thinkin' to pad your coffers even more with her dowry."

I laughed, barely restraining the urge to shake my head at the ridiculous statement. "First, Her Grace is aware of my mission for Cartwell. I had no choice but to tell her. We are old acquaintances, and she recognized me despite this." I gestured to my beard.

A wrinkle formed on Thomas's forehead. "You thought that was a good idea? Acquaintance or not, she could jeopardize everything. What if she tells all of Bath society what you're up to?"

"She will keep my secret. I have her word, and I trust her."

Thomas hardly looked convinced. "Very well. What of my second accusation? Are you hoping to claim her dowry?"

Again, I fought to keep still. "She would have to have one for me to claim. I cannot say I know the state of her finances in great detail, but the ducal family essentially cast her out after the Duke's death. Regardless, there is nothing between us."

I could explain the extent of the issue to Thomas, tell him that Sabrina was intent on helping bring Westmore to justice, but I disliked the idea of others learning of her involvement. Even servants were prone to gossip, and Sabrina didn't need more scandal attached to her name.

Thomas hummed. "I should meet this woman, I think. Lord Cartwell will want to know about her."

My stomach knotted. Cartwell would likely believe Sabrina was a distraction. I couldn't deny he would be right, but that did not mean I would fail at my task. Fortunately, Thomas was not going to meet Sabrina, so it did not matter. I had the perfect deterrent.

"Well," I said with a slight shrug, "you are welcome to join me, Her Grace, and *my mother* in the drawing room before dinner."

Thomas paused from styling my hair. "No, I think not."

"What do you have against my mother?"

The man refused to look at me, focusing his attention on my head. "I've nothing against your mother. She is perfectly amiable, to my knowledge, and given she has kept your secret, I can have no qualms against her."

I scoffed. "You avoid her like she carries the plague. Bounding out of rooms before she can enter, hiding below stairs—what is it you are not telling me?"

"Nothing, sir. I have nothing to hide."

Lies, but what could I do about it? I could not force the truth out of him.

Thomas finished with my hair and then helped me dress for dinner. I arrived over an hour early to the drawing room, just as I had intended. This afternoon, I had escorted Sabrina to the door and, before she left the house, whispered my request for her to come early as well. She had given me a look of suspicion but agreed, no doubt persuaded by her curiosity.

And I would. I had intended to pull her into another discussion about Westmore and finally convince her to stay out of my schemes, but with the conclusion that nothing I said would alter her course, our conversation would take on a different note.

With any luck, we would come to an agreement.

Ten minutes later, my butler announced her arrival. Sabrina entered the drawing room unaccompanied, her midnight black hair pinned fashionably with short ringlets framing her face. She rarely went without a bonnet. Did the hat save her from feeling self-conscious about her short hair or did she simply wear one to keep people from asking too many questions? There was nothing wrong with short hair on a woman, after all, albeit it was far less common, but Sabrina had always had long locks styled in the most elegant of coiffures. Would she grow it back out once this fight for justice ended?

"You seem rather deep in your thoughts."

Her soft voice pulled me from my musings, and my ears warmed. Since when did I think so much about a woman's hair? What did it matter what she decided to do once Westmore was convicted?

The Duchess was gorgeous either way, and I certainly had more important things to worry about at present.

"Forgive me," I said, dipping a bow to her.

Sabrina crossed the room to where I stood near the empty hearth. "What were you thinking about?"

You. I am always thinking of you.

The thoughts sent a rush of heat up my neck and into my ears. I cleared my throat. "Nothing of great import."

Did I imagine the disappointment that crossed her features?

"Well then, shall we cut directly to business?" she asked. "I assume you have asked me to come early in hopes of talking me out of utilizing my disguise come next Friday."

I chuckled, both at her blunt words and cleverness. "I had intended to do that when I asked you to come early, I admit, but have since changed my mind."

"Indeed? You are no longer opposed?"

"Oh, rest assured, Your Grace, I am exceptionally opposed to your late-night activities. Whole-heartedly and thoroughly opposed. But as I have known you for quite some time, I realized hours ago that any effort to discourage you was rather pointless."

At this, she smiled, taking what should have been a jab at her character as a compliment. And it was one coming from me; not that I would tell her how much I admired her stubborn nature at times.

"So what are we to discuss for the next hour, then?" she asked, her dark eyes sparkling. "I am glad to hear you've come to your senses, but a note would have prevented you from having to entertain me for so long before dinner."

"And give up extra time in your company? You must think me quite the fool, Your Grace."

That had sounded far too flirtatious, and I silently chided myself. Why could I not retain my focus around this woman? Distraction, indeed.

Sabrina tilted her head to one side, her eyes narrowed. "I suspect, Mr.—"

"Carrow." I glanced toward the open door. "Mr. Carrow."

She nodded, understanding smoothing her features. "Mr. Carrow, I suspect you still have a plan where I am concerned. You are too intelligent of a man not to, and besides, I cannot imagine that you truly wish to be in my company."

"You keep correcting my aunt and me, but I assure you, it is the truth. I certainly enjoy your company."

Her brows furrowed with frustration. "But *why*? After all I've done, why would you want anything to do with me?"

I considered her for several moments. No, I considered how much I should tell her. The words I wished to express were nothing if not vulnerable, a reflection of feelings I still did not comprehend.

"You are not the same person you were four years ago," I said softly. "Just as I am not the same man. We are all forever changing. Is that not the mark of humanity? To continually learn and grow, despite our imperfections and despite no chance of ever being fully without fault? None of us are free from making mistakes. I certainly am not. But it is clear to me that you are doing all you can to right the past—to become a better person than you were—and I find that remarkably admirable."

And attractive, but I had said more than enough already.

"I've made recent mistakes too." Her voice dropped to a whisper, and I had to lean closer to hear her. "A few nights ago, in fact."

My pulse pounded in my ears. Did she mean her adventure to The Bottom Ale? Imbibing too much brandy? There were other things she could easily regret about that night.

Sabrina looked up at me, and the moment her gaze fixed on my lips, I *knew*. She remembered.

"I must beg for your forgiveness." My words came out choked and rushed, my stomach twisting. "I should not have...it was a moment of weakness. I acted like a cad, and—"

"You?" Sabrina reared back, but the distance was brief. She glanced toward the open door and took a step closer, bringing with her a subtle floral scent. It was like a meadow of wildflowers in the first days of spring, erupting in full bloom to welcome the warmth of the coming days, and it addled my mind.

"You are not to blame," she whispered, though there was still force behind the words. "I initiated that kiss, not you."

"And I responded. You were foxed, and I took advantage of it. I forced my attention on you without proper consent."

Sabrina fought a chuckle. "Advantage? You and I have wildly different definitions of forced attention if you think yourself guilty of it that night. I spent a year married to a man whose attention I had no desire for. Believe me, I know what that is like. This was not it. I was not opposed to your response."

"But you were not in your right mind, either," I protested. Why was she not furious with me? And had she just confessed to wanting to kiss me? I liked the idea of that far too much.

Sabrina turned away with a heavy sigh. "We shan't agree on this, it seems. I suppose it would be best to forget the incident completely."

I was not likely to forget, but Sabrina obviously considered that kiss a mistake, and I would honor her wishes as best I could. "Very well. Let us lay the subject to rest. It would not do for my mother to overhear the conversation anyway. She would demand we wed."

"We wouldn't want that, now would we?" Sabrina smiled, but it wasn't genuine.

Did she want to marry me? That was absurd...was it not? My heart didn't seem to think so. Or my arms, which even now fought the desire to pull her against me. My lips, too, struggled to maintain the distance between us.

Sabrina took several steps back, breaking the spell and ensuring my body did not act on any of those impulses. "Since we have that decided, are you going to tell me your new plan? You must have one."

"Yes," I said, only half grateful for the change in topic. "I have a proposal."

Sabrina's eyes rounded, and she sucked in a sharp breath.

"Not that sort of proposal," I added quickly. "I propose an alliance. Between the two of us."

"An alliance?" Sabrina asked slowly, and I realized I was not making my intentions clear. The devil take it, all this talk of kissing had me completely befuddled.

"Not of matrimony," I said. "An alliance in bringing Westmore to justice."

Sabrina's shoulders relaxed. "Oh. Thank heavens."

So, she did not like the idea of marrying me? I was more confused than ever, and blast it all, her comment stabbed me with more disappointment. I should not care in the least. Mother wanted me to marry, and soon, but I wasn't ready. My life was a disaster that needed fixing before I could consider the notion.

"We work together to bring Westmore down," I said, ignoring the agitating confusion. "I can help keep your identity a secret, and you mine."

Sabrina nodded. "It wasn't until we played cards together as friends that we finally gained his attention."

"Precisely. He'll be expecting us both, come Friday. Working as a team is our best shot." My best shot of keeping this woman safe, but Sabrina needn't know my reasoning.

"I could do this on my own," she mused aloud, tightening a noose around my hope. "But I suppose you have been helpful. Unfortunately, that makes an alliance with Gregory Carrow a smart move, and I feel I must accept."

Sweet relief washed over me, but I did not let it show for fear she would change her mind. Sabrina offered her hand to me, and I shook it with a wide grin. "We are in agreement then, Your Grace. An unfortunate alliance to bring Arthur Westmore to justice."

Chapter Eighteen

SABRINA

I shifted in the chair while Helen pinned my curled hair into a tidy coiffure at the base of my neck. It had been some time since I had the luxury of gentlemen callers, and even longer since one had asked to take a walk with me. Still, I did not believe the passage of time was the only reason for my nerves, though it did little to help.

"Yer anxious," said Helen, a knowing smile pulling at her lips.

"Yes," I agreed. There was no sense in lying; Helen knew me too well. "I am going to ask Mr. Davis to help me locate Mr. Barton."

"Do ye think he has the resources?" Helen asked.

I shrugged. "I cannot say, but he certainly has a better chance of finding the man than I do. It pains me to even ask for his assistance, but Mrs. Barton needs her husband. I can only help so much, especially without an investment with Mr. Westmore."

Mr. Davis had told me everything—about how Mr. Westmore was a fraud. I wished it wasn't true. I had won a decent sum the other night at The Bottom Ale, but the money would only go so far. I had done little more than replace what I had spent the first night there, leaving me right where I had started weeks ago.

Since securing a new investment quickly was nearly impossible, I had decided that finding Mr. Barton would be a better pursuit. He could help his family far more than I could. But I also had little resources to make much progress in the endeavor. Hiring someone to track the man down would prove costly.

"Is that all that bothers ye?" Helen asked, still working on my hair.

"No, I am nervous to see Mr. Davis. It has been an age since I did this."

"What, walking?"

I shot her a pointed glare over my shoulder. "You know what I mean. I haven't gone on a walk with a caller since we left London. Years, Helen. It has been *years*."

Helen shrugged. "I imagine it will not be difficult to remember how to go on a walk with a fine man. Pretend he is me."

I laughed, but there was little humor in the sound. "You? And do what? Spill all of my secrets and lay bare my insecurities?"

Helen's grin only grew. "I do not think Mr. Davis would mind so much. He knows most of yer secrets already and still likes ye despite yer dressin' like a man."

My stomach fluttered, but I would pay it no attention. Mr. Davis liked me as a friend; nothing more. That was all I wanted anyway.

Memories of our kiss flooded my thoughts, and I squashed them down. Again. It seemed no matter how often I did so or how deep I buried them, they were determined to rise to the surface. It would not do, not when that kiss had been a mistake.

I had silently repeated the sentiment since the moment I recalled that night in my bedchamber. It *had* been a mistake—that I would own. The trouble was, I did not regret it in the slightest. Confessing how much I admired his eyes, on the other hand, was something I'd just as soon forget. What an embarrassment that was. No woman with any kind of poise complimented a man's eyes and confessed she dreamed of them, never mind that it was the truth.

"Whether ye agree or not," said Helen, "Mr. Davis has been good for ye. I'm glad he has taken notice and is callin'."

My brows furrowed. "What do you mean he's been good for me?"

Helen glanced at the empty breakfast tray resting in front of me on the vanity. "Ye've eaten more lately, but that aside, I think ye've been happier. Any man who can accomplish one of those things gets my favor, but both? He must be an angel."

This time I laughed genuinely. "I do not think Mr. Davis would consider himself an angel, especially given how much time he spends gambling. But, I will admit, it has been nice to have another friend besides you and Penny, and one that has looked out for me as he has. Though I hate that I put myself in a position to require his assistance at all."

Helen shook her head. "I hope ye learned yer lesson. No more brandy."

"No more brandy," I agreed. "That was more adventure than I ever wished to experience."

Well, perhaps parts of it might be worth repeating, but certainly in the absence of alcohol.

Once Helen had helped me dress, I made my way down to the drawing room to await my caller. *My caller.* How the words thrilled me. I'd experienced the feeling before, during my debut in London. The thrill of catching a man's attention and having him beg for my company had felt victorious then. Like a conquest of sorts.

But today, the thrill carried a different tone altogether. I felt no victory, but rather an eager anticipation and nerves that insisted I consider all that might go wrong. I had never rehearsed conversations or obsessed so much over where to rest my hands. Those things had always come so naturally to me. Why could they not now?

I knew why, though. It was not as though I hadn't cared for my callers' opinions before. Father had expected me to make good impressions with anyone of significance.

Father was not here now, however, and my caller was not here for a business venture. There were no agreements or schemes. Just me. Today, I cared to gain Gregory Davis's good opinion because I simply cared about him. His thoughts, his life, the way he saw me—it all mattered, and I could not rely on a title or my Father's money to hand me Mr. Davis's attention. No, it must be earned, and I feared I was not worthy of it—that my past would tarnish any chance I had of keeping his friendship.

I drew in a deep breath with the faint knock at the front door and Fox's deep voice welcoming Mr. Davis inside. Fox appeared in the drawing room entry. "Mr. Carrow is here to see you, Your Grace."

I winced slightly, and Mr. Davis seemed to notice, a smile lighting his eyes. I cleared my throat. "Thank you, Fox."

My butler bowed, and once he had left the room, Mr. Davis crossed to greet me. He offered none of our normal pleasantries, instead surprising me with a question. "That is your fox, then? The one we could not wake?"

At first, my brows drew together in confusion, but then, the memories returned. My cheeks filled with heat. "Good heavens. I am never touching brandy again."

Mr. Davis laughed, the sound soft and deep, stirring the flutters in my chest. "I'll admit, the mystery has nearly driven me to madness. I could not fathom what you were on about that night nor why you were so insistent about your fox. Now, I understand."

"I pray you will forget everything about that night," I said, embarrassment still warming my face.

Mr. Davis's smile shrank but did not disappear completely. "I agreed not to bring up what happened but made no promise to forget. I am not in the habit of making promises I cannot keep."

I blew out a slow breath. "If you intend to flirt with me throughout our walk, I may need to grab a fan to take with us, sir."

"Best grab your fan, then." His eyes crinkled with amusement, and the wrinkles only made his green eyes seem to shine all the brighter. Years ago in London, I had never thought Mr. Davis a charming man. An obvious flirt and one driven to win at the card tables, yes, but never charming.

How had I not seen it? Ever since our time together at his house party, I had come to see beyond the gambler. Beyond the titleless gentleman my Father would never approve of. I had been blind to a great many things, not the least of which was this man's worth, and I vowed to never make the mistake again.

"Shall we?" Mr. Davis offered me his arm, and despite a few more rounds of teasing, we left my house without my fan. Helen followed at a distance behind us as we made our way down the street.

"Where are we walking to?" I asked after we had gone several minutes in silence.

"I confess I am not as familiar with the most pleasurable places to walk here in Bath," Mr. Davis answered. "I thought we might venture to Queen's Square today, and you can tell me of more preferable locations for next time."

"Next time? Is that your way of asking me for another walk, sir?"

"I am not very subtle, am I?"

"Not at all," I said with a light chuckle. "But I am glad for it. Things are much easier when intentions are understood. Perhaps you might be blunt in this answer as well. Why have you called on me today?"

Mr. Davis laughed again. I enjoyed the sound far too much.

He sighed dramatically but placed his gloved hand over mine where it rested on his arm. "The truth, then?" He continued when I nodded. "My mother made me promise to call on you twice and to take a walk after the picnic. You see, I was desperate to attend Mrs. Anderton's event in hopes of gaining more information on Westmore, and the only way I could get invited to the event was if my mother requested the invitation for her nephew, Gregory Carrow."

Disappointment tugged on me, heavy as an anchor cast into the sea, but the feeling was short-lived.

"A second truth," Mr. Davis continued, "is that I protested the idea at first. My mother wishes to see me wed, and I feared her matchmaking attempts. I still do, in all honesty, but her scheming is far less bothersome when I enjoy doing her bidding." He looked at me, and his handsome smile reappeared. "I'm quite content to call on you, Your Grace. More so, to escort you anywhere about town."

"Truly?" I asked, my voice little more than a whisper.

"Truly." He leaned closer to me, bringing the scent of his masculine soap with him, his breath tickling the hair near my ear. "But I beg you will not tell my mother. She takes great pleasure in provoking my ire, and should she learn I'm not opposed to her plan, I might lose my one form of retaliation."

Laughter bubbled out of me. I knew enough of Mrs. Davis to understand his sentiments. "I do wonder why she would initiate any matchmaking scheme involving me."

"She likes you," he said easily. "Is that not obvious?"

"Heaven knows why."

"I can think of many reasons, but if it is the past that causes you to wonder, you may put it from your mind. My mother has always been forgiving, and I believe she can see how much you have changed since then. I certainly can."

Warmth blossomed through me at his words. He was in earnest, and I hardly knew how to respond. I wanted people to see that I had changed. I had worked hard to become a person I could live with, a person who was not so self-absorbed and conceited, but oftentimes I wondered whether I would ever truly succeed. After all, wanting to change and executing it were two entirely different things. I feared I might never be enough.

For him to acknowledge a change in me so openly made me feel as if I had finally found my way. It wasn't about recognition; I didn't need that or any sort of praise. I simply wanted someone to believe I could be a better person. If this man, whom I had hurt in the past, could believe it, then perhaps so could I.

A curt *quack* pulled me from my thoughts, and my feet stopped of their own accord. Mr. Davis did so as well, and from the corner of my eye, I saw him looking at me in confusion. We had reached Queen's Square now, and directly ahead of us within the shade of the trees, a feathered form waddled about. It required only a few moments of observation to recognize the creature that so frequently terrorized the streets of Bath, for I had scarcely seen a more ill-tempered duck.

"We had best go around," I said, nodding toward the mallard.

Mr. Davis followed my line of sight, and his brows drew closer. "To avoid the duck? Are you afraid of them?"

I chuckled. "Not usually. Ducks are pleasant enough, generally speaking, but Lord Duckworth is cut from a different cloth."

"Lord Duckworth?" Mr. Davis asked with amusement. "He has a name?"

"Well, we must call him *something*. There have been so many incidents that the papers have named him. He is certainly as conceited and ill-mannered as some of the lords I've met."

"An ill-mannered duck." Mr. Davis shook his head, his smile wide. "Surely he cannot be so bad?"

"He is. I've seen him chase several people outside The Pump Room. And just last week, there was an article detailing how Lord Cavenaugh had attempted to feed him. The man needed a doctor to stitch him up after the attack."

Mr. Davis's brows raised. "Truly?"

"Indeed. Lord Duckworth is a menace."

The mallard, apparently recognizing his name and highly offended by my insult, quacked and eyed us. Two short seconds passed, and the duck waddled forward. Mr. Davis and I retreated, and when Lord Duckworth's waddle shifted into a charge, the two of us turned and ran, following the path around the square.

It was not until we had gone some distance that I realized Mr. Davis had grabbed my hand. He tugged me along behind him, and once we were certain Lord Duckworth had given up his pursuit, we slowed to a stop, laughter pouring from us. Helen, too, had followed and failed to keep from laughing.

"I can see now that I must be on my guard when I go out," said Mr. Davis, slightly breathless. "I never imagined I would need to worry about ducks."

"Lord Duckworth is one of a kind, to be sure."

Once we had both regained our breaths, we continued around the square in the opposite direction of the creature. Our conversation lulled into silence, offering me the perfect opportunity to finally make my request. My insides twisted, or perhaps it was more my rebellious pride, but I needed to do this.

"At the picnic," I began, "you said I could request a favor from you if you did not find any berries I had missed."

Mr. Davis peered down at me, his curiosity piqued. "I did say that. Did you have a favor in mind?"

I drew in a deep breath. This man had done me enough favors; I did not like asking him for another, but this was not for me. "Do you remember the family I visited? Mr. Barton has been gone a long while and still has not returned. I am worried about what will come of them if he stays away much longer. I do what I can, but having him back would do them more good than I ever could."

"Do you have any idea where he has gone?"

I shook my head. "It has been over two months. Penny said he had gone away on business, which I took to mean he had finally found work. But Mrs. Barton also told her he was not to be gone for more than a week. What if something has happened to him?"

"Well, firstly, you mustn't blame yourself for any of this. I can tell it weighs on you, but none of this is your fault, regardless of Mr. Barton's circumstances."

"But it is my fault they had to leave London." I swallowed. It was time I explained everything to him. I did so as we continued our walk, insisting that if Mr. Barton had never assisted in convicting my father, he would not be destitute now. He had gotten his freedom, but it had come at a cost. Meanwhile, I suffered very little. None of it was fair.

Mr. Davis listened without interruption. Once I had finished, he stopped and turned me to look at him directly. "Sabrina, you cannot control everything that happens in life. Not in yours or the Bartons'. I understand your father is to blame for much of the family's troubles, but it is not your responsibility to take care of them. To fix it all."

I blinked back tears. Mr. Davis had told me something similar that night in my bedchamber. I wanted to toss the burden I had carried for so long aside, but it was not easy when I felt part of the situation was my fault. I had coaxed Mr. Barton into providing evidence against my father, thus revealing to all of England his involvement.

"Regardless of who should carry the blame, I cannot stop until I know Mr. Barton is safe at home." A lone tear trickled over my cheek, and I swept it away. "I must see to that much. I cannot bear the idea of leaving the family without a husband and father."

A soft smile pulled at Mr. Davis's lips, and he stared at me with an unreadable expression. I looked away, uncomfortable with the attention. It felt too much like praise.

"If you are determined to find Mr. Barton, then I will assist you," said Mr. Davis. "I owe you a favor and will look into the matter, but you must promise me that, once we have found him, you will start taking care of yourself first. Charity work is a wonderful thing,"—he tucked his knuckles under my chin and brought my gaze to his—"but you are important too."

I blinked back more tears. I had spent years basking in a sense of self-importance and thought change meant becoming completely selfless. Had I taken things too far?

"I will try," I said, putting the notion away for later review. "It may take time for me to accept."

Mr. Davis lowered his hand, his smile broader than before. "Good. And I will do what I can to help find Mr. Barton."

"Thank you."

"You needn't thank me." He tucked my hand back around his arm, and we continued down the path. "I promised you a favor, and this is a fair request. Though, while we are on the topic of requests, might I ask one of you?"

"You may," I replied with some hesitation.

"I would like to call on you again tomorrow," he said. "We can discuss a plan for Friday."

"Ah. That would be wise, and it would fulfill your mother's stipulations. Two calls and a walk?"

Mr. Davis chuckled. "Indeed, but I did not ask for my mother's benefit."

"No, you asked so we might make a plan."

He nodded slowly. "I suppose that is true if we pretend it is not, in part, an excuse to see you."

My cheeks heated. Mr. Davis had never been this flirtatious with me in the past. Perhaps he had not been bold enough to do so, knowing I would not have accepted his attention then. Did that mean he realized I was open to it now?

Was I open to it? I had thought myself finished with the idea of courtship and marriage, but what if I was mistaken about that also?

I cleared my throat. "Very well, you may call on me."

"Good. And I lied before. I have another request." He stopped, again turning so we might face one another. His green eyes bore into mine, all humor gone from them. "I am not certain if you recall, but you gave me permission to call you Sabrina. As you did not object to my doing so earlier, I hoped you might extend the privilege to me again…without the brandy as an influence."

If my cheeks had been warm before, they were a blazing fire now. "Oh. Yes, I do remember granting you that permission, and I…well, I was honest about disliking being called by my title. I do hate it. I would prefer you call me Sabrina. We are friends."

"And allies," he added with a satisfied grin. "So you must call me Gregory."

I bit my lip, attempting to fight the incessant flutters in my stomach, before allowing his Christian name to pass from my tongue. "Gregory. Unless, of course, we are undercover at some gaming hell, then I will call you Carrow."

"Much obliged, Blyth." He winked at me, and drat it all if my body did not respond to his flirtation. I had not blushed this much even during my debut Season. Regardless of whether my feelings on courtship and marriage were shifting, I needed to get my reactions under control. We had a mission to fulfill, and neither of us could afford to think of anything else until it was over.

Chapter Nineteen

GREGORY

The man sitting across from me in the study was an interesting character with a curled mustache and bald head. Mr. Feathermore, a private investigator, had listened with quiet intensity as I told him everything I knew about Mr. Barton. Occasionally, he nodded and scribbled notes on a long piece of foolscap, while other times his gaze would grow distant as he stared seemingly at nothing, lost to his thoughts.

I hoped those thoughts meant he believed we might locate the missing man.

"Very good, Mr. Carrow. I will look into this matter and send word the moment I have any news." Mr. Feathermore stood and straightened his coat. "Expect a note within the next few days."

"That soon?" I asked, standing as well.

Mr. Feathermore grinned, a cocky sort of smile. "Indeed. I have a great deal of experience in finding people. Presuming they wish to be found, the matter is often quickly resolved."

I nodded, though part of me wondered if that was the case. Sabrina hadn't any idea why Mr. Barton had not returned. What if the man had simply given up on his old life and taken up a new one someplace else? I hated to think anyone would leave their wife and children to suffer in destitution, but I was not acquainted enough with the man to make anything of his character. Sabrina, though, was adamant something was amiss and keeping Mr. Barton from his family.

"I thank you," I said, offering Mr. Feathermore my hand.

He shook it, and with a final curt nod, left me alone in the study. I had no idea whether hiring Feathermore would prove fruitful, but Sabrina had asked for my help, so I would give it. I owed her a favor, but in truth, I would have been glad to assist regardless. We had gained Westmore's attention, which meant there was no need to drop more money at the tables at present. I had more than enough to do this for her.

Besides, I wanted to see her happy, and finding Mr. Barton seemed a step toward that.

A light tap drew my attention to the door, and I waved Thomas inside.

"Tonight, then?" he asked.

"Yes," I answered, not needing him to clarify. Thomas and I had been discussing my course of action for the meeting with Westmore for days. When I was at home, that was. I'd been gone more often than not.

"Remember to tread cautiously," said Thomas. "One sniff of disloyalty, and Westmore will cast ye out."

"I shall. I know what is at stake. And anyway, I want justice served as much as Cartwell does."

Thomas's expression eased. "Yes. I sometimes forget the man did ye wrong as well. Ye need closure as much as his lordship."

"And we shall both have it. I am determined."

A smile flitted onto Thomas's lips, but it quickly faded with the sound of Mother's voice carrying up the stairs. They cracked and squealed as she headed in our direction, and Thomas's eyes nearly bulged out of his head.

Without a word, he raced to the other side of the study, tripping over a chair in the process. The furniture overturned as Thomas's feet entangled with the chair legs, and my valet scrambled to right himself. He barely made it to the door adjoining the room with the small library before Mother appeared, and Thomas yanked it open with such force he almost tipped backward. Mother gasped, and her jaw hung slack until the man had escaped into the library and shut the door behind him.

"What the devil was that?" Mother asked.

I gave her a pointed look. "Language."

"Oh, posh! Don't you dare chide me. I've heard far worse out of your mouth, and besides, who do you think you learned it from?" She lifted her skirts slightly and crossed the room. Pulling the door open, she peered inside. "He's gone. What sort of valet have you hired, Gregory?"

I lifted my brows and shook my head. "I haven't the faintest idea, to be honest."

"Surely you asked for character references before bringing him on?"

"Not precisely, no."

Mother's eyes narrowed. "Well, you ought to have. Strange, that one. Who knows if he can be trusted. Why is it every time I enter a room he scurries off like a rodent with a hunk of cheese?"

"I do not believe he appeared so gleeful as that during his escape."

"Panicked like a thief," Mother corrected. "He is up to something. I am determined to discover what it is."

I shrugged. "By all means. It will give you something to do. I, for one, am at a loss for why he so pointedly avoids you."

Mother retreated from the library door and sat down in the seat Feathermore had vacated not quarter an hour ago. She pressed the back of her hand to her forehead, slumping into the chair. "Heaven knows I need something to sustain me. I will die of boredom before you catch this criminal for Cartwell. I am withering away from lack of socialization, Gregory. The life drains from me even as we speak. I cannot live like this!"

I rolled my eyes at her dramatics. "With any luck, we will be one step closer after we meet with Westmore tonight."

Mother snapped upright. "We? We who?"

"Not you, if that is what you mean to ask."

"Of course not me. I am not daft. I have no patience for men deep in their cups acting as fools. So, who is it?"

"I..." Telling Mother I was involving Sabrina in my schemes was...well, I had intended to keep that particular detail a secret. She would not approve. *I* did not even approve, but the Duchess had given me little choice.

"Spit it out, Gregory. I can tell when you're lying, so do not bother attempting to pull the wool over my eyes."

I sighed, resigning myself to the oncoming beratement. "Her Grace is assisting me."

Mother pursed her lips. "Though it hardly surprises me, I do not like it. Dangerous, what you're doing. The hells are no place for a woman of her position." Her lips lifted on one side. "Then again, she has the gumption and intelligence to take care of herself. She will handle things just fine."

I didn't dare mention Sabrina had already entered at least one gambling establishment. Twice. Disguised as a man. I would keep that information to myself, and not because I feared Mother's judgment. No, I was afraid she would encourage Sabrina to continue.

Or worse—join her.

I shuddered at the image of Mother wearing breeches. *That* I must prevent at all costs.

Chapter Twenty

SABRINA

A disguise was good at hiding one's identity but not one's nerves. Waiting in my drawing room for Gregory to arrive was perhaps the worst sort of torture I had ever experienced. I had promised I would not run off to The Bottom Ale on my own, and quite frankly, had little desire to break that promise. My body was a ball of nervous anticipation. Tonight, there was far more at stake.

The first two times I had gone into the gambling den, I had been determined to gain Mr. Westmore's favor. Investing with him was the only way to get the funds I needed. But now, I knew the truth of things. Mr. Westmore was a fraud, and the stakes were far higher than I imagined. It was not just my reputation at risk.

Was it wise for me to go tonight?

Of course, it wasn't, but I refused to bow out like a coward. I wanted to help.

I pulled back the curtains enough to glimpse the darkened street below. There were few people wandering about Bath this time of night. Anyone traveling to and from social gatherings or entertainments would take a carriage, leaving the streets largely without pedestrians.

The drawing room door creaked open, and Helen peeked inside. Her gaze searched the room until it found me before she whispered. "He's here. Are ye ready?"

I crossed the room but still kept my voice low. "I am. Where is Fox?"

Helen's lips twitched. "He's below stairs, rummaging through his chamber in search of his glasses. Again."

I reached up and adjusted those missing glasses to sit evenly over my nose, feeling a mixture of amusement and guilt. Fox had no idea his spectacles had seen his mistress at card tables and completely inebriated.

"Very well, I should go while he is thoroughly distracted," I said.

Helen nodded and preceded me down the stairs, checking to ensure the foyer remained absent one gray-haired Fox. I left the townhouse and found Gregory waiting for me outside the door. His hair was neatly combed to one side, and the emerald green of his waistcoat matched his eyes with impeccable perfection. He greeted me with a smile that embellished his already handsome face, creating a swirl in my stomach that I struggled to ignore.

"Are you ready?" he asked softly.

"As ready as I can be."

Gregory looked me over as if to evaluate my response and heat crept into my cheeks. His gaze settled on the cravat tied about my neck, and his expression softened. His fingers lifted to it, and he loosened the fabric. "Allow me to tie this properly for you."

"Helen is not accustomed to tying cravats," I said, though the words were choked as his gloves brushed against my skin. I could still feel his warmth, and a shiver wracked my body. Whether Gregory noticed the reaction or not, he said nothing.

"When did you learn to tie a cravat so well?" I asked. "Is that not what a valet is for?"

"Perhaps, but I've spent a year without a valet, which required me to learn. Though I would not consider myself an expert in the art." He peered down at me with a grin. "There you are. A proper gentleman."

I scoffed and shook my head. "I may be the least proper gentleman in Bath. I cannot claim to even qualify for consideration."

We began our way down the street.

"Fine, then. You are the most adorable gentleman in Bath." His grin grew at my display of exasperation. "But it is only because I know your true identity. I assure you, no one else will think you are adorable. Certainly not with those exceptionally large spectacles and that cap."

"What is wrong with my cap?"

"I believe it went out of style a decade ago, but that is no matter. It lends you an air of naivety that Westmore will believe he can exploit."

"Well, at least I am not growing a rug suited for a hunting lodge on my face. What sort of air do you think that offers?"

Gregory's nose scrunched. I might have even called it adorable. "I've no notion of what he makes of my beard, but I can assure you, the moment we finish this mission, I will shave it off. I cannot stand it." His head dipped close to my ear. "Unless you secretly like my beard, in which case I could be convinced to keep it."

"I do not like it, though I cannot imagine why my opinion would convince you to keep it even if I did."

He looked at me, his green eyes considering. My pulse raced under his intent gaze, and I couldn't help wondering where his thoughts had gone. No man had ever studied me as Gregory did. It went beyond the admiration of my outward appearance. It was searching and intense, probing in a way that left me wrought with vulnerability.

I cleared my throat and turned my attention ahead of us. "You really ought to stop flirting with me."

Gregory seemed to shake himself free of whatever thoughts had held him prisoner. "I will agree to do so for tonight. I will say nothing of tomorrow."

Somehow that still sounded rather flirtatious, but I let it go.

"Have you eaten today?" he asked with the lull in our conversation.

I had grown to expect that particular question. Gregory had called on me every day since escorting me home intoxicated—despite having already met his mother's requirements—and he always asked after my eating habits. At first, it had irked me that he would insert himself into my daily affairs, but as the days passed, the memory of Mrs. Davis's words soothed my agitation.

He cares very deeply for those he calls friends.

Gregory cared for me, and that information was enough to douse any anger I might have felt, though my mind had begun to wonder if the depth of his concern came from more than friendship. I never allowed myself to ponder on the thought for long.

"It will please you to know that I had a very hearty breakfast," I said. "I even had two strawberry tarts with tea this afternoon."

"Brava, Sabrina, but while I trust you on a number of things, this is not one of them. I will check with Miss Colewater later." He raised his brow, indicating my opportunity to correct my statement.

I merely laughed. "I promise it is the truth. I am trying, you know. To take care of myself."

It had been hard to admit that my neglect had become substantial, and changing my habits was no simple task. At times, I still felt guilty for having so much while others did not.

"I know," said Gregory. There was a hint of something I couldn't discern in his tone, but he gave me little opportunity to consider it. "Look, there is a hackney ahead. Let us make haste to Beau Street."

We arrived at The Bottom Ale not long after, and I followed Gregory into the establishment. The card room was fuller than usual, which meant more smoke and chatter. When prompted, a maid led us to a private room where Mr. Westmore sat at a round oak table. He welcomed us with a nod and gestured for us to join him and several other men already seated.

"Thanks for joining us, gentlemen. Before we begin, I would like to relay some of my experience and recent successes. I know investing is risky business and prefer to set you at ease as best I can."

He spent the next ten or so minutes describing his many ventures. I had even heard of several of them, having seen articles in the papers or overheard the gossip. Mr. Westmore was not all smoke and mirrors, it seemed.

"Does anyone have any questions?" Mr. Westmore asked.

A portly gentleman lifted his hand to catch his attention. "What sort of returns are we looking at for this new venture?"

Mr. Westmore chuckled. "Ah, straight to it. We will get to that, I assure you."

"I have a question," Gregory said. I covered my surprise. I had thought we would play things safe at this meeting to not jeopardize things.

After a nod to proceed, Gregory continued, "I mean no offense by this, but I heard a rumor that Westmore is not your legal name. I only wished to give you an opportunity to clear up the confusion or, perhaps, alleviate concerns with an explanation. Might I assume that an alias would provide you with...certain anonymity to keep lesser men from cashing in on your expertise?"

My heart pounded. Gregory had worded things with polite curiosity and a subtle compliment, but it might arouse suspicion all the same.

Mr. Westmore cocked his head, a pensive look about him. "May I ask where such rumors circulated?"

Gregory shrugged, chuckling lightly. "Honestly, I cannot say. I may have been in my cups at the time, even. Might have imagined it all, but I thought to ask as it would be a rather intelligent play. You seem the sort to take advantage of such an idea."

The man took Gregory's words with pride that might have been humorous under different circumstances, lifting his chin with an air of superiority. "You are not wrong. I do tend to use an alias until I am certain those around me can be trusted."

"Brilliant," Gregory confirmed. "A strategy we could all learn from. I presume you will sign your legal name on any documentation, then?"

"Of course, of course. Speaking of which." Mr. Westmore passed out sheets of paper. A contract, I noted, after glancing it over.

"I've intended to invest in West Indies trade for some time now," Westmore continued, "but I've never been one to go at ventures like this alone. My last one was highly profitable, and I thought to share this opportunity. There are several others already onboard, and should you decide to join us, we will have a formal meeting in two week's time."

This was it—we'd gotten our invitation to the investment meeting. All we had to do now was pretend genuine interest. I looked at Gregory, expecting to see relief in his expression, but instead, his entire body was stiff, his jaw clenched tightly. He stared across the table at Westmore with an almost murderous look...which was certainly not conducive to accomplishing our mission.

Beneath the table, Gregory's hand tightened into a fist on his thigh as Westmore continued to describe the venture. Something told me that if I didn't act, our cover might be blown.

With as much subtlety as I could, I reached for him. Gregory's gaze shot to me, his brows furrowed in question. I squeezed his hand, and the tension in his expression eased. We both wore gloves, but even so, I could feel his hand relax beneath mine.

I hadn't any idea what had gotten him so worked up. We both wanted justice, but Gregory's reaction seemed to run deeper than that. It seemed...personal.

But how could it be when he was doing this at Lord Cartwell's request?

I shoved the question away for later and focused my attention on Mr. Westmore. The meeting lasted approximately an hour, and when the other men took to ordering brandy, I heartily refrained. Mr. Westmore gave me an amusing but understanding grin, which rankled my pride. I didn't let it show, though. So long as my actions weren't suspicious, that was all that mattered.

When Mr. Westmore stood to leave, Gregory and I did so as well, then followed the man at a distance from the establishment. Tension radiated from Gregory, and I prayed I had been the only one to notice. It wasn't until we had climbed into an enclosed hackney that I dared ask him what was the matter.

"It's nothing," he responded with a dismissive wave.

"It is not nothing," I insisted, removing Fox's spectacles and tucking them away in my coat pocket. "You glared daggers into Mr. Westmore tonight. You do realize that sort of fuming animosity could ruin everything, do you not?" I reached for his hand again, this time with both of mine, and cradled it between them. "Please tell me. I have never seen you react that way to the man before. What about tonight was different?"

Gregory's gaze dropped to our hands, but he made no effort to pull away. "I was duped once by a man named Daniel Whitticker, just after my father's death and I inherited. Whitticker convinced me to invest in a venture in the West Indies, and..." He swallowed. "And I nearly lost everything. My finances, as you are likely aware, have never recovered."

"I thought you had lost your family's fortune to cards?"

He shook his head. "I have lost much to cards, and indeed, I did nearly lose what I have left to your father four years ago, but the bulk of my failure comes down to one poor decision to trust a man I should not have. I was not a gambler before that. I only went to the tables in hopes of winning back enough to keep my estate afloat. Or to pay off creditors when my luck was low. I've been teetering on the edge of ruin for years.

"But that is not the worst of it. The reason I am so willing to do this for Lord Cartwell is because Arthur Westmore is another alias of Daniel Whitticker. He is the same man, still cheating people out of their money."

"Which is why you asked after his name," I guessed.

"We need the information to bring it to the courts." He shook his head. "It needs to end. I will not allow him to hurt anyone else. I know what happened is largely my fault. I should have been more proactive in checking the contracts, in requesting character references, but it had all sounded so legitimate. I knew not to offer such blind trust to a stranger. Father taught me better than that, but I still went through with it. All I saw was easy money. I am a disappointment and failure."

"It was not your fault. You had just lost your father and stepped into your inheritance. No one would expect you to recognize a fraud with so little experience."

"You are wrong. The blame sits on my shoulders, and my mother has suffered for it. I made a mistake. That will always rest on me."

Guilt swirled in my stomach. I had not known any of this years ago when I had manipulated Gregory into doing my bidding. I had thought him like so many men of my acquaintance—addicted to cards and eager to toss away a fortune with abandon. But Gregory's actions were born out of desperation, and from the way he spoke, out of guilt.

"I am sorry," I whispered. "So sorry for what I did to you before the house party. I had no idea..."

I shook my head. Knowing the extent of Gregory's troubles then would have changed nothing. The woman I had been would not have cared for his plight. In fact, I would have used him worse than I had.

"You must think me such a fiend." The words came out cracked, and my eyes brimmed with tears.

Gregory turned his entire body toward me, and with so little room in the hackney, his leg pressed into mine. "I might have thought that once, but not for some time, Sabrina."

He said my name with such soft tenderness, an almost reverence that tethered my soul to his. I realized how dearly I wished that cord to never be severed. I had never trusted a man the way I trusted Gregory, and I desperately hoped he truly saw me as a woman who had changed.

As a woman who had fallen in love with him—with his goodness. His kindness. With all of him, right down to the way he looked at me now, those haunting green eyes filled with a longing I understood.

"Sabrina." His hand lifted to my cheek, and his fingers glided to the base of my neck. I leaned into his touch, my eyes closing, willing time to freeze so that I might memorize every detail. Every feeling. Was it possible his sentiments matched mine?

My eyes flitted open, and I found Gregory staring at my lips. When he met my gaze again, it was with an unspoken question, one I seemed incapable of voicing an answer to.

So, I answered without words, grabbing the lapels of his coat and gently tugging him closer. Gregory's lips met mine, tentative at first, but responding with more vigor to match my enthusiasm. The hand cupping the base of my neck slid into my hair, dislodging my cap. It fell into my lap and then onto the floor, but I was too impassioned to care. Too wrapped up in feeling, for perhaps the first time in my life, loved.

I had kissed the duke. I had kissed Lord Emerson, and even other suitors. But none of those kisses had ever felt like this. I wanted this man, and with how soundly he returned each brush of my lips to his, he wanted me too.

The hackney stuttered to a stop, and Gregory ended our exchange with reluctance, a groan rumbling from deep in his chest. He rested his forehead against mine, his chest rising and falling beneath my hands. How I wished Beau Street were much farther from my townhouse.

With a sigh, Gregory leaned away from me and retrieved my cap from the floor. He placed it on my head and then tucked my stray hair into it. His expression had turned so passive I wondered if I had imagined the passion he'd exuded moments before.

"Goodnight, Sabrina," he whispered.

"Goodnight." I opened the door of the hackney and climbed out.

"May I call on you tomorrow?" Gregory asked.

The hope lacing his voice restored my spirits. I nodded. "Tomorrow."

And I caught a glimpse of his boyish smile before closing the door.

Chapter Twenty-One

GREGORY

My fingers drummed against the desk in my study, and Mr. Feathermore eyed them with a grimace. It was difficult to have patience, even if I did understand that finding missing people often took time. Thus far, Mr. Barton's whereabouts were still unknown, but Feathermore had caught wind of a few rumors that the man remained in town.

What I could not understand was, if the information were credible, why the man would stay away from his family. The situation filled my stomach with unease, but I would not lose hope just yet. For Sabrina's sake, and the Bartons', I wanted to get to the bottom of it.

Mr. Feathermore stood. "I know it is frustrating, but this is a good sign. A few rumors may not seem like much, but any indication he is alive is always a positive."

I winced at the implication. No doubt Feathermore had been hired to find people in the past and found them dead. I should be grateful that Mr. Barton at least seemed to be among the living.

"Keep me informed should you discover anything more," I said.

"Of course, sir. I expect to have something for you in the next few days."

With my nod of approval, the man left my study, leaving me to my thoughts. I had hoped our meeting today would end on a more promising note. Sabrina was meant to visit this afternoon so we could go over Westmore's contract again. It had been a week since our last excursion to The Bottom Ale.

A week since our kiss.

My ears warmed with the thought. I had been unable to concentrate on anything since that exchange, the memory a constant shadow. Neither of us had brought it up, but there were glances and smiles, discreet touches and unspoken conversations, each time I called on her. I welcomed all of it—craved it, even—but it all served to torture me. While pleasurable, none of it compared to kissing her.

I had reminded myself that my attention, for now, needed to revolve around finding evidence against Westmore. Once this was all over, I could afford to allow my feelings to dictate my future.

And there were feelings. Until that moment in the hackney, I hadn't dared admit it to myself, but now that I had kissed Sabrina—well and truly kissed her—I could think of little else. I loved her, and it seemed she might share my regard.

This was all Mother's fault.

I growled, rising from my chair to cross the room and peer out the window. I had been perfectly content in my bachelorhood until she insisted I spend time with the Duchess. Look at me now. I was considering marriage—nay, planning a proposal. None of this would have happened had Mother not come to Bath.

Perhaps that was not entirely correct. My time with Sabrina outside of Cheltenham was where it had all begun for me. That rare glimpse of her true self had started me down this path, and meeting her here in Bath, learning of all the ways she had changed, only pushed me further toward this inevitable conclusion. I had always been attracted to her, but now, that attraction went so much deeper than her dark hair and engaging eyes. I worried about her more than I did myself, and every display of her kindness increased my admiration.

I leaned forward, and my forehead thumped against the window. Gads, I was completely besotted.

Regardless, my affections needed to be placed aside for the time being. I wanted to bring Westmore to justice, but I also needed

Cartwell's promised payment if I were to have any chance of a future with Sabrina. I would not take a wife with my finances in shambles. It would not be fair, nor would my pride allow it. Being dependable as a husband mattered to me.

Sabrina arrived late that afternoon, joining me in the drawing room with Mother serving as our chaperone. Mother sat in a chair on the opposite side of the room, embroidering a handkerchief. Or, pretending too. I wasn't oblivious to the way she watched my interactions with the Duchess, and while I would tell her of my plans eventually, I was in no rush to give her the satisfaction of declaring how right she had been.

"I cannot see anything to implicate the man." Sabrina slumped back against her chair with a frown. "We've been over this contract a hundred times. There is simply nothing here to prove Mr. Westmore is a fraud."

I hated to admit it, but she was right. The contract was our only piece of evidence, and nothing within its lines marked the man a criminal. It was standard documentation.

"I'm not certain where to go from here," I said. "The meeting is next week, and Westmore will expect us to sign the contract if we attend. We were too eager at The Bottom Ale to back out without raising his suspicions, and besides, if we don't sign it, we will lose all access to the man."

"What more can we do? Surely there is something. The man must have close associates helping him in all of this. Fraud at this scale requires more than two hands. Father paid several people to assist with his operations."

I nodded. She had a valid point, and if anyone understood how deep this kind of criminal activity ran, it was Sabrina. According to rumor, she had been instrumental in bringing her own father's crimes to light.

"Even if we discovered who was working for Westmore, they wouldn't hand information over to us when it put them at risk too," I said. "Getting them to turn on him is unlikely."

"Perhaps, but we've nothing else to go on at present. Were you in contact with anyone else when you invested with him the first time?"

Sabrina looked hopeful, and I hated disappointing her. I shook my head. "It was only Whitticker I spoke with. There were probably more working the scheme, as you said, but I was never made aware of their identities."

"Drat," she spat. "It is most frustrating when criminals are too intelligent to leave bread crumbs."

I smiled at the way her nose scrunched with her irritation. We were once again without a lead, and all we could do is wait until the meeting. Hopefully, evidence would present itself then or Westmore would make a mistake. It seemed unlikely given how long he had gone without being caught, but I refused to give up.

My butler, Jenkins, cleared his throat from the doorway, drawing our attention. "Forgive the interruption, sir, but a Mr. Angston is here to see Mrs. Davis."

Mother sat straight and tossed her embroidery over the back of the chair, her eyes alight with excitement. Who on earth was Mr. Angston?

"Show him in," I said with some reserve, keeping a watchful eye on Mother. When Mr. Angston entered the room, she stood and smiled wide. I, on the other hand, had possibly never frowned so deeply, for the gray-haired man standing in my drawing room was none other than Lord Cartwell.

Why was he showing up now, and under a false name no less?

Had Thomas written to him of my difficulties? Was he here to withdraw his payment? I had spent half of what he had given me before, and while Cartwell had assured me he would not ask for it back, I couldn't help but feel nervous. Our agreement had been verbal only. In my eagerness to get justice, I hadn't thought to request more than that, and now, I saw the error.

Lord Cartwell fully entered the room, his attention focused solely on Mother. He approached where she stood, scooped up her hands, and brought them to his lips, all with a tender smile that furthered my confusion. There was almost an air of adoration in the way he greeted her.

I crossed the room, only vaguely aware of Sabrina following me. I stopped in front of Cartwell and dipped a bow. "My lord, I was not expecting you."

Cartwell grimaced.

"*My lord*?" Mother asked. "What are you on about, Gregory?"

I glanced between the two of them. Mother appeared as confused as I felt, but Cartwell looked...guilty. I narrowed my eyes. "Someone explain to me what the devil is going on."

Cartwell rubbed the back of his neck. "Perhaps we ought to be seated for this."

"Fine." I turned and took a step forward, but paused before proceeding. "Forgive me for not introducing you to Her Grace, The Duchess of Rochester, but as I am uncertain I even know who you are at present, you will excuse me."

I reached for Sabrina's hand and guided her to the nearest settee. She followed without a word, and once we had sat down, I learned close to her. "That man introduced himself to me as Lord Cartwell. Have you ever met him?"

"I'm not sure," she whispered. "My father introduced me to a great many people after my debut. Lord Cartwell may have been one of them, but I cannot recall. He does not look familiar."

We would have to rely on the man himself to tell the truth then.

Cartwell—or whoever he was—and Mother took their seats. The man sighed, resting his elbows on his knees. "I hope you will forgive my deceit, but I am not Lord Cartwell as I led you to believe. My name is John Angston."

Mother gasped. "You pretended to be Baldwin? Whatever for?"

He patted her arm before continuing. "It was not my idea, I assure you. Baldwin asked me to be him for a meeting, and I agreed before I had all of the details. You know how convincing my nephew can be."

"Your nephew?" The question slipped from my tongue with an undertone of accusation. "Does that mean you enticed me to do your bidding with a wealth you do not possess?"

"Not my bidding," Angston replied. "As I said, it was all my nephew's idea. You were hired by Lord Cartwell. I am simply not him."

I massaged my temples. This entire conversation was giving me a headache. "So, you are not Cartwell, but the real Cartwell hired me. Why have you pretend to be him? What purpose could that possibly serve?"

Angston cleared his throat. "I suppose he wanted to keep a close eye on you without adding too much pressure. The scheme seemed harmless enough, so I went along with it. I had thought...well, I had thought since he summoned me here that you had discovered the truth. Or he had given up the charade."

A close eye on you.

I had been reclusive for the majority of my time in Bath. The only way anyone could have kept a close eye on me was if they were living under the same roof. That could only mean...

"Thomas," I spat. "*He* is Lord Cartwell?"

Chapter Twenty-Two

GREGORY

"**G**uilty." Thomas's tenor voice rang from the doorway, and we all turned to face him. My valet had the decency to color in embarrassment. He stepped into the room and closed the door. This was a conversation best had without the rest of the servants overhearing.

"I am Lord Cartwell," said Thomas. "It is as John says; I wanted to keep a close eye on you without adding to the pressure you must have already felt. At the time, it seemed like a good idea. And it was...until your mother arrived."

Mother's lips were pursed, and she glared at him with unveiled disapproval. "Now I know why you were always scrambling out of my presence. Here I thought you feared me. I am not some tyrannical monster. Shame on you for deceiving me so."

"I am sorry," Thomas said with a genuine plea. "But you would have recognized me, and I was not ready for Mr. Davis to learn the truth."

I stood and held up both of my hands. "So, you pretended to be a servant while all along you were the man who hired me. You also implemented your uncle in the scheme by having him pretend to be you. I suppose I must cease calling you Thomas, then."

"You may call me Thomas. I prefer it to Baldwin, in fact. I've no notion what my parents were thinking to dub me so horrifically. When is being bald ever a win?" Thomas shook his head. "My father passed eight months ago, and due to your absence from higher social circles, my plan relied on you being unaware of that fact. I did not know if you had ever met my father, but since he and John are so similar in appearance, I hoped he would pass as convincing."

"And my mother? I assume she is familiar with your family, which is why you avoided her?" My attention shifted to her, and this time, Mother blushed. Had I ever seen my mother do that? I couldn't recall a single time.

"Quite familiar," Mother said shyly. "Especially in recent months."

Mr. Angston reached for her hand, encompassing it in his own, and gave her a soft smile.

Gads, I was not ready for what those gestures implied. "I need fresh air. Or...or a stiff drink. Perhaps both."

I took one step toward the door before a hand grasped my wrist, stopping my escape. Sabrina stared up at me with concerned eyes. Pleading ones that begged me to stay. I was torn between sitting back down and dragging her out the door with me. The latter held far more appeal because I was sorely tempted to find a private nook and kiss her senseless, as I had wanted to do for days, but it would give fodder to gossip.

Well, it would give fodder to Mother's suspicions. I wasn't ready to face those yet either.

I sat down next to her with a sigh, and Sabrina took my hand. She gave it a little squeeze, similar to the way Mr. Angston had comforted Mother, but Sabrina never let go. I didn't want her to. I wanted to do more than hold her hand, and if I had any say in that matter, I would once this was all over. Until then, this would suffice.

I intertwined my fingers with hers. Fodder be hanged.

"Why did you decide to end your façade?" I asked, turning my attention to Thomas, who was staring at my and Sabrina's hands with a barely concealed grin. I didn't dare look at Mother.

He shrugged. "With Mrs. Davis here, I was bound to be discovered sooner or later. Besides, you are close to finishing this. You've managed to gain Westmore's trust. All we need now is evidence against him and his true name to bring up the charges."

"Which we are no closer to finding," I added. "The contract states nothing incriminating."

Thomas grimaced. "Yes, I know, but we will have our evidence. I am sure of it."

He was far more confident than I was.

The meeting with Westmore approached, and with less than a day to find the much-needed evidence, everyone was gathered in the drawing room. We had all scoured the contract dozens of times, and Thomas had even provided the paperwork and details of his previous business with the man. There was nothing condemning to be found, and no amount of tea and cakes could soothe my growing agitation.

Fortunately, Sabrina's presence did what no beverage or sweet could. Merely having her at my side lessened my anger, and I found the hours of nighttime, when she returned home to rest, were most unbearable. I grew antsy and struggled to sleep. I longed for Sabrina the moment she left, and it showed in my eagerness to greet her each morning. While Mother had kept her words to herself, her smirks had not concealed her thoughts on this development.

Someday, I might thank her for meddling, but I was in no hurry to do so.

Next to me, Sabrina yawned, and she swept a strand of her dark hair away from her face as she peered down at the paper in front of her.

"Perhaps we ought to take a break," I whispered.

She looked up at me with droopy eyes but smiled. "We haven't the time for that, which you know."

I did know, but I was also tired of sitting in this room. "Our remaining time might be better spent making a plan for tomorrow."

I had considered asking Sabrina not to come to the meeting at all. She risked her reputation each time she stepped foot outside in her disguise. But I also knew she would not back down, and asking her to would do more harm than good. I preferred keeping her close over pushing her to act rashly, which would undoubtedly happen were I to attempt to persuade her.

"A plan is a good idea," she said with another yawn. "Though I do not think I'll be much help in making one."

She leaned over and rested her head on my shoulder with a sigh. Holding my hand the day Mr. Angston arrived seemed to have dismantled a barrier between us. We hadn't kissed again, but neither of us had been particularly careful with our exchanges. Everyone in the house likely surmised a proposal was forthcoming.

They were not wrong to expect it. I anticipated that very thing myself.

"Sir?" Jenkins spoke from the doorway, and Sabrina sat up as we both turned to face him. "Mr. Feathermore is here to see you...and he's brought a Mr. Barton with him."

"What?" Sabrina whipped around to look at me, her eyes wide. "Mr. Barton?"

"I told you I would do all I could to find him, did I not? I owed you a favor."

Her lips lifted into a bright smile that quickened my pulse. Without warning, Sabrina threw her arms around my neck, and her breath tickled my skin, sending a thrill through me.

"Thank you," she whispered.

"Do not thank me yet," I said as she pulled away. "We need to question him."

Sabrina nodded, and I instructed Jenkins to see the two men inside. Cartwell, Angston, and my mother watched the entire affair from the other side of the room with intrigued expressions, but there was no time to explain the whole of it just now. Feathermore entered, his clothing an impeccable display of mute browns and greens, while Mr. Barton looked much worse for the wear. The man could not have been more than a few years my senior, but he possessed an almost gaunt figure, and dark circles rested beneath his eyes.

His gaze settled on me for a moment, not a touch of recognition, but once it shifted to Sabrina, his entire countenance changed. Surprise, concern, and possibly fear all flitted across his face.

Sabrina stood and clasped her hands in front of her. "Mr. Barton, we've been terribly worried about you."

"We?" he repeated, taking in the other occupants of the room, his confusion intensifying.

"Yes. Your wife and daughters...and me." Sabrina attempted a smile, but it was hesitant.

Mr. Barton's focus returned to her, and upon her warm gesture for him to enter, he crossed the room with eager steps. "You've been to see them? How are they?"

Genuine concern laced his tone, and I quickly tossed away any notion that he had abandoned his family. Still, it did not explain his absence.

"They are, but I am certain they will be better once they see you," said Sabrina.

Her words did nothing to comfort the man. Indeed, he winced. "I cannot see them. Not yet."

"Why not?" I asked.

Mr. Barton looked at me, his distrust clear. I could not blame him. He and I were not acquainted.

"I hired Mr. Feathermore to find you," I continued. "On Her Grace's behalf. You can trust that we did this in the interest of your family. We mean you no harm, Mr. Barton, but if we are to truly help you, then you must explain yourself."

Barton glanced at Feathermore, who nodded his reassurance, and then looked me up and down. "You are a gentleman of means?"

Means? Very little at present, but I suspected he would be less forthcoming with the entire truth. "I hired Feathermore, did I not?"

Barton pursed his lips, but in the end, my vague response was good enough for him. "I was ordered to assist with a scheme. Suppose he heard about my dealings with Mr. Perry and thought I'd know what I was about. Which is unfortunately true. I oversaw Mr. Perry's lesser business practices for years. Experience, whether I like it or not. I wanted no part in doing it again, but my family was threatened. Said he would hurt them if I refused."

"He?" asked Sabrina.

Barton hesitated again, and now that I understood the situation, I could hardly blame him. "You may trust us, sir. I will bring your family here if I must to protect them, but we cannot help you without all the information."

"You give me your word on that?"

"I swear it."

Barton nodded. "Man goes by the name of Westmore at the moment, though it's not his real name."

Sabrina gasped, and my stomach tightened. Westmore had employed Barton because of his experience with fraudulent business practices? And under threat, to boot. Our evidence, it seemed, was within reach.

Cartwell joined us, his expression filled with the same excited hopefulness. "Do you have any physical proof of Westmore's plans? Or know his true identity?"

Barton retreated a bit, staring at the Earl with a guarded look. "Perhaps."

"I think introductions are in order," I said. "And we may need to explain ourselves as well."

I gestured to the empty chair behind Cartwell. Introductions were made, and then everyone found comfortable seating. Cartwell explained how he had been tricked out of a great deal of money by the man presently known as Arthur Westmore, and when he had concluded, he looked a question at me.

Sharing my past would not come without ramifications. The only people who knew about my lost fortune, besides Whitticker, were Sabrina and Cartwell. I had kept the information from Mother for so long, and though I knew the time had come to tell her the truth, I struggled to form the words.

To my surprise, the information did not shock Mother. She listened with rapt attention, and her brows furrowed, but she said little, interrupting only to ask a question or two. She had likely known something of the sort had happened—she was too intelligent and observant not to have. Still, it wounded me to see the disappointment in her eyes.

I had failed her, and that was a difficult thing to live with.

"With your help, we can put a stop to all of this, Mr. Barton," said Sabrina. "But I won't pressure you into this. My request brought your family much pain last time. I shan't do it again. I owe you a great apology."

Mr. Barton smiled softly at her. "I appreciate the sentiment, Your Grace, but I am glad for your persistence."

"How can you be glad? You've been unable to find employment because of me."

"Aye, that is true, but not because of you. I made a choice years ago, agreeing to do your father's bidding. He paid me well for it, and I was desperate to pull my family out of poverty. That choice had a consequence, and the longer those dealings went on, the more I regretted it. I tried to quit a number of times, but your father threatened me. I was in a prison of my own making. Then you came along and asked that I help put a stop to his crimes. I knew it was time. I don't hold you accountable for what happened. I owe you my gratitude for unlocking my shackles and for keeping me from a death sentence. Without your testimony to the courts, and that of Mr. Montfert's, I doubt I would be here."

Sabrina sighed, as if his words brought her a great deal of relief. She had blamed herself for so long, I imagined they did. She needed this closure, and I was grateful to have been able to provide it for her.

"His name?" Lord Cartwell prompted. "We need his legal name to proceed with the charges."

Barton shook his head. "I've kept documents over the past several months. Learned my lesson from working with Mr. Perry and hoped to find a way out of this. But he never signs the forms as anything other than Westmore."

"I asked him about it at the meeting," I said. "Told him there were rumors and wished to be put at ease. Insinuated his intelligence for using an alias. The man preened under the flattery and promised this venture would have his true mark."

Cartwell sighed. "Let us hope he keeps his word on that front. Whatever documentation Barton possesses will go far in providing evidence, but if we cannot link them to the man because the signatures are different, we will be hard-pressed to convince the courts."

"So we wait for him to sign the papers, then have him arrested."

The Earl nodded. "Not the best plan, but for now, it is all we have."

Chapter Twenty-Three

SABRINA

The moment had come for justice. The meeting with Mr. West-more would occur within the hour, and I could not have been more anxious. I was eager to put this all behind us, though I had no idea what my future held.

Only hope that had not been there a month ago.

Mrs. Davis descended the stairs to where I stood in the foyer of Gregory's townhouse, disguised and all, her eyes twinkling with happiness. She and Mr. Angston had been inseparable since he arrived, and it was surprising not to see her on his arm.

"Where are you off to?" I asked, taking in her dark blue satin gown and feathered hat.

"The theater. John and I are having an evening out. I thought it better than sitting here…waiting." She grimaced. "I will still worry all night, but at least I do not have to do so alone."

"I am glad you will have John." I lifted a brow. "He is rather besotted with you. Shall we expect an announcement soon?"

Mrs. Davis smirked. "Possibly, and I expect your attendance at the wedding. Though come dressed as a lady if you do not mind."

I laughed, but emotion crept into my eyes, and despite my attempt to blink it away, a tear broke free. Mrs. Davis rushed forward, her brows knit with concern, and placed her hands on my upper arms. "My dear, whatever is the matter?"

"Nothing," I said with a slight shake of my head. "Truly. Nothing is *wrong*. I am simply overwhelmed with how happy I am. You've made me feel so welcome, and I can hardly account for my good fortune. It was unexpected."

Mrs. Davis pulled me into an embrace, one of the few I had ever received, nearly displacing my cap. I could not recall ever getting a hug from either of my parents. Helen, on occasion, had hugged me, but this...this was different. It felt warm and accepting—the way, I realized, a mother's embrace should feel.

"You are always welcome in our home," Mrs. Davis whispered before pulling away. "In fact, I rather hope you will soon be included in that *our*."

My face heated, and Mrs. Davis's knowing grin did little to cool it. It would be a lie to say I did not hope for the same thing, but Gregory and I had not spoken about anything of that nature.

As though we had summoned him, Gregory descended the stairs in a dark green waistcoat that brought out the color in his eyes. His hair was styled to keep his curls out of his face and his beard was neatly trimmed. I still disliked the facial hair, but he was utterly handsome.

What would it be like to marry such a man? One that stole my breath upon entering a room and made me feel more cherished than I ever had? Such bliss sounded impossible, yet it stood before me as a bright hopefulness within reach. I wanted Gregory. I wanted a future with him. Children with him. Gone was my desire to live out my days as a widow in near solitude.

Gregory bowed. "Sabrina, Mother." He spared me a smile before fixing his attention on Mrs. Davis. "Have the Bartons been sent for?"

"Yes," replied Mrs. Davis. "Mrs. Barton and the children should arrive in the next quarter hour. I've instructed Cook to see to it they have a proper meal tonight. I had considered staying to ensure they were comfortable, but I think after not seeing Mr. Barton for so long, they will appreciate some privacy."

Gregory nodded. "Of course."

Mr. Barton had not returned home yet. We'd wanted to ensure it was safe before he did so. True to his word, Gregory had offered to bring the family to his townhouse. They would finally be reunited.

Lord Cartwell joined us, as did Mr. Angston, and we bid the couple farewell before climbing into Gregory's carriage. I listened in silence as the two men discussed our course of action. I was not to interfere tonight, and while I suspected Gregory had wished to ask me to stay home, he had not, likely knowing I would refuse.

Instead, I would watch the entire thing unfold. I did not particularly welcome the idea, but if Mr. Westmore became violent, I was better off in some darkened corner. After all, dressing as a man had not given me the ability to fight like one.

"Have The Watchmen been informed?" Gregory asked.

"Yes," Lord Cartwell answered. "I convinced three of them to meet us at The Bottom Ale. They've passed the evidence along to the constable. Once Westmore is arrested, he'll be taken to the Watch House on York Street until morning." He placed his hand on Gregory's shoulder. "You've done well. Let's finish this tonight, arrest this fraud, so I can send your funds."

Gregory gave him a curt nod, determination blazing in his eyes.

When we arrived, three men waited outside the building, and Lord Cartwell immediately went to speak with them. Before I could follow him, Gregory stopped me with a gentle hand on my arm. "Are you certain about this? You promise to stay away from Westmore?"

The concern in his voice released flutters in my chest. "I promise."

His expression shifted to something more somber, and he reached up to brush his knuckles over my cheek. "Sabrina, after this is over, I—"

"It's time, gentleman," Lord Cartwell interrupted. His gaze flicked to me, and he smirked. "Let's put an end to this."

GREGORY

Entering The Bottom Ale knowing Westmore would soon be brought to justice was more satisfying than I anticipated. One peek into the same private room we had used before alleviated any concern he wouldn't show tonight. Westmore sat at the table, a dozen men or more surrounding him.

I claimed my seat. Sabrina, along with Cartwell and The Watchmen, would remain in the main card room. Once Westmore had signed the agreement, I was to whistle, a signal that the time to make the arrest had come.

"Mr. Carrow," Westmore greeted. "Good to see you. Where is your friend Mr. Blyth?"

"Urgent business has taken him from town," I said. "He sends his deepest regrets."

Westmore pursed his lips in a pout. "A shame. I was hoping to have him on board. Perhaps if he returns swiftly, we can make arrangements to meet."

To steal more money, I thought. I forced a smile. "He would appreciate that, I am sure."

"Good." At this, he dove into the details of the investment. To any without knowledge of the man's schemes, the entire thing sounded lucrative. Convincing. Hearing him speak with such enthusiasm, such persuasive charisma, and answer every question with promptness healed something inside me. I had been taken by this man, but I was not as foolish as I had allowed myself to believe. Indeed, he was skilled in the art of deceit, and I could no longer fault myself for falling victim.

"So, if everyone is satisfied and has no more questions, let us proceed." Westmore placed a contract onto the table—the same one we had spent days going over to no avail. We had evidence; all that remained was to link it directly to Westmore. Mr. Barton's name had been sullied too thoroughly for the courts to act on his testimony alone. We needed Westmore's name, his true name, on this document.

The contract was passed around the table, each man signing their name. When it came to me, I utilized my alias for what I hoped was the last time. Then, the paper returned to Westmore. I held my breath, watching as the quill hovered over the paper. Waiting for him to mark his fate.

He signed with a flourish, and I grinned.

The moment he lifted the quill, I lurched forward and snatched the document. Westmore startled, his eyes wide. I gave him no time to question my actions, bringing two fingers to my lips and whistling as loud as I could manage.

"What are you doing?" Westmore asked, standing abruptly.

"Putting an end to all of this."

"What?" Westmore leaned back, his brows drawn tight.

"This entire venture is a hoax, and I can prove it."

Murmurs echoed from the other occupants in the room. Westmore's eyes flashed, and his hand pressed against his side. He might have a gun hidden beneath his coat, which was why I had instructed Cartwell to ensure Sabrina was kept out of the way. Westmore would not go quietly.

I stood, clutching the contract, my eyes fixed on the hand at his waist. "You've been running schemes for years. I have evidence of your fraudulent activity." I glanced toward the door and noted that Cartwell and The Watchmen stood there, waiting.

Westmore followed my gaze, and his face paled. "You've no evidence. You lie."

"I assure you, I don't."

"Tread cautiously, Carrow. Your next words might be your last." His voice dripped with warning, which did nothing to ease the pounding of my heart.

"And allow these men to become victims of fraud?" I spat the last word loudly, ensuring all attention was on us. Witnesses were always beneficial in court. "I think not. They deserve to know the kind of snake they are dealing with and that any money invested with you may as well get dumped into the sea."

One of the men stood, his voice gruff. "What's this about?"

I cut Westmore off before he could respond. " I have physical evidence to prove this man has, over the last several years, tricked many out of their fortunes. The constable has looked over that evidence and is in agreement." I nodded toward The Watchmen, and they moved forward.

Westmore reached into his coat and withdrew a pistol. I ducked beneath the table, losing my hold on the contract. It flitted away from me just as a shot rang through the air. The room erupted into chaos as the occupants scrambled for the door, knocking over chairs, and screams sounded from inside the main card room.

"Block the door!" one of the watchmen shouted.

I crawled under the table. Westmore had retreated to the back corner of the room, cowering but still armed. If I could reach him without being seen...

Another shot rent the air, and I jumped at the sound before pressing forward. Once at the end of the table, I peered up at Westmore, careful to keep hidden. His gun was aimed at the door, his finger resting on the trigger. He breathed heavily, a frenzied look in his wide eyes.

"Stay back!" he demanded.

I doubted even The Watchmen would approach the man in this panicked state, but surely Westmore realized he could not escape? He had nowhere to go.

Of course, such desperation could make a man entirely illogical. And dangerous.

"This is a misunderstanding," Westmore pleaded.

"The evidence suggests otherwise," one of the watchmen said. "Lord Cartwell has brought up these charges against you, as well as Mr. Davis. They've provided enough documentation to warrant an arrest."

Westmore's brows furrowed. "Davis?" His eyes swept the room, searching for me, and his hold on the pistol loosened. This was the precise distraction I needed.

I kicked a chair, toppling it over. Westmore fired at it. I crawled out from beneath the table and scrambled to my feet. Barrelling into him, we both crashed against the wall. The pistol fell to the floor with a heavy *clack*, and Westmore swung his fist at me. I evaded the punch and lunged forward, using all of my body weight to pin him against the wall.

Two of the watchmen rushed to assist me, each of them taking one of Westmore's arms.

"Unhand me!" he shouted, fighting their hold to no avail.

"They will," I said, taking a step back. "Once you're behind bars."

Westmore's attention shifted to me, and his eyes roamed my face. They narrowed slightly as if he were digging deep to recall a memory. His study was interrupted when the two watchmen dragged him forward, and he resumed his fight against them, shouting as they led him out of the room. The third collected Westmore's weapon and left with a curt nod.

"That was quite the tussle," said Cartwell. He still stood by the door, now leaning against the jamb, his arms crossed over his chest. "Did he sign the contract?"

My gaze darted over the floor until I spotted it tucked against an upturned chair. I crossed the room and retrieved it. Holding it up to catch the flickering candlelight, I perused the list of names at the bottom. My heart lurched at the familiar scrawl.

Daniel Whitticker.

"He did not sign his real name," I whispered, my stomach sinking into unknown depths.

"What?" Cartwell came to my side and took the contract from my grasp.

"He signed it as Daniel Whitticker. I knew there was a chance he wouldn't, but... How can we connect him to any of the documents from Barton now?"

Cartwell's jaw clenched. "We cannot, and once the magistrate realizes it..."

Westmore would be back on the streets, free to continue his schemes. Or worse—free to track down those who had him arrested. There was no telling what he would do.

"What now?" I asked, feeling so depleted my tone carried the feeling.

"Now? Nothing. We go home. Perhaps there is something we missed. Perhaps..." Nothing in his voice suggested he believed it. All we had worked for the last few weeks had gone up in smoke. We had failed.

Cartwell shook his head, and without another word stormed from the room. My feet remained planted in place, still and unable to move. Unlike my heart, which beat faster now than it had during my scuffle with Westmore. We had failed, and failure meant I had not met Cartwell's stipulations. He had promised to pay me when Westmore was charged. Without all the evidence we needed, he would be released, likely as soon as tomorrow.

The future I had envisioned—the one where I brought Fallborn back to its former glory—sifted between my fingers like sand. It was in my palm, but I could not grasp it. Could not keep it. I had no funds to fix all that was broken, no funds to support my mother or a wife.

A wife. *Sabrina.*

I hastily vacated the room and searched for her in the card room. It did not take long to find her as she waited in a shadowed corner just outside the door. She passed me a look of sympathy as I approached, her dark eyes slightly glazed. Cartwell had likely informed her of everything.

"Are you well?" I asked, thankful she had not been in the room with bullets flying every which way.

In true character, she ignored my question about her health and responded in her deepened voice. "We can still find evidence."

"It is over. There is nothing more to be done."

"No. I refuse to give up. We can—"

I reached for her arm and tugged her closer. "It is over. We can do nothing more. The charges will be dropped. You must promise me you will never put on this disguise again after tonight. Should Westmore see you, he might assume you had a role in it."

She lifted her chin. "I did have a role in it."

I glared at her, and she heaved a sigh. "Very well. I shan't be Mr. Blyth ever again."

"Good. You should go home."

Her brows furrowed. "What of you?"

I looked toward the card tables. Several games had resumed now that the chaos had settled. I still had the money from Cartwell's initial payment. Perhaps all was not lost. If I could find my stride tonight, I might have enough to make some headway now that my debts were clear.

"You intend to stay?" Sabrina asked. "Then I will stay, too."

"No," I said firmly. "You have risked yourself enough. Please, go home."

"You could come with me," she suggested, a hopefulness in the words that nearly left me undone. "We could look for more evidence together."

A deep ache settled in my chest. How I wished to oblige the request, to spend more time with her. But without the payment from Cartwell, I could never give her the life she deserved. My finances would continue to dwindle, and I could not, in good conscience, ask her to bear that burden with me.

I shook my head, searching for the right words, but there were none.

Sabrina took a step back from me. "Well, then I wish you the best of luck, Mr. Carrow." Her voice cracked, and with it, my heart. The damage spread like a plague, shattering me piece by piece.

And every ounce of my willpower was tested as I watched her walk away.

Chapter Twenty-Four

SABRINA

The first signs of morning poured into the breakfast room, faint hints of orange penetrating the black curtain I had stared at most of the night. Sleep had eluded me until my tears left me exhausted enough to finally fall into a deep slumber, which hadn't lasted more than an hour before my mind was alert and thinking about everything that had occurred at The Bottom Ale.

Mr. Westmore would get away with his crimes, which bothered me deeply, but it was my conversation with Gregory after the arrest that prevented my peace. He had chosen to stay at the card tables rather than accompany me home. His choice had hurt. I had returned to my townhouse feeling lost and confused. Something had wedged itself between, an unspoken obstacle I could give no name, and I feared I had lost him.

I stepped away from the window, wiping a teardrop from my cheek. Why had I allowed myself to grow so attached to the man? Hadn't I been determined to never court again? To never marry?

Clearly, my resolve had not been as firm as it ought.

I filled a plate from the sideboard and took my seat at the round table. I had no appetite this morning, but I would eat. Regardless of how things had ended with Mr. Davis, I would not slip back into old habits. If nothing else had come from our friendship, he had at least made me realize the necessity of taking care of myself.

Our friendship.

Perhaps it was time I accepted the truth. I had thought Gregory could look beyond my past misdeeds, but maybe I had been wrong to assume. My actions in the past had ruined any chance I might have had at a happy marriage.

"Ye are up early," said Helen, entering the room with a tea tray.

I tried for a smile but knew it fell flat. Helen offered a look of sympathy in return. She was aware of everything that had occurred last night. I was grateful for her companionship, especially now. For years, Helen had been the only person I could confide in. I was uncertain what I would do without her.

Fresh tears glazed my eyes, and before I completely understood what was happening, Helen had taken my hands, pulled me up, and guided me into her arms. I had only sobbed in someone's embrace once before, and while some part of me rebelled against it, I let the tears flow.

Helen loved me, and while the realization served as a balm to the deep ache in my heart, I wanted more. I wanted a future with Gregory Davis. I wanted a husband and a family—one of support and comfort. Love had been absent my entire life, and until I experienced it firsthand, I hadn't known what I was missing.

How could I be happy without it now?

I drew in a deep breath and pulled away from Helen. I might never be completely happy, but I would appreciate the things I did have: a friend and a future open to possibilities. That would be enough.

"Thank you," I whispered. "For everything, Helen."

"Always, Your Grace."

I shot her a playful glare, and we both laughed. It felt good to do so.

"Will you join me?" I asked, gesturing to the table. Helen had long been more than my maid, but I had never asked her to dine with me. She hesitated for a moment before nodding. I sat down while she filled a plate at the sideboard and waited for her to join me.

"I think it's time I hired a cook," I said.

She blinked at me, a flash of hurt in her eyes.

"So you and I have more time together," I continued. "You may still serve as my lady's maid if you wish, but I…I was rather hoping you might be a companion of sorts instead. I know it is not customary for a servant to rise to that position, but you are my friend, Helen."

Helen smiled. "I would be honored and plenty happy to continue doin' yer hair." She reached out and touched the unkempt locks cradling my face. "I shall be happy to see it grown out again."

"As will I."

We finished breakfast, and my spirits were lifted by our conversation. Helen helped me dress and fixed my hair into something presentable before we left the townhouse. Helen had finished the new dresses for the Bartons, and as promised, I wore the one I had sewn myself. It was far from perfect, but I took pride in the finished product. I even considered giving sewing another go.

Not any time soon, mind, but someday.

When we arrived in front of the Bartons' home on Union Street, I found my feet cemented to the pavement. I had lost count of the number of times I had visited them, and not once had my presence ever been welcome. Things had changed—Mr. Barton had returned home—but I still hadn't any idea whether I would be slighted.

With an encouraging smile from Helen, we made our way to the door. I knocked, holding my breath at the sound of footsteps from within. The door swung open, revealing Mrs. Barton, her appearance still haggard and her clothing worn.

But there was a new light in her eyes, and as she took me in, her expression softened.

"Your Grace." The words were breathy and filled with emotion. "Please come in."

I swallowed against the lump in my throat. She had never invited me inside.

I clutched the parcels to my chest and entered the small house. The girls stood upon my entry and dipped a curtsy before greetings were exchanged. Mr. Barton joined us too, a smile pulling at his lips the moment he saw me. Both girls embraced me after opening their parcels, and my ability to maintain composure nearly shattered then.

"How are all of you?" I asked as Helen and I took a seat. There was little in the way of furnishings in the sitting area, leaving Mr. Barton and the girls to stand.

"Much better now," said Mrs. Barton, her voice still laced with emotion. "Thanks to you."

I shook my head. "You needn't thank me. In truth, I did very little. It was Mr. Davis who found your husband."

"At your request," Mr. Barton interjected. "And my wife tells me Adaline's doing much better thanks to the herbs you brought from the apothecary. Never mind the other things you have provided my family in my absence."

My face heated. "Please, keep your praise. None of it would have been necessary had you not helped me in the first place."

"Perhaps not," said Mr. Barton. "But I have never regretted it."

He had implied as much, but that had not stopped me from feeling guilty.

"The dresses are lovely, Your Grace," the littlest Barton girl said. She'd been holding it against herself since the moment she opened the package. "Green is my favorite color."

"I am glad you like it," I replied. "If there is anything more you stand in need of—"

"That is kind of you," Mrs. Barton interrupted, "but with William promised employment, I think we will manage quite well. We cannot take advantage of your kindness anymore."

"You've been offered employment? That is wonderful news!"

Mr. Barton grinned. "I have your Mr. Davis to thank for that. He's asked we return to Fallborn with him. Offered us a place in his tenant houses if I'd oversee the repairs for his estate. Given Westmore will go free, I think it best for my family's safety, and I do not mind the prospect. It will be a change but worth it to work for such a good man."

At this point, I might as well become a rain cloud with the amount of tears I was holding in. Gregory had done more than find Mr. Barton; he'd given him and his family a promising future and a haven.

"Yes, he is a good man." My gaze dropped to my lap.

"Will you be joining us there as well?" asked Mr. Barton.

"Me? Oh, no. Mr. Davis and I...that is...there is no understanding between us."

Confusion furrowed his brow, but he did not question my answer. "I see. Well, I do hope this is not a permanent goodbye for us, Your Grace."

Much as I shared his sentiments, I harbored no such hope.

GREGORY

One round. That was all I had managed to play last night at The Bottom Ale. I had not been able to focus on anything but the memory of Sabrina's distraught expression and retreating figure, and no matter how I had tried to shake the image, I could not.

Nor had my heart ceased to ache since.

Morning light poured in from the window, and I lay in bed, willing myself to move. Yet another failure rested on my shoulders, and it drained me. Spending half the night chiding myself for ever being so hopeful in the first place had done nothing to help.

Slowly, I sat up and rubbed my eyes. For so long, I had spent my nights at the tables. I'd convinced myself much of it was out of necessity—that I needed to play and win to pay down my debts. Most of the time, the reasoning was sound, but not always.

There were nights that I needn't win funds out of desperation. There were nights when I stayed far longer than necessary. It was those nights when my thoughts inevitably wandered to Whitticker and my foolish decisions.

I wonder what it is you need distracting from. Mr. Carlisle, my frequent tablemate in London, had once said that. I hadn't thought of myself as needing to be distracted then. Now, I realized the man had seen through my act, even through my desperation. Part of my gambling habits were born from a desire to forget. What better way to bury my failures than by succeeding at the tables?

Except, last night's game had not proven enough of a distraction, and I suspected cards might never hold that power for me again. I had lost more than money, and no amount of wins in a gambling hell could repair a broken heart.

Perhaps I ought to tell Carlisle as much. He had said he gambled to forget the loss of his wife.

I shook my head. There were more important matters for me to see to at present. Preparations to leave Bath and return home needed to begin right away. My estate was floundering, and the sooner I returned, the sooner I could contrive a plan.

Or try to. Hiring Mr. Barton when I had no money might prove a regrettable decision, but I needed help and he needed safety for himself and his family. We would look out for one another, at the very least.

I descended the stairs and entered the small parlor that served as a breakfast room. Mother was already there, sipping at her morning coffee, a tray of ham, eggs, and sweets before her.

"Good morning, Mother," I said, helping myself to a plate at the sideboard.

Mother harrumphed, and I turned to look at her with raised brows. She crossed her arms, her expression foreshadowing her belligerent tone. "It is not a good morning at all!"

"I am as displeased as you are about Westmore," I said, calmly stacking slices of ham onto my plate.

"Do not play with me, Gregory. Lord Cartwell told me you stayed for the games after that fraud was arrested. What do you mean by such actions? I knew our finances were dire, but you never told me how rotten they were. Why did you not mention it? I am your mother. I deserve—"

"Mother!"

She snapped her mouth closed, and I heaved a sigh. The last thing I wished to do was yell at her, but sometimes her dramatic personality got in the way of reason. I took a seat next to her at the table, allowing myself to calm before I spoke again. "I should have told you, but I cannot change that now."

"Why did you not?" she asked softly. "Do you not trust me?"

"It is not that at all. I was ashamed. Everything Father worked for had slipped through my fingers so quickly. I knew you would be disappointed, as would Father were he alive. I could not face it."

She reached for my hand. "It was not your fault. You think you are the only one to fall for that man's schemes? Hardly. There are dozens of victims. Do you think less of Lord Cartwell for having been fooled?"

"No, but regardless, I cannot fix things. My agreement with Cartwell was not fulfilled; therefore, financially, we are no better off than we were before this entire ordeal, save for what remains of his initial payment to me."

"Surely he will still pay you for all this trouble?"

I shrugged. "I cannot hold him to it when I did not keep my end of our deal. Regardless, I am sorry. For all of it. I acted too swiftly when I inherited and without due diligence. I fell for the lies, and you have suffered because of it."

Mother swatted at the air. "Suffered is a strong word, Gregory. Have I gone without some luxuries? I suppose. But nothing that I could not live without. Besides, you are what is important to me. I should hope you know that."

I nodded, warmth spreading through my chest.

"Now"—Mother speared a piece of her ham—"what about this gambling last night? I had hoped you would break the habit. We can find another way to sustain the estate."

"I played one game and...well, I realized that cards have been a form of distraction." I tilted my head and grimaced. "A distraction that no longer appears viable. I shan't return to the tables; I give you my word. Although, I haven't much of a plan to fix our income at present."

"You will get us righted," said Mother. "I have faith in you. What you lack is faith in yourself." She shifted in her chair, her chin lifted. "Which is why having two women in the household who believe in you will be just the boon you need."

"Two women?"

Mother's brows furrowed, an incredulous look filling her expression. "Of course, two. Me and the Duchess."

My stomach twisted with some mix of eagerness and disappointment. "Mother, the Duchess will not be joining us at Fallborn."

"Why not?"

"Because that would imply that I intend to court, and eventually, marry her."

Mother stared at me.

"I cannot marry her, Mother."

"*Why. Not?*" She enunciated each word with barely controlled aggravation. "You are in love with that woman. Do not attempt to convince me otherwise."

"I shan't lie to you. I love her and want nothing more than to take her as my wife." I quickly continued when a spark of hope lit her eyes. "It is asking too much. The estate may never be profitable. How can I beg her to take such a risk? To raise a family with the threat of financial ruin hanging over our heads. It is unfair and selfish, Mother. I cannot do it."

"And how does Her Grace feel about this? Did she agree the risk is too great?"

I wet my lips, considering ways to excuse myself without answering. Which would do no good. Mother would follow me to the privy if I denied her an answer to this question. There was no escaping it. "I have not spoken to her about the matter."

"Did you intend to leave Bath without even talking to her about this?"

"I...I have not yet decided what I will do if you must know. I owe her an explanation, but would a conversation not make everything more difficult for both of us? We would not suit, Mother. I cannot give her what she deserves."

"Gregory Andrew Davis!"

I winced. She never used my full name unless she was particularly peeved.

"You would not *suit*?" She flapped her hands about dramatically. "And here I thought you were intelligent! Hah! Would not suit. You keep this monstrosity on your face for weeks when it does not suit."

"That is different," I countered.

"You're right; it is different because you and Sabrina suit one another perfectly. What that lady deserves and needs is *love*. The only person who cannot see that is you." She stood, muttering under her breath. "I am going to fix this."

"Mother."

"Must I do everything myself?" she continued to mumble as she headed for the door. "Completely stubborn, just like his father. Ridiculous."

"Mother!"

She disappeared from the room, and all I could do was stare after her, my heart pounding. What was she going to do? Mother was nothing if not mischievous. Her words should always be taken at face value, for she despised pretenses. When she said she intended to fix something...

I swallowed, terrified she might do something drastic, yet also foolishly hopeful she would.

It required less than an hour of worrying what Mother might do to motivate me to take things into my own hands. She was right; I loved Sabrina, and I should not allow the state of my finances to keep us apart. At a minimum, she deserved to know how I felt.

Still, I was not about to give up entirely on ensuring our future together had the best chance of security first. If Mother could take drastic measures to prompt me to act, then perhaps I could do the same to Westmore.

The Watchmen agreed to my request for a private audience with the man, and as I entered the watchhouse, I drew in a deep breath, hoping to ease my nerves. Regardless of the outcome, I had to try.

Westmore glanced up from the wooden bench he sat on behind the bars of his cell, meeting my gaze. Anger flickered across his expression, but there was also an element of curiosity within his eyes. He stood and approached the bars with a façade of confidence.

"Well, what to do I owe the pleasure, Mr. Carrow?"

"Davis," I corrected.

He looked at me then, truly looked. His eyes roamed my face, and I knew the moment recognition took hold. I had shaved before coming here, which must have aided in jogging his memory. "Davis. I remember you."

"How flattering."

The grin that filled his face was smug, almost evil. "Revenge, was it? So angry with how I deceived you that you've pursued me all this time? Well, congratulations. You finally caught me, but from what I hear, your holdings are...in shambles, putting it kindly. You may blame me all you like, but it took very little to convince you to hand over your inheritance."

I fought to keep anger from showing in my expression. "You have heard correctly. Ever since you swindled me out of money, I have struggled. But that is why I am here. The charges brought against you can be dropped. I can convince Cartwell to do the same."

"And why would you do that?"

I leaned closer to the bars. "Because I want my money back. I want in on your schemes. Once I've been repaid, you can go on your merry way. All I care about is restoring my estate."

Westmore studied me. "Why should I believe anything you say?"

I gripped the bars, my frown deepening. "I am tired of living on the edge of ruin. Tired of feeling desperate. Tired of looking over my shoulder and wondering when my creditors will strike. I have all the evidence compiled against you. I can make it disappear. In exchange, all I want is my life back. No more threats of debtor's prison. No threats of destitution. We can work together, you and I, and both get what we want."

Westmore considered this. It was all a bluff, as I had no intention of letting him escape justice, but bluffs sounded convincing when they were rooted in true emotion. I was tired of living this way, and I did want my life back. What Westmore didn't know was that the evidence against him was not enough for a conviction, and I saw no need to inform him otherwise.

He rubbed a hand over his chin. "I let you in on my schemes, and we part ways once you have regained your money?"

"Yes," I said firmly.

"How do I know you will not bring up charges again? Or double-cross me?"

I shrugged. "You do not, but if I become involved, why would I turn myself in for crimes committed?"

His brows raised. "That would be rather foolish."

"Indeed."

I held my breath while he studied me again. "Get me out of here, and I will agree to your terms."

I shook my head. "Forgive me for not trusting *you*. If you want this to happen, I need something from you. I want your name—your *real* name. I am not stepping into this without it. You owe me that much after everything."

Westmore scoffed. "An odd request, but if that is all you require to move forward, then so be it. My name is Alfred Hitchins."

Lies. That was the name he had used when swindling Cartwell. I remembered it from the documents we spent hours going over.

"Another alias," I said. "You are testing my patience. I have proof of several names you have used over the years and will not be tricked. Perhaps I will chat with Lord Cartwell and have the charges magnified instead. He is an earl. His influence surely can see you face death rather than transportation."

Westmore blanched, and he dropped his voice to a low whisper. "Fine. My name is Frederick Harrowood. I was born in Northampton to Margaret and Alfred Harrowood. The local vicar there will attest to my identity, as he practically supported me and my siblings. I grew up with nothing."

"Anyone else who can confirm?"

He spat off a short list of names, and I made note of them in a small book I had brought along for such an occasion. Until verified, I could not know if he told the truth, but something in me believed Frederick really was his name.

"I will return in a few days once I know you are telling the truth. Until then, I wish you comfort in these...accommodations."

He responded with a wry smile, and I left the watchhouse far lighter than when I had entered.

Chapter Twenty-Five

SABRINA

A week had passed since I had seen or spoken to Gregory Davis. I had foolishly thought my heart would heal after a few days without his company, but that could not have been further from the truth. I missed him, and I hated feeling so despondent without him in my life. I had never allowed any man to dictate my happiness.

Well, perhaps that was untrue, but this pining and heartache were new to me. I disliked it greatly, and I cursed Gregory for ever opening my mind to the possibility of love, only to rip it away from me.

Which was why the letter I presently held had incited a mixture of emotions in me. Anger, confusion, hopefulness—drat the man! If he intended to step out of my life, then why should he send me such a note? Why did he even remain here in Bath?

I tossed the note next to me on the sofa cushion. Gregory Davis would drive me to madness.

"Ye look particularly frustrated this mornin'," said Helen, entering the room with a tea tray. "Somethin' the matter?"

Everything. Everything was the matter, and I felt torn as to what to do. I gestured to the note. "Read it and tell me what you think."

Helen set the tray on the oak table and then snatched the paper from the cushion. Her lips lifted, and her eyes lit with excitement. "'Tis from Mr. Davis."

"Unfortunately," I muttered. "Go on. Read it."

"My dearest Sabrina, I have spent much time this last week in deep thought and have come to a conclusion you may find most unwelcome. The truth is that I love you. It is my greatest desire to spend whatever remains of my days with you, but I fear I have ruined any chance of such a future. Can you ever forgive me, my darling? Can you look past the man who has made so many mistakes, who has disappointed you so deeply? My time in Bath is nearing its end, but I must see you one more time. If nothing else, allow me to deliver my regrets in person and beg your forgiveness.

"I shall attend the assembly on Thursday and hope that I might find you there. Please meet me in The Octagon Room at half past nine. Until then, yours, GD."

Helen looked up at me, her smile still in place. "It is very romantic."

"No." I stood, shaking my head. "It is not romantic. Have you forgotten we have not spoken in over a week? That he dismissed me from the pub? We were to never see one another again. I had resigned myself to it. I shan't go."

"Now ye don't have to be resigned," said Helen.

"I...no, Helen. I cannot do this. What if this changes nothing? I do not know if my heart can stand another goodbye."

Helen's expression softened. She placed the note on the table and scooped up my hands. "Mr. Davis is a good man. He has made mistakes, I will grant, but it sounds as if he wishes to make amends. I think ye will regret it if ye do not go. Always wonder. Besides, he never truly told you goodbye. We only assumed it."

I groaned. "Why must you be right? And when did you become so persuasive?"

"Persuasion is easy when it is what the heart already wants." Helen grinned. "So ye will go to the assembly?"

"Do not get your hopes up. I am agreeing to go and meet with him. Nothing more."

"My hopes are exceedingly high," she admitted. "But I will do my best to conceal my anticipation."

As would I.

GREGORY

"How do you know she will be at the assembly?" I glared at Mother, and the way she lifted her chin in defiance was concerning.

"I saw to it. Never mind how. You can speak with her there."

After spending days with Cartwell attempting to verify Westmore's true identity, and having found success in the endeavor, I had awoken this morning with the intention to call on Sabrina. I had not seen her in a week, and the ache to be in her presence had grown unbearable. I wanted to tell her all that had happened—that Westmore would pay for his crimes and that, with Cartwell's payment, I could potentially provide for her, should she accept me as her husband.

The relief had nearly overwhelmed me, but Cartwell had also deemed me a fool for thinking he had not intended to pay in the first place. He'd had the money ready the moment I went to him with Westmore's name.

"What if I do not wish to attend the assembly?" I asked. "I would rather go to her now."

"And ruin everything I planned?" Mother scoffed. "A few hours will not kill you."

They might, given how much I longed to march to Gay Street this very minute.

"You promised I could be social once this was all over," she added. "I am holding you to it. I want to attend one assembly before we leave."

"Fine, I will wait, but you could at least tell me what scheme you have orchestrated. It is no longer necessary."

"Nothing terribly wild, I assure you." She swatted the air and scurried past me.

I heaved a sigh and headed to the study. The hours dragged on as I dove into paperwork and ledgers. Twenty thousand pounds was a great sum, but it would not cover everything to restore Fallborn.

I needed to pick and choose what repairs and improvements to prioritize. The ones that would enhance Fallborn's income were of utmost importance, but that meant neglecting other things. The desire to rush into it all—to restore my childhood home to what it should be—was difficult to ignore.

And I fought that desire until night had descended upon Bath and I readied myself for the ball. I met Mother in the foyer and escorted her to the carriage. The drive to Bennett Street seemed to last an eternity.

Minutes. It lasted minutes, but how could I be blamed for the way anticipation distorted time?

"There is John," said Mother with a tone of tenderness when we arrived. "Just there by the door."

Sure enough, Angston waited near the entry to the assembly hall, but his attention was not on the arriving carriages. Instead, he stared wearily at the waddling form of Lord Duckworth, who was making a nuisance of himself, honking his displeasure as he chased those exiting their carriages.

A smile tugged at my lips as I remembered my stroll with Sabrina through Queen's Square. The mallard truly was ill-tempered.

I handed Mother down from the carriage, and we gave Lord Duckworth a wide berth as we approached Angston. He escorted Mother inside, with me following close behind. A crush already filled the ballroom by the time we had shed our coats and gloves, and with so many people in the room, the heat quickly grew unbearable.

Our group perched near the refreshment tables, and Mother made her requests to John, which he happily obliged. The two of them fell into a soft exchange, one filled with significant looks and smiles. While the idea of my mother remarrying felt foreign, I did not oppose it. John made her happy—that much was clear—and my Mother's happiness was my top priority.

James Heaviside, the Master of Ceremonies, welcomed us all, his lively speech marking the start of the evening. The orchestra began to play the first set of the night, and I found myself surprised Mother and John did not immediately take to the floor.

"I thought you intended to dance?" I asked, leaning close to her.

"I shall, but there is something else I must see to first." She did not spare me her attention, and I followed her gaze to where Miss Colewater stood on the opposite side of the room. My stomach leapt. If Miss Colewater was here, surely that meant Sabrina had come as well.

Miss Colewater gave a firm nod, though it did not seem like one of acknowledgment. I turned to Mother, my brows furrowed, just in time to catch her return the gesture. When I glanced back, Miss Colewater had gone.

"What was that about?" I asked.

"Hmm? Oh, it is time for your meeting."

"My meeting?" I repeated.

"Indeed, Her Grace is waiting for you in The Octagon Room."

"What?" I spluttered. "What do you—"

"I wrote her a letter on your behalf. It was very charming and romantic, so I expect you to not make a liar out of me."

Uneasiness crept in. This morning I had been ready to propose, but now that the moment was here, I hesitated. I wanted Sabrina, but I feared condemning her to a life fraught with financial insecurity. I had Cartwell's payment, yes, but I had mismanaged funds before. What if I did so again? What if I made another mistake that cost us everything?

"Hold this for me, will you, John?" Mother passed John her tray of treats and her beverage. Without warning, she pulled me into an embrace. Frustration kept my posture stiff, but after a few seconds, the emotion drained out of me.

"What if I fail again?" I whispered. "What if she comes to resent me?"

Mother's arms tightened around me. We were likely making a scene, but Mother had never cared for such things. "She will not resent you. She cares for you, and doubt prevents you from seeing how much. You've punished yourself for long enough. It is time to forgive yourself. To move on."

Forgive myself?

Had I not told Sabrina that her efforts to rectify her past misdeeds were more than enough? Had I not told her to forgive herself so the past might be put to rest? Yet here I stood, a hypocrite guilty of ignoring my own advice. I had berated myself for my mistake with Whittaker for years. I had thought bringing the man to justice would satisfy my guilt, but it hadn't. It still raged within me because I had never faced the monster it created.

"I don't know if I can." My voice cracked.

Mother's expression turned stern. "I do not blame you for what happened, Gregory, and neither would your father were he alive. Do you think he did not make his share of mistakes? I can promise you he did; I stood by his side through all of them. Marriage is not about two perfect people coming together. It is rather the opposite—two very *im*perfect people agreeing to weather life's storms and face the disappointments together in hopes that they will both be a little better, a little stronger, when the sun returns."

"Not everyone sees marriage that way," I said, smiling slightly. "Especially among the *ton*."

Mother's nose wrinkled. "That is their loss. But you have the opportunity for a love match. Please do not throw it away because you fear the storm. Do not choose to face it alone."

I tapped a finger against my thigh. "The Octagon Room, you say?"

Mother grinned. "Go get her, son."

With a curt nod, I turned, unable to stop my lips from rising.

Chapter Twenty-Six

GREGORY

The Octagon Room was an enormous, two-story suite with several fireplaces embedded in its angled walls and a giant, candle-lit glass chandelier dangling in its center. Chairs adorned the walls between the doors and fireplaces, and several paintings hung on the upper level between tall windows that, during the day, filled the room with light.

The wallpaper itself was a mixture of intricate greens and blues, patterned with ornate lines of gold. Lovely as the room was, it paled in comparison to the creature who stood near one of the four hearths, her dark hair woven into braids pinned to the top of her head and her pastel yellow ball gown perfectly fitted to her figure.

My heart jumped at the mere sight of her, and when our eyes met, the air left my lungs in a sudden whoosh. Sabrina Stafford was the most beautiful woman I had ever met, and while I had once assumed that beauty existed merely on the outside, I now knew better. Away from her father's expectations, she shined, much like her yellow dress and the candlelight reflecting off the glass of the chandelier. Her light penetrated me, guided me, and I knew for certain I would be forever lost to it now.

How had I ever thought to let her go?

I swallowed and crossed the room to her. Much as I knew my heart, I did not know hers. Sabrina may still reject an offer of marriage from me, and she would not be wrong to do so. Uncertainty still surrounded my future, and I was no one of great importance.

Gads. Was I truly about to propose?

Good heavens, I was.

I bowed to her, and she returned a curtsy with a hesitant smile. "Good evening, Mr. Davis."

"Good evening, Sabrina."

Her brows furrowed, and her words surprised me. "You shaved."

"I did," I responded with a chuckle. "Do you approve?"

"I do."

Silence fell between us. Where did I begin? An apology? Or should I lay my feelings bare before her first?

"You hired Mr. Barton," said Sabrina before I could come to a decision.

"Yes. You told me of his difficulties after the last scandal, and I did not wish to see him or his family suffer again. I owe him, besides. Westmore would still be at large were it not for him."

Sabrina nodded. "All the same, it was kind of you to offer him employment."

"I've seen firsthand similar kindness. The Bartons are good people, and I'm honored to help them. To know them."

A slight blush tinted her cheeks. "Well, if you are to take them from me, I suppose I will have to find a new family to focus my efforts on."

My lips twisted to one side. "Perhaps not, though I am certain there are many in need near Cheltenham."

Her eyes met mine, wide and full of question. My heart pounded against my chest at an unhealthy pace. Was it hope I saw hidden in her expression or fear?

"You said you wished to meet with me," she whispered. "I cannot continue as we are, Gregory. My heart is near breaking one moment and filled with joyous hope I know not what to do with the next."

I took a step closer to her. "Hope for what, my dear Sabrina?"

Her chin lifted to keep our gazes connected. "Hope that I may have what I want—no, what I *need*. What I feel for you is far more than desire. It is safe and warm and bright. It is everything I never had and everything I never knew I wanted. Do not torment me by dangling hope within my grasp."

I smiled, reaching forward and wrapping an arm around her waist. We were not alone in The Octagon Room, and there was a real possibility that any onlookers would spread rumors about us, but I found it difficult to care. Not when this woman had as good as confessed.

"I believe you've described what my mother would call love," I said softly. "Do you love me, Sabrina? For I have certainly fallen madly in love with you."

She gasped and pulled out of my arms, sending my heart plummeting into my stomach. Doubt flooded my thoughts...until she squealed, pointing past me, a great deal of fear twisting her expression. I turned in time to glimpse a feathery form flying in my direction. Lord Duckworth collided with my body, nearly toppling me to the ground, and began pecking at my legs, feet, and hands.

I retreated, my arms flailing in an effort to block its violent attack. It did no good. The fowl followed each step backward, voicing its frustration. I yelled for help, hoping a footman would hear or someone in the room would take pity and alert one. Sabrina seemed too shocked to move, her back pressed against the wall as she watched my dance with Lord Duckworth with some mixture of worry and amusement.

The mallard began an aggressive assault on my coat. I swatted the animal away, rotating out of its reach, only for it to follow each movement with unrivaled determination.

"Your coat!" Sabrina called. "I think he is after your coat!"

Twisting away from the bird, I shrugged out one arm and then another before tossing the fabric to the floor in a heap. Lord Duckworth ceased chasing me and began a mad attack on it instead. I backed away, my chest heaving, until I reached Sabrina's side.

"What the devil is wrong with that thing?"

A giggle escaped the woman beside me. "He is hungry, it seems. Look! He has found something in your pocket."

My brows furrowed. "Are those biscuits?"

"They were, I think. Now they appear to be biscuit crumbs."

I faced her, my expression serious but my tone failing to hide my amusement. "I do not carry biscuits around in my pockets, just so you are aware. I haven't any idea where"—my jaw dropped—"*Mother.*"

"Your mother hid biscuits in your pocket?" Sabrina asked. "Whatever for?"

"Heaven only knows. That woman is always up to no good and more dramatic than the duck. She was eating a biscuit when she embraced me earlier. I would not put it past her to also sneak Lord Duckworth in here simply for the pleasure of watching the scene unfold or creating gossip."

Two footmen entered the room and frantically raced toward the rogue duck. Sabrina and I watched as they struggled to capture the creature, and once they had, a pile of feathers lay scattered over the floor.

"Well, that was unexpected," said Sabrina as they carried the screeching creature away.

"Indeed. Much about tonight has been unexpected, including our meeting."

"What do you mean?" She tilted her head and plucked a stray feather from my shoulder. Once released, it fluttered to the floor.

I cupped Sabrina's cheek and brushed my thumb over her smooth skin. She deserved the entire truth. "My mother is the one who wrote that letter to you, though I wish I could claim to have been so bold. I haven't any idea what it contained, but if there were any declarations of love, know that they reflect my sentiments. I do love you, Sabrina, and I want nothing more than to marry you. I propose another alliance between us, and I hope beyond measure that you will not consider this one so unfortunate. We make a good team, you and I, and nothing would please me more than to have you at my side."

Her eyes glazed over, and she leaned into my touch. "Even with my egregious past? I know I have apologized, but—"

"Your past was never what kept me from you. I cannot promise you luxury, Sabrina. I cannot promise that I will succeed in my endeavors to fix my income or restore my estate. All I have to offer you is my heart. If that is not enough—if the risk is too great for you—then I understand. But you must know that any future with me has its financial uncertainties."

Her expression softened, and she reached up to touch my face. "I married a duke, Gregory. It never made me happy. It never made me feel loved. In the past few weeks, you have given me both of those things, and I can only imagine how much more fortunate I shall feel when I am your wife."

My wife. The words made me grin wide enough my cheeks ached. "Then I will post the banns with haste."

She chuckled, her slender fingers stroking over my cheek. "I do have one stipulation."

"What is that?"

"No more beards."

A hearty laugh escaped me, and I pulled her closer. "No more beards. You cannot have hated it more than I did."

"Debatable, but let us agree to put the argument to rest. I'd prefer you did not grow it out again to settle it."

"Agreed. Hardly worth the trouble. Or irritation. Besides, my mother might put me in the grave if I ever allow that beaver on my face again."

"And I would hold the shovel," she said teasingly. Her smile faded, replaced with a genuine tenderness that stoked the already glowing fire within me. "In case it was not completely clear, I love you, Gregory. I think I have loved you for quite some time, in fact. The difficult part was allowing myself to admit it."

"A bit of brandy saw to that. After all, why else would you dream of my eyes?"

Her nose wrinkled adorably. "Shush, you. I never want to speak of that embarrassment again."

"I did tell you I would not forget it. I do not want to. That said, I hope our kisses from here on out are more like our time in the carriage."

Sabrina pulled away from me, her smile smug. "Then perhaps you ought to offer to escort me home, Mr. Davis. Helen would allow us a moment of privacy, I think." She raised her brows suggestively and turned around, heading for the main entry.

I followed with several quick steps to catch up. "While I do like this plan, you've forgotten my mother will also be in the carriage."

Sabrina shrugged, dropping her voice to a whisper. "Given her willingness to send love notes on your behalf, I cannot think she will mind, but perhaps you are right. You will need to call on me tomorrow instead."

"Indeed, I intend to, but first"—I grabbed her hand and entwined our fingers—"I should like to dance with my bride-to-be."

Epilogue

SABRINA

The overgrown vines that had once adorned the walls of Fallborn were now gone, and the unkempt shrubs and gardens surrounding the carriageway were trimmed into submission. It had been years since Fallborn looked so welcoming. At least, that was what Gregory led me to believe. Having been here only once before our marriage, I had little choice but to trust him on the matter. Regardless, I looked up at our country home with a sense of joy, merely for the fact that it was ours.

I had never felt such a sense of peace. Never felt more accepted. Home had taken on an entirely new meaning in the last few months.

"What do ye think he's been up to today?" Helen asked, walking next to me on the road leading to the house.

I swung the empty basket in my hand, pondering her question. It was much lighter now that we had delivered fresh tarts and bread to the Bartons, who had taken up residence in one of the tenant houses. Two more families had moved in just this week, and I had been so eager to meet them that I'd begged Cook to make them a treat as well.

"I'm not certain," I answered. "Now that the roof is repaired, perhaps Gregory has moved on to replacing the floors in the guest wing? There was a bit of damage due to the leaks."

Helen nodded. "Does that mean Fallborn might see visitors in the future?"

"I should hope so. What use is it to fix the guest rooms if we've no intention of ever having guests? Although, who I will invite, I haven't any idea." There was always Penny and her new husband, but no, they were surely too deep in newly-wed bliss to come. That only left Phillip and his family. Would they make the journey if I invited them?

A burst of warmth flooded my chest at the idea. They would come. "I will speak to Gregory, but I think I shall invite my cousin."

"That's a wonderful idea," said Helen. "Always did like Mr. Montfert."

I gave her a playful glare. "You mean you like his children. Do not think I'm unaware of how you spoiled them during the wedding. Children have a tendency to tattle, you know. Often unintentionally."

Helen shrugged, but she grinned back at me. "I shan't deny it. I will spoil them until ye've yer own little 'uns runnin' around. Then I'll spoil them instead."

I shook my head, but the idea of having children of my own gave me an even greater sense of contentment. A family—that was what I had gained since the start of summer. Not only had Gregory become my closest friend and the keeper of my heart, but I had found refuge and acceptance with his mother and even the staff at Fallborn, who had welcomed their new mistress without judgment. Mrs. Davis had remained with us until her marriage to John Angston a fortnight ago, and I found I already missed her company. Perhaps that was why I was so eager for guests.

We entered the house, and the butler took our hats, coats, and gloves. Winter was settling in, the sky a somber gray with the threat of snow.

"I think I will see if Cook needs help with anything," said Helen. I had brought her with me to Fallborn as a friend, not a maid, but Helen insisted on helping with things. We were still operating on minimal staff, which gave her plenty of argument about earning her keep, though neither I nor Gregory would ever press her to do so.

Since she refused to abandon her position and had such an affinity for children, I thought to offer her the position of nurse.

When the time came, of course.

I bid Helen goodbye and climbed the stairs. I followed the sound of pounding into the guest wing where I found my husband on his knees, prying out a rotted plank with a hammer. Mr. Barton worked next to him, as did two other men. Despite the hard labor, they all wore smiles and conversed easily, as friends might.

I cleared my throat, gaining their attention. "Forgive me, but may I steal Mr. Davis for a moment?"

The other men nodded, and one even winked. They had learned that my stealing generally meant more than a conversation.

Gregory followed me into the corridor, pulling the door closed behind him to muffle the bangs of the hammer and afford us a little privacy. He wiped the sweat from his forehead, replacing it with a streak of dirt.

"You are back early," he said. "I did not expect to see you until well after noon."

I lifted onto my tiptoes and brushed the dirt away before pressing a kiss to his cheek. "It is well after noon, my love. You are working yourself too hard."

Gregory chuckled, wrapping an arm behind my back and pulling me close. "Maybe so, but I intend to stretch our money as far as I can. If that means doing a good chunk of the work myself, then so be it."

"With twenty thousand pounds, you can afford to give yourself time to rest."

"Is that why you steal me away?" he asked, dipping his head closer. "To force me to take a moment to rest?"

"Not at all. Since I helped you complete your mission from Cartwell, I demand some benefit from the funds. Payment, as it were."

He hummed, fighting back a smile. "I see. And having a house that does not leak and floors that do not creak is not enough?"

I tilted my head from side to side, and Gregory tweaked my nose playfully. The man was pouring so much energy into fixing the estate, and I admired him dearly for his hard work. On occasion, I had to remind him that, while I appreciated his diligence to provide for us, I had not married him for the house or any worldly possessions we might fill it with.

Gregory smirked, as if reading my thoughts. "I know. My heart is your only desire."

"Not my *only* desire. I like a great deal more of you than simply your heart."

He laughed deeply, enfolding me in both arms. Wrapping me in a cocoon of safety and happiness. Gregory's lips met mine as a soft rumble echoed through the house and the patter of rain tapped against the windows. We had faced more than one storm since exchanging our vows, and we would certainly face more in the future.

But with his lips tenderly chasing mine, I knew without doubt we would weather them all.

Thanks for reading! I hope you enjoyed Gregory and Sabrina's story. If you have a moment, please leave a rating/review on your preferred platform.

Gregory and Sabrina often speak of their shared moment outside of Cheltenham. While that scene did not make it into this book, you can get the bonus scene here for FREE! https://BookHip.com/XSNHGSK

Be sure to check out the next book in the series, An Unclaimed Heart.

My Books

HISTORICAL ROMANCE

The Time Pearls

In Time With the Duke
The Future with the Marquess
Courting A Modern Lady

Apsley Family

Saving Miss Scott
Matching Mr. Montfert
Evading the Lieutenant

Standalones

An Unfortunate Alliance

Romantic Comedy

I Heart New York

You Wish
If the Suit Fits
White Picket Defense
Saved By Mistle Tow

Acknowledgments

I've written quite a few books, but this was—admittedly—one of the hardest ones I have ever written. Writing a series with a group of brilliant authors was new and challenging, and I certainly faced my share of doubts about my own writing throughout the process. But I am so grateful to have been invited to join these ladies. They've become dear friends, and I'm blessed to have had the opportunity to get to know them. So, a big thank you to my series buddies for keeping it fun, no matter how many crazy ideas we bounced off each other, and keeping me motivated to get this book finished! Michelle, Amanda, Teah, Miranda, and Brooke—thank you for being so wonderful to work with!

A big shout out to my critique partners, Justena and Miranda, for wading through the rough draft of this thing. Your initial feedback was beyond valuable.

A huge thank you to my beta readers: Brooke Hampton, Amanda Panhorst, Leigh Walker, Beba Andric, Heidi Stott, Jessica Albano, Janice Green, and Molly Stratford. This book is much more polished thanks to all of you, and I appreciate your feedback.

Have you seen the map of Bath?! And the adorable headers?! I cannot go without thanking Amanda Daley for making it so beautiful. She was amazing to work with, and I can't wait to collaborate with her again in the future.

With how difficult this book was for me, I have to thank my family for putting up with my often sour mood. There were days where I wanted to chuck this book out a window or light it on fire—I may or may not still feel that way about it, but never mind that. My wonderful husband and kiddos are always supportive, and even though I don't always have the quiet atmosphere conducive to writing, they keep me going and encourage me more than they even realize. I also gotta shout out to my husband for accompanying me on a trip to England last year. Our visit to Bath really helped with the inspiration for this book, and I am so grateful he's willing to be my travel buddy.

I'd also like to thank my Heavenly Father, as none of my books would have even been completed without Him. I would not be on this path at all without His prompting guidance, and I'm grateful every day I choose to follow that prompting.

Thank you to all my readers! To every person who has purchased, reviewed, and read my stories, to anyone who has liked or commented on my posts or sent me sweet messages, YOU give me the motivation to keep going. I thank you from the bottom of my heart.

About the Author

Brooke Losee lives with her husband and three children in central Utah where she enjoys fishing, gardening, and gathering as many rocks as her pockets can hold. Brooke obtained a BS in Geology from Southern Utah University but has always had a passion for all things books.

Brooke began her journey to authorhood in 2020 with the notion of publishing one novel. That book turned into a series of seven, and the Pandora's box of ideas was unleashed. Her works range from fantasy to historical, all featuring a sweet and clean romance.

To follow her writing journey and keep informed about upcoming stories visit http://www.brookejlosee.com.